Murder at Buxley Manor
A British Cozy Mystery

By Leena Clover

Copyright © Leena Clover, Author 2023

All rights reserved. No part of this publication may be reproduced, stored in a retrieval system, or transmitted, in any form, or by any means (electronic, mechanical, photocopying, recording or otherwise) without the prior written permission of the author.

This book is a work of fiction. Names, characters, places, organizations and incidents are either products of the author's imagination or used fictitiously. Any resemblance to actual events, places, organizations or persons, living or dead, is entirely coincidental.

First Published March 9, 20223

CHAPTER 1	**11**
CHAPTER 2	**23**
CHAPTER 3	**36**
CHAPTER 4	**48**
CHAPTER 5	**60**
CHAPTER 6	**73**
CHAPTER 7	**85**
CHAPTER 8	**97**
CHAPTER 9	**109**
CHAPTER 10	**121**
CHAPTER 11	**132**
CHAPTER 12	**145**
CHAPTER 13	**157**
CHAPTER 14	**168**

CHAPTER 15	179
CHAPTER 16	191
CHAPTER 17	203
CHAPTER 18	215
CHAPTER 19	227
CHAPTER 20	240
CHAPTER 21	252
CHAPTER 22	265
CHAPTER 23	277
CHAPTER 24	290
CHAPTER 25	302
CHAPTER 26	313
CHAPTER 27	322
CHAPTER 28	333

CHAPTER 29	**345**
CHAPTER 30	**358**
CHAPTER 31	**369**
CHAPTER 32	**378**
EPILOGUE	**389**
RECIPE – BUXLEY MANOR KEDGEREE	**392**
ACKNOWLEDGEMENTS	**396**
JOIN MY NEWSLETTER	**399**
OTHER BOOKS BY LEENA CLOVER	**400**

NOTE: This book uses British spelling.

THE EARLS OF BUXLEY

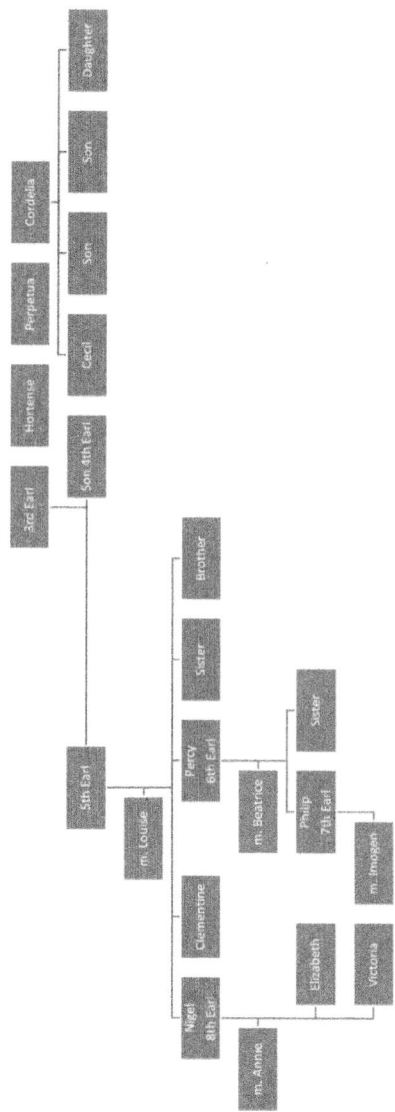

TEXT VERSION

Hortense

Perpetua

Cordelia

    Cecil

3rd Earl

    4th Earl

    5th Earl - married to Louise

        Clementine

        6th earl - Married to Beatrice

            Philip (7th Earl)

            Nigel (8th earl) - married to Annie

                Elizabeth

                Victoria

RESIDENTS OF BUXLEY

At Buxley Manor

Upstairs –

Nigel Gaskins – 8th Earl of Buxley, second son of the 5th earl

Clementine Barton – Nigel's widowed sister. She runs the manor with a firm hand, or tries to.

Hortense and Perpetua Gaskins – Nigel's great aunts

Imogen, Lady Buxley or Momo – Youngest Dowager Countess, widow of Nigel's nephew Philip, the previous Earl.

Gertrude Ridley or Bubbles – Imogen's unmarried sister, more or less a permanent resident of the manor.

Elizabeth Gaskins or Bess – Nigel's daughter

Downstairs –

Barnes – butler

Mrs. Jones – housekeeper

Mrs. Bird – cook

Wilson – lady's maid

Marci – scullery maid

At the Dower House

Louise, Lady Buxley – Nigel's mother, Dowager Countess

At Primrose Cottage

Beatrice, Lady Buxley – Nigel's brother's widow, Dowager Countess

At the Vicarage

Cordelia Chilton – Nigel's great aunt

Cecil Chilton – local vicar and Cordelia's son

Chapter 1

The old Vauxhall sped along the undulating country lanes, eating up the miles under a cornflower blue sky. The rolling hills of the Cotswolds presented a serene picture that May afternoon in 1921. Sheep grazed in the distance and daffodils nodded in the gentle breeze.

Lady Elizabeth Gaskins patted her new bob and allowed herself a smug smile as she thought of the radical step she had taken.

"They are going to love you, Vicky."

Her companion didn't share her optimism.

"Even the great aunts?"

"Especially them. Aunt Hortense and Aunt Perpetua are the cat's pyjamas. Now Aunt Clem I'm not sure about."

"What about the Dowager Countess?" Vicky's voice was full of awe.

"Which one?" Elizabeth smiled mischievously, her voice full of mirth. "Tell me about them."

Vicky was nervous but resigned.

"Lady Buxley, your grandmother, Lady Imogen and ..."

"Aunt Beatrice, silly. Actually, they are all Lady Buxley. And Momo's the bee's knees. She's like the mother I never had but don't tell her that. Makes her feel old."

Neither of them mentioned Lady Elizabeth's father though they were both thinking of him.

"Are you sure I won't be discovered?"

The car slowed as they reached the outskirts of Buxley. Elizabeth warned her companion to duck and stay out of sight. She didn't want any eager villager to spot Vicky. Unlike the servants at the manor, they were anything but discreet, hungry for gossip about their lord and his family. Dozens of locals had been hired for the upcoming house party and excitement ran high as guests from London and the surrounding estates arrived in style, prepared to spend a week or more at Buxley Manor.

"We can hide you for two days, darling. I can handle my maid. Barney's the one I'm worried about. He can read my thoughts before I think them."

"I thought you lot didn't care what the servants think."

"On the contrary, my dear," Elizabeth laughed. "The servants rule us. I wonder how the old guard hasn't realized it yet."

The car drove through a set of ancient stone pillars and went around a bend. Vicky looked around in awe as they traversed several acres of park land, studded with ancient oaks and beeches. A brook gushed down a small hill and disappeared in the bowels of the earth.

"That meets the river Severn somewhere down the line." Elizabeth stifled a yawn. "The stream's wider on the north side." She waved a vague hand over her head. "We have plenty of trout and Papa likes to fish."

Formal gardens began, with meticulously kept flower beds and topiaries. The car swung into a barely visible lane and travelled under a canopy of trees before pulling up in front of a side door. Minutes later, they were rushing up a flight of uncarpeted stairs.

***

The Butler Barnes watched the car pick up a cloud of dust and come to a screeching stop outside the side door. He watched Lady Elizabeth step out and beckon someone in the passenger seat. Curious, he leaned forward in anticipation although his face did not betray an ounce of emotion. He was a fourth generation butler and being inscrutable was ingrained in every fibre of his being. His ancestors collectively rolled in their graves when he dropped the crystal decanter he was holding, spilling expensive whiskey over the ancient Persian carpet. A loud gasp escaped from his mouth and his eyes popped while his mind tried to make sense of what it was seeing.

"Mrs. Jones." He roared, almost running to the green

baize door that led below stairs. "Mrs. Jones!" His knees protested but were ignored as he almost tumbled down the steps to the kitchen."

"Mr. Barnes?" The statuesque housekeeper came out of her room, looking bewildered. In thirty four years of service at Buxley Manor, she had never seen the butler show more excitement than a raised eyebrow. "You look white as a ghost! Let's get you some tea."

Barnes entered his own office and collapsed in his chair.

"It's because I have seen a ghost." His brow furrowed as he questioned his eyesight. "I think."

Mrs. Jones lingered at the door, torn between fetching tea and asking for an explanation. She rang the bell on the butler's desk. A young scullery maid arrived almost instantly.

"A pot of tea, please, Marcy, " she ordered and took a seat herself.

Barnes had pulled out a bottle of port and was pouring a hefty amount in a glass. He slid it across the table.

"You are going to need this, Mrs. Jones."

"That's enough drama for today, Mr. Barnes. Are you going to tell me what's amiss? And no more guessing games, if you please. There's a mountain of work waiting for me and it's almost time for lunch."

The butler gave her a broad grin.

"She's here. Lady Victoria. Saw her myself a few minutes ago."

"You poor thing," the housekeeper clucked. "How much of this port have you tossed back today?"

Barnes ignored the sarcasm.

"They both pulled up outside the back door a few minutes ago. Lady Bess brought her."

"Impossible!" The housekeeper placed her hands on her cheeks, shaking her head in disbelief. "You mean she knows?"

"Apparently," Barnes sighed. "And I say it's time."

The housekeeper gave a shrug, reminding him it was none of their business.

"Lady Bess has made it so. Why didn't they come in through the front door? What am I supposed to tell my lord?"

"You will say nothing, of course. Lady Bess is up to something. We must look the other way and play along."

Barnes gave an approving nod.

"Exactly my thoughts. You will make sure they have what they need?"

"A little extra food won't be missed in this house. Now I wonder what that minx has planned."

Barnes felt the weight of his sixty some years on his shoulders.

"I just hope Lady Victoria is here to stay. Lord Buxley will be ecstatic."

Mrs. Jones allowed herself three minutes to sip the wine. Then she rose to get back to her duties. She opened the door and paused as a thought struck her.

"How did you know it was her?" She turned around and asked the butler.

"You couldn't tell them apart, if they weren't dressed in different clothes. I thought I was seeing double."

Mrs. Jones smiled and gave a nod before heading out.

***

Two middle aged women sat in a cosy room in the east wing of the manor, engaged in idle chit chat. Although they had the same green eyes and fiery auburn hair, they couldn't have looked more different. Widowed in her twenties, the youngest Dowager Countess at Buxley Manor was a picture of restraint. Her dress was old fashioned, almost Victorian in its severity. Her hair was arranged in a sedate bun. Imogen, Lady Buxley, had suffered loss several years before the Great War. She scarcely mentioned her husband so it was easy to forget she hadn't been born at Buxley.

"Say yes." Her companion urged. "It's taken me ages to convince the pater. He agreed on the condition that you will accompany me."

With her short hair and a sleeveless frock that barely skimmed her calves, Gertrude Ridley was nothing like her sister. She had never married but could not be accused of being a dried up old spinster.

"A flat in London is out of question, Bubbles. Buxley is my home."

"I know, I know, Momo. You are attached to this old pile." She rolled her eyes, twisting her mouth to show her disdain. "But what's the harm in living a little? You can come back here any time you want."

"And what am I supposed to do in your den of iniquity?"

"Have a life! Enjoy yourself for once." Gertrude cried. "The world has changed in the past twenty years. Don't you ever want to go to a dance club? Listen to some jazz? Even have dinner at a swanky restaurant?"

"Mrs. Bird is an excellent cook," Imogen replied.

"Let your hair down for a night, Momo," Gertrude pleaded. "Once you dance the Charleston, you'll set aside all these ridiculous notions of yours."

Imogen took a sip of her tea and realized it was cold. She rang the bell to ask for a fresh pot.

"You're a middle aged woman, Bubbles. Not one of these bright young people we hear about. Aren't you a little long in the tooth to be doing all this?"

Gertrude's eyes hardened for an instant. She pasted a smile on her face and tapped her foot, biting into a biscuit.

"I won't give up, you know. At least come flat hunting with me. We can go shopping and be back here for dinner."

There was a knock on the door and the butler came in.

"You rang, my lady?"

Imogen pointed at the cold tea. "Can we get a fresh pot, Barnes?"

He cleared his throat and nodded.

"Luncheon is about to be served, my lady."

Imogen's eyes darted to a clock by the window. She hadn't realized how late it was.

"Thank you, Barnes. We'll be there soon. Have any more guests arrived today?"

"Mr. Miles Carrington and his family came an hour ago. His brother, Mr. Trevor, is on his way and hopes to make it for lunch."

Imogen thought for a minute.

"Why don't you delay lunch a bit? That way, we can eat with Mr. Trevor Carrington."

The butler bowed his head.

"Lady Clementine forbade it."

"Of course I did." A tall, well built woman strode in, bringing in a burst of energy. "We can't let the house party disrupt our meal times."

"Of course not," Gertrude piped up, mimicking her.

"No cheek from you, Bubbles!" Lady Clementine snapped. "We have a whole bunch of people arriving at their whim. I have asked Mrs. Jones to set up a cold buffet in the breakfast room. The guests can eat when they arrive."

"You think of everything, Aunt Clem." Imogen looked uncertain. "Can we eat now or should I order a pot of tea?"

Clementine's face softened.

"Of course we can, my dear. There's pork pie and jam roly poly for dessert, with custard. It's your favourite, isn't it?"

"Are you still in the nursery, Momo?" Gertrude teased.

Imogen ignored her and followed her aunt out of the room. She liked being taken care of. She shuddered at the thought of living on her own in London. Regardless of what her sister said, she had no wish to be independent.

***

Nigel Gaskins, Earl of Buxley, stood in a babbling brook in the woods, somewhere at the south of his property, waiting for the fish to bite. Polo, his chocolate brown poodle, sat on the shore beside him, snoozing in the warm sunshine. The stream was languid and reduced to half its usual force, thanks to the drought they had been facing for the past few months. But it was the only way he could escape the rush of people who were about to descend on his home. You could say one thing in favour of the fish. They didn't talk behind his back. And they did not expect him to utter any inane cliches.

The second son of a second son, he had never expected to inherit the earldom. A peculiar turn of events had landed the title in his lap. Twenty plus years later, the mantle sat heavy on him. Swatting a bee that was buzzing close to his ear, he wondered what life would have been like if his father had never become the earl. Would he still be in India, working in some dusty office for the Raj? Maybe he would be a diplomat, traveling to exotic lands as an emissary of His Majesty.

"What are you thinking about, Nigel?" Ian Lowe, Viscount Cranford, sought his friend's attention. "Shall we head back for lunch, old boy?"

The earl snapped out of his reverie and stared at his friend. The Spanish flu had left him a shadow of his former self but the blue eyes staring back at the earl were full of life. The Viscount put on a brave face and had insisted on accompanying his friend that morning, trying to hide how he struggled to take every breath.

"Mrs. Jones packed a few sandwiches for us."

"Surely you won't deny me a spot of lunch?"

Nigel hesitated. He knew what the Viscount was leaving unsaid. He needed to be on hand to welcome his guests.

"I suppose Bess will be waiting for me, eh, Ian?"

The Viscount leaned on his cane and quirked an eyebrow.

"If I had a daughter like Bess, I would move heaven and earth to see her smile. It's not every day she turns twenty one."

The duo started trudging back to the manor.

"I suppose the time has come to tell her everything." Nigel scratched the day old growth on his face. Clemmie would make a fuss if she saw him like that. "I think Polo agrees." He took the stick the poodle brought him and flung it as far as he could.

"Bess is the most sensible young one I know," Ian reassured him, laughing at the dog's antics. "You don't have a thing to worry about."

Nigel's eyes burned with unshed tears.

"She will hate me for what I did, Ian. What if my own daughter believes I'm a murderer?"

Ian stopped to catch his breath. His chest heaved with effort as he shook his head.

"If you think she hasn't heard the rumours, Nigel, you are deluding yourself."

Chapter 2

Barnes led a stately procession across the lawn, ten minutes before 4 PM. It was the time tea was served at Buxley. The afternoon was hot and the atmosphere stifling in the absence of a breeze. Clementine Barton presided over a table set under a towering oak, swatting a persistent fly that hovered around her.

"Where is the Victoria Sponge, Barnes?" she demanded, making two footmen stumble as they placed trays of sandwiches and scones on a table. "You didn't forget it, did you? Viscount Cranford is partial to it."

"I will bring it out momentarily, my lady." Barnes bowed and dispatched one of the footmen with a sharp nod.

Guests began to trickle down from the house. Clementine's face softened when she spotted her niece, accompanied by one of the Carrington girls. She had just turned eighteen and worshipped Bess.

"I say, Aunt Clem, this is quite a decent spread." Bess popped a cucumber sandwich in her mouth.

Mabel Carrington followed, eager to mimic her actions.

"Girls, girls …" Clementine sighed. "A little decorum, please. When are you going to start acting like proper young ladies?"

Bess managed to smuggle a couple of scones into her skirt pocket.

"How many times have I told you?" she laughed. "Times have changed, Aunt Clem. Women are bolder than before, more assertive."

"We can blame the War for that," Clementine muttered. "Is our way of life really lost, Bess?"

The girls giggled and Bess took a seat next to her aunt.

"Not really. Where do you think I learned to speak my mind, dear aunt?" She placed her arms around the ample woman and gave her a quick hug. "Not from Momo. You are my inspiration."

Clementine smirked. "Momo can't say boo to a goose." She patted her niece on the cheek. "I did my best, my pet. You are the daughter I never had."

Bess knew what her aunt expected her to say in return. She might have obliged a few years ago but the deception the entire family had been part of was fresh in her mind. Despite the abundance of aunts and great aunts in the manor, she had grown up yearning for her mother and it rankled.

"Papa depends on you," she replied. "You know how much he values your advice."

Miles Carrington arrived with a strapping young man at his heels. They proceeded to fill their plates while Clementine poured the tea.

"Who is this, Mr. Carrington?" Bess flashed a smile at the young man. "I don't think we have met."

"Phipps is my secretary," Miles dismissed. "Pay him no heed."

"Gordon Phipps, at your service." The young man bowed.

Bess judged he was just a few years older than her.

"You must know Mabel?" She turned toward her friend and was surprised to see a rosy tint across her cheeks.

Miles didn't look happy. Bess perused Gordon over the rim of her cup. He seemed well mannered but he was trying hard to ignore Mabel, paying particular attention to piling jam on his scone.

"Isn't your brother joining us?" Bess asked Miles.

Mabel leaned forward. "Clara and Uncle Trevor should have been here by now, Papa. Do you think Grandfather has taken a turn for the worse?"

"How is Lord Shelby?" Clementine was concerned. "Mama would like to visit him before …" She didn't complete the sentence. "So would Nigel and I."

Miles waved a hand in the air, shaking his head. "The baron's fine. As fine as he can be, that is. You know how unorganized Trips can be. He must have forgotten they were supposed to be here for lunch."

"He got caught up in some estate business," Gordon Phipps spoke up. "But they will be here for tea."

Barnes cleared his throat.

"That's right, Mr. Carrington. Mr. Trevor telephoned an hour ago. Mr. Phipps talked to him."

Miles did not look pleased. Bess saw him shoot a glare in Gordon's direction.

"What about Nigel?" he asked. "Isn't he joining us for tea?"

"Papa and Viscount Cranford were out fishing this morning," Bess explained. "They are probably dozing in his study."

The sponge cake finally made an appearance and was given full justice. Trevor Carrington arrived with his daughter in tow.

"Clara!" Bess hugged her friend. "We have been waiting for you."

"Mary wanted to come," she laughed. "Papa almost gave in but Nanny put her foot down. Fifteen is too young for a house party."

"You mean a weekend?" Bess laughed. "That's what people our age are calling it now, old bean."

Clementine asked after Trevor's wife.

"Visiting her sister in Bath," he told them. "We expected her yesterday but she decided to stay another week."

"Why am I not surprised, Trips?" Miles drawled. "You have no control over her, do you, old boy?"

Trips pursed his lips but didn't take the bait.

"Where is your wife, Miles?" Clementine asked. "The lovely Rose?"

"Mother has a headache," Mabel answered readily. "She is resting now but hopes to feel better in time for dinner."

Trips gave a hearty laugh. He said nothing but the look he directed toward his brother spoke volumes. Bess had heard about the rivalry between the brothers but this was the first time she was actually witnessing it. She decided to ask Aunt Clem about it later.

"What are you wearing for the party?" Clara asked Bess. "I got a new dress in Chipping Woodbury but it will pale before anything you bought in London."

The girls walked back to the house, arm in arm.

"I just got back from Paris this week," Bess revealed, working the girls in a frenzy. "My boarding school friend introduced me to a designer called Coco Chanel."

Mabel wanted more details.

"Did you get everything? Shoes, hat, bag?"

"And more …" Bess nodded. "Just wait until the party tomorrow night, girls. Everyone is in for a big surprise."

Clara pestered her for more details but Bess was having none of it.

"You will have to be patient. Now how about going for a ride? I can send a message to the stables to get some horses saddled."

They entered the solarium and began the long trek under the glass enclosure that led to a side entrance. Barnes sprang to attention as soon as he saw them.

"Lord Buxley would like to see you in his study, my lady," he informed Bess. "I would not keep him waiting."

"Of course not, Barnes." Bess gave her friends an apologetic look. "Sorry girls. I have to go see what Papa wants."

Mabel decided to skip the ride and Clara agreed with her.

"Maybe tomorrow morning, before breakfast?" Bess promised. "Where have you put them, Barnes?" she turned to the butler.

"The two Miss Carringtons are in the pink room." He gave them a slight bow. "I trust you are comfortable? Just ring for the maid if you need anything."

They giggled and assured him they were fine. Mabel and Clara had visited Buxley Manor since they were little girls and were well acquainted with the staff and the house. Barnes had given them many piggy back rides and looked the other way when they sneaked into the kitchen to beg jam tarts off Mrs. Bird.

"Thank you, Barnes," they chorused before heading for the stairs.

Bess followed the butler down the hall, wondering what her father wanted from her.

"Lady Bess." Barnes opened the door of Nigel's study and announced gravely.

Polo rushed to welcome her, springing up to her knees. Bess picked him up and scratched his ears, sending him into raptures. The little poodle had been a gift on her fourteenth birthday and the two had become inseparable. But Polo transferred his allegiance when Bess ran off to the war.

"Thank you, Barnes." Nigel waved him off. "That will be all."

"Perhaps some tea?" he suggested, looking around, spotting a pot that sat untouched on a side table.

Nigel quirked an eyebrow and looked at Bess.

"Marvellous idea, but we are fine. I can ring if I want something."

Barnes was not pleased but he refrained from saying anything.

Bess flung herself in a chair opposite her father and placed her legs on an arm.

"What ho, pater? I was about to go for a ride with Mabel and Clara."

Nigel fiddled with the ink pot and straightened a few papers on his desk.

"You can go riding tomorrow, Betsy."

Bess sat up straighter and stared at her father.

"I say, is everything alright? You haven't called me that since I turned eight."

Nigel got up and walked to a large hunting scene on the wall. He pressed a hidden button to reveal a safe. Bess watched as he turned the handle clockwise and anticlockwise and unlocked it, pulling out a velvet box.

"Your mother wanted to call you Betsy." Nigel opened the box with a flourish, revealing the box's contents and set it before Bess. "Aunt Cordelia and Clementine insisted we call you Elizabeth."

Bess gasped at the ruby necklace within. It contained a rare pigeon's blood ruby in the centre, framed with diamonds and smaller stones. Polo yipped, cross at losing her attention.

"The king's necklace!" she gushed. "I thought this belongs to Aunt Clem."

Nigel didn't respond immediately. Bess looked up, waiting for his reply.

"It was a gift from the Maharajah of Burma to my grandfather, for saving his life from insurgents. And no, Clemmie never had it. Your Uncle Percy gave it to me when he became earl. I gave it to your mother as a wedding present."

Bess ran a hand over the stones, still in awe.

"So it belongs to me now."

Nigel cleared his throat.

"Err, not quite, my dear. But you can wear it tomorrow for your party."

"But I'm an only child, Papa. Who else can lay claim to this glorious piece of jewellery?" Her eyes twinkled with barely suppressed mirth.

Nigel walked to a window and stared over the grounds.

"There is something I have to tell you the day you

turn twenty one." He took a deep breath. "You must prepare yourself."

"Am I coming into a fortune?" Bess teased. "Come on, Papa. You are not making any sense."

She set the gems aside and walked to the window, taking her father's arm. "You are not sick, are you?"

Nigel sighed deeply.

"I have wronged you, my dear girl. Will you ever forgive your old Papa?"

Bess had a good idea what her father was talking about so his words did not have a big impact on her. She wondered how she would have dealt with the shock had she been completely unaware of Vicky.

"What nonsense! Stop being maudlin right now. We have a house full of guests who expect to be entertained. Where is your stiff upper lip, eh?"

Nigel grabbed her arms and pulled her close, planting a kiss on her head.

"Darling Bess. I remember the day you were born, like it was yesterday. I held you in the crook of my left arm and …"

"I say, that was careless."

"Your mother and I created a trust for you," Nigel told her. "You will come into a tidy amount tomorrow. Enough to say goodbye to this old pile, by Jove."

Bess led him to a chair by the fire and insisted he sit. Polo scurried over and deposited himself at Nigel's feet.

"This old pile is the only home I have known," she reminded him. "I will be happy to spend the rest of my life here."

"I hope not!" Nigel cried. "This place is Bedlam. Sometimes, I can hardly hear myself think."

"If you insist," Bess teased. "Maybe I will go to America. They say it's the land of opportunities."

Nigel turned ashen.

"I met some girls from there during the war, you know," Bess confided. "They crossed an entire ocean to come and help those in need."

"You were equally brave. The whole village is proud of you."

"Fiddlesticks! Are we done here? I have to take a bath before dinner. Drinks at seven in the great hall, Papa."

Nigel told her he was looking forward to it.

"And by the way," Bess turned around and gave a broad wink. "I have a surprise for you too, Papa. Just wait until tomorrow."

Chapter 3

Dawn skirted the horizon, painting it in a faint apricot shade. A cock crowed on the home farm and birdsong filled the air. Bess woke a few seconds before there was a knock on the door and Wilson, her lady's maid, came in with a pot of tea.

"Big day, my lady." She greeted as she opened the curtains to reveal dust motes dancing in the light of the morning sun.

Bess almost flung off the covers before she realized Vicky lay next to her.

"Thank you, Wilson. I say, can I have some coffee? And some eggs, bacon and toast? I'm starving."

Wilson raised her eyebrows.

"Mrs. Bird is laying on a breakfast with all your favourites. They will be expecting you to join them, my lady."

Bess stretched her arms over her head and gave a wide yawn.

"I could eat a horse now, Wilson. I am that hungry.

Maybe I will join the others later?"

Like any good lady's maid, Wilson gave in and promised to return with some sustenance.

Vicky flung off the covers as soon as the door closed and rubbed her eyes.

"You think she suspects?"

"Doesn't matter," Bess grinned. "They will know everything tonight anyway."

"Why do you get to go down and not me?"

Bess's eyes gleamed with mischief.

"Are you suggesting we switch places? That's a rum idea, Vicky. I didn't know you had it in you."

Vicky was scandalized.

"I never said that. They will spot my accent a mile away."

"I dare you."

"No need to," Vicky laughed. "I admit I am a scaredy cat, Bessie. Now how exactly are we going to pull this off tonight?"

There was a knock on the door.

"One minute, Wilson," Bess cried and shooed Vicky behind a screen. "You can come in now."

Wilson entered with a dress slung over her arm, followed by a maid bearing a loaded tray.

"Eggs and bacon, toast and marmalade and some kedgeree. That should get you started, my lady. And coffee, of course."

Bess thanked her and made a show of picking up her knife and fork, her eyes following the maid around the room.

"I pressed your dress for the party," she explained. "It's really beautiful, my lady, although …"

Etta Wilson was only six years older than Bess and had grown up on the Buxley estate. She and Bess had been friends of sorts before they became master and servant.

"You can speak your mind," Bess urged. "Don't you like it? It's all the rage in France."

"A bit ahead of the times, my lady." Wilson cleared her throat. "Are you trying to scandalize the dowagers?"

"Maybe I am," Bess winked. "We are going to shake things up tonight, Wilson."

Wilson wished her luck and warned her to be in her room by five to dress for the party.

Vicky emerged from behind the screen after Wilson left and started buttering her toast.

"What are we going to say, Bess? Should we just tell them how we met? And what if our father refuses to talk to me? He did send me away all those years ago."

"You think too much!" Bess complained. "Imagine the look on their faces! I just want to know how many of them were in on it."

Vicky tapped a spoon on her soft boiled egg and dipped a piece of toast in it.

"I can see that gets your goat, sis. But what if they turn me out?"

Bess's eyes turned to stone. It was the same fierce expression her ancestors had used for generations to rule over their land.

"They wouldn't dare. Anyway, Papa said I will receive my inheritance today. I am going to be a rich woman, my dear. We can get a flat in London and paint the town red."

Vicky's face fell.

"But I came to Buxley for a reason."

Bess munched on a piece of bacon.

"All in good time, old girl."

***

Sir Dorian Ridley attacked the mountain of kedgeree on his plate and took a hearty bite. His once red hair was peppered with grey but the large mutton chop whiskers still boasted a vibrant hue. There was no doubt his girls took after him. His wife Viola sat beside him, crumbling a piece of bread. She was a mousy woman who rarely spoke in company but was plugged into the local gossip. Their daughters Gertrude and Imogen sat on either side of their parents, spreading marmalade on toast.

Miles Carrington and his brother Trevor sat as far away from each other as possible. Clementine Barton presided over the table, watching everyone with a hawk's eye. Viscount Cranford was absent but Gordon Phipps sat alone, working his way through a mound of eggs.

"I say, Nigel." Sir Dorian spoke with his mouth full. "Your cook deserves a bonus for this kedgeree. I cannot get enough of it."

"You can come here for breakfast every day if you want." Lord Buxley was magnanimous. "This is your daughter's home, old boy." He took a bite of his own kedgeree and nodded in approval, slipping a piece of fish to Polo who sat on his feet under the table. "Mrs. Bird is a whiz. She butted heads with the *khansama* when she was younger, you know," he said, referring to the Indian cook who had accompanied his father to England. "But now she makes the best curry in the region."

"Did someone say curry?" Bess strode in, accompanied by the Carrington girls. "I hope there's some kedgeree left for us."

Mabel and Clara were looking a bit dazed. Bess had accompanied them on a morning ride as promised, then scandalized them by riding astride.

"You are looking smart, birthday girl," Gertrude Ridley complimented her jodhpurs. "Is this your way of announcing your independence?"

Bess looked pleased. "Let's get one of these for you too, Bubbles. You don't know what you are missing."

Sir Dorian mumbled under his breath.

"Please don't give her any more crazy ideas. Do you know she wants to get her own flat in London? And do what, pray tell?" He turned toward Nigel. "These girls will be the death of us."

Lord Buxley was lost in thought.

"Papa's a modern thinker, Sir Dorian," Bess stated. "Isn't that right, Momo?" She started loading her plate from the buffet, serving herself a hefty amount of everything. "What ho, Peter?" She sat next to another new arrival, a young man in a sober brown suit and thick horn rimmed glasses. "When did you get here?"

"Just in time for breakfast," he replied. "To be honest, Lady Bess, this is not my kind of thing." He looked around the table with hooded eyes. "The company is quite exalted for the likes of me."

"What a load of rubbish. It is my birthday and you are my guest. And what did I tell you about this lady nonsense?"

Clementine cleared her throat.

"Peter is a well mannered boy who is following all the proprieties. Which is more than I can say for you."

"Come on, Aunt Clem. Our way of life is coming to an end. Admit it."

"Over my dead body," Clementine huffed. "Sir Dorian is right. You girls need an iron hand to whip you in shape."

Gertrude and Bess burst out laughing. Mabel and Clara hesitated for a second before joining in.

"She means a husband," Gertrude chortled. "Better watch out, girls."

Clementine wanted to know how many eligible men had been invited to the party that night.

"You know, the usual crowd," Bess shrugged. "Most of them are idiots, living off their allowances and trust funds. My kind of man will not be cruising from one party to another, Aunt Clem. He will have a purpose in life."

Miles Carrington looked offended. "Do mind what you say, Bess. Mabel and Clara hang on to every word you speak. No daughter of mine will marry a working man."

"What's wrong with earning an honest living?" Gordon Phipps joined the fray. "A self made man is better than one who flits about drinking and gambling, making silly bets."

"Gordy's right," Mabel blurted. "I thought you would appreciate hard work, Papa. Rosehill would never have flourished without your efforts."

Miles sprang to his feet, red in the face.

"You know what your problem is, Nigel? Too

many blasted women about the place. I don't know how you stand it, old man."

Clementine told him to go for a walk in the grounds.

"The staff is busy setting up the ballroom and the caterer's people will arrive soon. I suggest you men go into the village and have lunch at the Buxley Arms."

Sir Dorian was pleased with the idea.

"A pint or two of ale sounds like the perfect way to beat this heat. What do you say, chaps?"

Nigel declared he was going to his study to take care of important business.

"Come along, Peter."

Polo trotted after them.

Chairs scraped and footmen scrambled to clear the table. Barnes came in with a fresh pot of tea and placed it before Bess.

"Coffee is not tea, is it, my lady?"

"A cup of Darjeeling is just what I need now, Barnes." Bess poured the tea and added milk and sugar, a smile lurking at the corner of her mouth.

The servants always knew everything.

***

Ian Lowe, Viscount Cranford, sat in the cosy parlour of Primrose Cottage, sipping broth. Beatrice Gaskins, one of the Dowager Countesses of Buxley, perused him with a frown.

"What kind of doctor do you have at Cranford Hall, Ian? You should see our man while you are here."

"You are such a dear, Bea. But nobody can help me now. It's a wonder I survived so long."

They talked about him going to a resort town like Bath or Harrogate to take the waters. Ian wrinkled his mouth in distaste.

"What a foul idea. I would rather enjoy Nigel's hospitality." He rubbed his hands in anticipation. "You will be there for Elizabeth's party tonight?"

"That girl's running wild. Takes after her mother."

"Come on, Bea, old girl. That's a bit harsh, don't you think? She had a rough time growing up without one."

Beatrice reminded him there had been plenty of feminine influence on offer.

"Nigel spoils her enough. And Momo and Bubbles do their bit. She should have been married with a brood of kids by now."

Ian dissolved into laughter which turned into a violent cough.

"You are so old fashioned. This is 1921. Girls are thinking about careers now."

"What did I say?" Beatrice sniffed with disapproval. "Just like her mother. I hear she sits on the board of some railroad company. How unnatural!"

Ian was surprised. "Does Nigel know this? I thought the family had cut all ties with his wife?"

Beatrice poured a cup of tea for herself and stirred it with a vengeance.

"One hears things." She did not elaborate the source of her knowledge.

Ian dabbed his brow with a snowy handkerchief. The sun streamed through the cottage windows, warming the delicate French furniture. Inspite of the pleasant weather, Beatrice had insisted on lighting a fire. Pink and yellow roses climbed the ivy covered walls of the cottage, creating a picture postcard scene.

"I wish Mabel took after Bess," Ian sighed. "But

she seems intent on getting married at eighteen."

He didn't mention what he suspected or the looks he had seen pass between Mabel and Gordon Phipps. Beatrice would be shocked at the idea of hobnobbing with a secretary. Ian was tired of listening to her caustic remarks.

"She is not your daughter, you know," she taunted. "If only you had listened to me then."

Ian's eyes burned as he remembered Mabel's mother. Marion had been the love of his life but by the time he worked up his courage to declare himself, it was too late. Miles Carrington beat him to the punch.

"My Marion would be alive now." He swallowed a lump. "I am going to avenge her death, Bea, if it's the last thing I do."

Chapter 4

The formal dining room at Buxley Manor sat thirty. Every chair was filled and the table was set to Clementine's precise instructions. Champagne flowed as the canapes were served and guests partook of the caviar and oysters, trying their best to appear nonchalant. Some, like the great aunts Hortense and Perpetua, couldn't stop smiling. Lord Buxley sat at the head of the table, stunned. Among the dowagers, Beatrice wore a sullen expression but Imogen and Grandma Louise, Nigel's mother were tickled pink.

Lady Clementine Barton, self proclaimed hostess, was furious.

A bus full of noisy young people had arrived after tea, full of bonhomie, eager to shake a leg at the party. Bess didn't actually know all of them. There were girls she knew from school, of course. They had brought brothers and cousins. Others had tagged along, lured by the prospect of lavish victuals. Clementine put her foot down and restricted entry to dinner.

"But why, Aunt Clem?" Bess cried. "Surely we

have enough to feed the village?"

"I have been working on these place settings for months," Clementine replied. "Your hooligans are not going to upset it. Be happy I am accommodating a few."

Bess folded her arms, a light dawning in her eyes.

"I see what's going on here. You picked out those who have a title."

Clementine thought she was doing everyone a favour.

"It's bad enough I have to entertain that secretary Miles brought with him. Not to mention Peter Osborne. I will not have any more riffraff at my table. What will Sir Dorian think? Not to mention Viscount Cranford."

"Peter went to Eton with your son," Bess reminded her. "He spent many summers at Buxley. And have you forgotten the Osbornes have served this family for generations?"

Clementine had brushed her off, urging her to get dressed.

"We eat at seven sharp, remember? Your party guests will start arriving at nine."

"What about those who are not allowed to enter the dining room?" Bess persisted. "Are they to eat stew with the servants?"

Clementine told her she had arranged a meal for them at the pub.

"They will get some hearty pie at the Buxley Arms. And there will be plenty more at the party."

Bess went back to her room to dress. She had contrived to get another dress pressed, flustering Wilson in the process.

"I could swear I pressed this in the morning, my lady," she mumbled.

Bess apologized, taking pity on the poor woman.

"I couldn't wait until the evening, I am so excited. So I wore it and strutted around the room, admiring myself in the mirror."

The maid's face softened.

"You are not the only one, my lady. Mrs. Jones is having a hard time controlling all the young maids. They can't stop giggling. And everyone wants a peek at those jazz musicians you hired."

The dress had been pressed again and delivered to Bess.

"Wasn't this a swell idea?" she asked Vicky after Wilson left. "I had to beg and plead with Mademoiselle Chanel to make two of these. Something about each piece being unique."

The girls stared at each other, admiring themselves. Dressed in knee length, sleeveless black frocks studded with sequins, wearing several strands of pearls that came up to their waists, they were poster childs of a new decade. Both sported short bobs, with brown eyes that sparkled as brightly as the rope of diamonds around their heads. They held hands and jumped up and down, unable to control their excitement.

"I say, Bessie, are you sure about this?"

"Of course, old bean. It's time to confront them so you can claim what belongs to you. I am so tired of this beastly subterfuge."

Vicky took a deep breath, coming to a decision.

"Okay then, lead the way, little sis."

They stepped out of the room, hand in hand, running into Wilson. She dropped the basket of sewing she was holding, her eyes growing wide with shock. Bess realized she had also been kept in the dark.

"My lady ..." she sputtered. "But ... how is this ...

who is this, my lady? Are you playing some kind of trick at the party?"

"Not a trick, Wilson." Bess patted her arm. "Ask Barnes. Or Mrs. Jones."

The girls did not encounter any more servants on their way to the dining room. There were no predinner drinks since cocktails would be served at the party later. Bess had hired an expert from a top London club, determined to serve the colourful, frothy libations that were all the rage.

Barnes saw them first. His eyes widened for a split second but his expression remained inscrutable. He gave a deep bow and placed his gloved hand over Vicky's, as if to make sure she was real.

"May I say you are a sight for sore eyes, my lady?" He sighed softly. "Welcome to Buxley Manor. Or should I say, welcome home."

And so it began. Vicky surprised the butler with a hug, proving she was American. Bess walked toward the head of the table, sidestepping Clementine.

"What ho, Papa?" she beamed from ear to ear. "Meet Vicky, my twin. Your other daughter."

Nigel's mouth opened and closed like a fish and his face drained of colour.

"I warned you, Bess," Vicky hissed. "He's going into shock."

Barnes appeared with a snifter of brandy and placed it before Nigel. A bald man with a pencil moustache sprang up from his seat and came around.

"That's excellent thinking, Barnes. Down the hatch, my lord."

Bess picked up the glass and held it to her father's lips. She wondered if she had acted rashly. What if she gained a sister but lost her father?

"Is it apoplexy, Doctor Evans?" She watched him check Nigel's pulse.

Clementine told her to be quiet.

"Have you had your fun?" she snapped. "How could you be so insensitive, Elizabeth?"

Vicky pulled out a chair and sat down next to her father. She squeezed his hand and waited for him to say something, her eyes filling with tears.

"Bbb ... But ... but ... how?" Nigel sounded helpless. "Bessie?"

She sat next to Vicky, feeling an outburst of emotion for her poor parent. This was a scene she had replayed in her mind hundreds of times. How she would rant and rave and accuse her father of separating her from her twin. All the pent up emotions of the past few years dissolved into nothing at the thought of losing him. The moment of triumph she had envisioned never came. Instead, she felt her cheeks grow wet with the stream of tears she had never shed.

"We met at the Somme," she explained. "In 1918."

"1918." Nigel whispered, all his questions loaded in a single word.

"It was a few minutes before three in the morning," Bess continued. "We had just returned from the battlefield and I was holding one end of a stretcher as we transferred the wounded to the nurse's tent."

It had been a bad night for the Allies. Bess had been up for thirty six hours, ready to drop from exhaustion. But so was everyone around her.

"She was cauterizing a man's thigh. I thought I was losing my mind, Papa."

The girls had managed to grab a cup of weak tea an hour later. They talked a bit, remarking on the astounding coincidence, too dazed to think clearly. Vicky got her transfer orders the next day and the Armistice happened a few weeks later. The girls did not meet each other again until they were demobbed and sent home.

One blustery day in the February of 1919, on a snow covered bench in Hyde Park, they had figured out the truth.

"You are a nurse?" Nigel's eyes lingered over Vicky.

"She wants to be a doctor," Bess told him. "Vicky's terribly brave, Papa. She joined the Red Cross and trained to be a nurse."

"You're no milk and water miss," Vicky argued. "You ran away from home at sixteen to become an ambulance driver."

"My dear," Nigel pumped Vicky's hand. "I am happy. Pour the champagne, Barnes," he bellowed. "My little girl is home, where she belongs."

Everyone started speaking at once, fawning over the girls, bombarding them with questions. Bess took Vicky around, introducing her to everyone, starting with their grandmother.

"I hope you have a backbone, Victoria." Louise Gaskins, Dowager Countess, gave her the once over, shooting a glance at Bess. "You are seven minutes older than this minx and you have my permission to pull rank as needed."

The great aunts twittered and blushed but were sincere in their welcome.

"Did your mother send you here for a handout?" Beatrice glared at Vicky, her mouth set in a sneer.

Vicky frowned and let Bess pull her away.

"Aunt Bea loves to be nasty," Gertrude laughed. "One can always trust her to be true to character." She stood up and enveloped Vicky in a hug.

"Hush, Bubbles." Imogen tapped her sister on the shoulder and shook Vicky's hand. "Welcome to Buxley. I say, this is quite a surprise."

Clementine frowned when a footman brought in a chair and placed it near the head of the table, next to Nigel.

"You might have given me some warning, Bess," she muttered, still obsessing over her seating chart.

The soup arrived, a creamy asparagus. Barnes presided over the footmen and the assembled guests finally shifted their attention to the food.

"By Jove!" Nigel exclaimed and laughed loudly, plunging his spoon in the soup. "You know how to shake things up, Bessie."

The conversation picked up over salmon mousse

and Barnes presented roasted duck drizzled with a blood red berry sauce.

"I say, aren't we going to have curry?" Bess exclaimed. "Vicky's dying to taste it."

Clementine rolled her eyes.

"Curry at a formal dinner? Don't be ridiculous."

"But it's our birthday, Aunt Clem," Bess insisted. "And I have never had a birthday celebration without Railway Mutton Curry."

Barnes cleared his throat, giving a barely perceptible nod. One of the footmen rushed to clear the dishes before Vicky and Bess. He returned with a platter heaped with saffron scented rice and a bowl of curry.

"I am having some of that." Nigel chose to be assertive after two decades and avoided looking at his sister.

Bess insisted on loading their plates. Vicky took a tentative bite and pronounced it was delicious.

Viscount Cranford raised his glass and proposed a toast. People around the table joined in.

"Your father never stopped thinking of you, my dear." He patted Vicky on the arm. "You make him proud."

Miles Carrington cut in.

"Just keep her away from my brood, Nigel. One wanton daughter is bad enough. I don't want this American anywhere near my Mabel."

Lord Buxley placed his napkin on the table and stood up.

"You will not sit at my table and insult my children, Miles."

Grandma Louise sprang to her feet and began clapping loudly. There was a flurry of activity as all the men at the table scrambled to join her.

"But we haven't finished dinner yet," Clementine cried. "Stop this tantrum at once, Nigel."

Bess and Vicky sidled close to their father, each taking one of his arms. Guests were beginning to look confused, not sure what to do next.

Louise, Dowager Countess, had the last word.

"You never knew when to shut up, Clem. Take the ladies into the great hall. Barnes can serve the cheese and fruit there. I presume the girls will cut their birthday cake in the ballroom so there is no need to serve dessert now."

She pointed a finger at Miles.

"If you had a shred of sense, you would let Mabel learn a thing or two from Bess, you ninnyhammer. Stop being in high dudgeon, drink your port and start acting like a second son."

Nobody dared to cross her. There was an exodus as the ladies left the dining room and the men began lighting their pipes and cigars.

"She's magnificent!" Vicky gushed as the twins made sure their father was fine and left the room. "I envy you, Bess."

"Isn't she the leopard's spots?" Grandma Louise encouraged me to join the war effort." Bess stopped at the door and turned around to shoot a glare at Miles Carrington. "She doesn't suffer fools gladly."

Chapter 5

Champagne flowed and the brassy sounds of the jazz band Bess had hired echoed through the cavernous ball room at Buxley Manor. Another bus load of twenty somethings had arrived as the sun went down over the woods, dressed to the nines in bright colours. They proceeded to the dance floor and started shaking their limbs in wild abandon, partaking of champagne and cocktails at an astonishing speed.

Several families from the region had been invited for the birthday party, although Clementine insisted on calling it a ball. They arrived with their young daughters in tow, expecting pre-war Edwardian grandeur, completely unprepared for the modern scene that met them. The looks on their faces were comical. Many of them had only read about such debauchery in the newspaper. Clementine stood by, helpless, as they gathered their debutantes and left in a huff.

"You have ruined my reputation," she wailed. "And your own. Who will marry you now, Elizabeth?"

Nigel danced arm in arm with his two daughters, having the time of his life.

"Put a sock in it, will you Clem? And stop being so beastly."

"I'm warning you, Nigel!" she stalked off without a word.

Bess ignored her aunt and tried to greet every guest. Many faces were familiar but she did not know everyone. That meant the party was a success.

"Try one of these cocktails, Papa?" she steered them to the two bartenders who were trying to keep up with the demand. "How about a Sidecar? Or a Hanky Panky?"

"Now, now, old bean." Nigel laughed. "Are you trying to scandalize your poor father?"

"Relax, Papa," Bess laughed. "It's mostly gin or brandy with a few more liqueurs or sirops thrown in."

Waiters moved around, carrying trays loaded with canapes of shrimp and salmon in mayonnaise, tartlets of onion and game, hearty sandwiches of fish paste or ham and much more. Buffet tables had been set up with platters of cheese and fruit and dainty cakes and pastries. In case anyone was still hungry, there were a few pies of chicken and veal and a joint of roast beef.

Mabel waved at them, trying to imitate a young man in a gold jacket with hair curling around his neck.

"Bess, who is that hirsute boy the Carrington girl is with?" Nigel inquired.

"Curtis Pierpont," she supplied readily. "Marquess of Turnbridge."

"What? Miles can't complain, can he?" He sipped the drink Vicky handed him and excused himself. "You don't want an old fogey spoiling all your fun, girls."

Vicky watched his receding back with a look of longing. A small part of her wondered when they would meet again.

"You will see him for breakfast tomorrow," Bess replied.

The sisters had an uncanny ability of reading each others' thoughts.

"How is he taking it?" Vicky wanted to know.

Bess paused before replying. "Papa has always pampered me, looked the other way when I threw a tantrum or gave Aunt Clem a hard time. He indulged me more than people of his class, took me riding and fishing. But I felt like he was a new person tonight."

"How so?" Vicky's eyes were full of hope.

"Did you not see how happy he was? It's like a part of him was missing and he found it now."

Barnes appeared at her shoulder.

"Ten minutes to midnight, my lady."

Bess clapped her hands.

"Time for the fireworks? Jolly good, Barnes. Start nudging them towards the terrace."

Vicky suggested giving the band a break, waving a hand at the hopping milieu.

"That's the only way to get their attention."

Barnes dispatched a footman to convey the message.

"What about Papa and the aunts and dowagers?" Bess wanted to know. "And the rest of our guests?"

Barnes told her the men were busy playing cards in

the library. One of the dowagers had left long ago. But the oldest was in the parlour with the youngest, chatting with the other guests.

"Bubbles is right here, dancing with that scrawny boy who Lord Ashford knows from Oxford." Bess waved at Gertrude. "The fireworks should not take more than fifteen minutes. Start herding everyone to the buffet after that, Barnes. And the servants do not have to stay up. Tell Mrs. Jones she can clean up here tomorrow."

"Are you sure, my lady?" Barnes frowned.

"This lot will hang around as long as there is a drop of alcohol to be drunk," Bess laughed. "No telling when they will leave, Barnes."

The music stopped and one of the men from the band told everyone to head to the terrace. After a burst of protest, the crowd shuffled to the French doors that had been thrown open.

"I say," one of the men complained. "What's the bally idea?"

Bubbles came over, slightly out of breath, looking several years younger in a trendy red frock and ropes of shiny beads.

"Why aren't you dancing, Bess? This jazz band is the cat's meow. When I get my flat in London, I'm going to a club every night."

The word about the impending fireworks had spread through the crowd. People began lining the stone balustrade, eager to grab front row seats.

"You can count on the toffs to put on a good show," a voice declared. "What a terrible waste, though."

"Shut up," another reprimanded. "Your uncle gives you an allowance, old man. You haven't worked a day in your life."

Bess and Vicky let Gertrude lean on them, almost dragging her outside.

"You weigh a ton, Bubbles," Bess moaned. "Lay off the pudding for a bit, will you?"

"I say, what the deuce …" the voice from earlier exclaimed.

Someone struck a match, dropping it with a curse. A couple of girls screamed, then mass hysteria ensued.

"Was that Mabel?" Bess freed herself from Gertrude's vice like grip and looked around, bewildered. "What's going on?"

The crowd began pushing. Vicky cried out in pain

as someone trod on her foot. Barnes appeared as if by magic, accompanied by two footmen.

"This way, my lady."

Fireworks exploded in the sky, illuminating the terrace for a split second.

Another woman screamed and a few more joined in, reluctant to be left out.

"By Jove, Bess!" A man exclaimed. "This is spiffing."

Vicky had spotted a shape on the floor and she rushed toward it, propelled by a sixth sense. Her experience on the battlefield kicked in and she fell to her knees when her feet struck the object, groping in the dark while hoping she was wrong. Was it some kind of gag for the party? The newspapers were full of the antics of the idle rich.

Once she determined what lay before her was human, helped by momentary flashes of light from the fireworks, she looked for a pulse. Her hand touched something warm and a metallic smell that was a bit too familiar surrounded her.

"Bess," she opened her mouth to cry out but barely managed a whisper.

A comforting hand landed on her shoulder.

"I'm right here with Barnes."

The fireworks stopped as suddenly as they had begun. Three footmen cordoned off the body and they waited for the people to go back in. Some opted to stay out in the fresh air. Bess put two fingers in her mouth and let out a piercing whistle, a trick a farm worker from Wales had taught her during the war.

"Supper in the ball room," she announced.

That spurred some of them on.

"Do we know who it is?" Vicky asked.

"In a moment, my lady," Barnes replied.

The terrace was almost empty when a maid arrived with a torch.

Bess gasped while Barnes belied years of training and swore under his breath.

"Mr. Miles Carrington," he said softly. "We must telephone the constable."

One of the footmen returned with Dr. Evans who had been about to leave. He shook his head, confirming Vicky's verdict.

"Get some smelling salts for the ladies, Barnes, " he

ordered. "And send someone for the constable."

"I was about to go and telephone, Sir," Barnes replied. "Will you stay here with the ladies?"

He didn't wait for an answer.

"We are not going to swoon, Dr. Evans," Vicky bristled. "You can rest assured."

"I forgot you have seen worse than this," he replied. "But those men on the battlefield were strangers, my dear."

Unlike the man lying cold before them, Bess realized. She had known Miles Carrington all her life. He was a bit old fashioned in his views but so were most men of his class and generation. Bess had spent a lot of time at Rosehill, the estate he had acquired through sheer hard work, inspite of being a second son.

"What's going on, Bess?" Mabel's voice bore into her, a bit uncertain. "Who is this?"

Bess stared back at her, speechless. Mabel clung to the Marquess who had somehow lost his jacket in the milieu. He was two sheets to the wind but he sobered up quickly, reading the situation.

Vicky took Mabel's arm and gently nudged her toward the ballroom.

"Why don't you get some food before it's gone?"

Mabel brushed her off, taking a closer look at the body on the floor.

"Wait a minute, what are you trying to hide, Bess?" She huddled closer to the Marquess. He placed an arm around her shoulder, holding her in a vice like grip. "Is that what I stumbled against?" She noticed the doctor for the first time. "And Dr. Evans ... looks like one of your guests is sick."

"Too much champagne, probably. Some blokes don't know their limits. Why don't we go in, darling?"

Mabel seemed trapped, her wide eyes darting over the form on the floor, taking in every detail. Her curious nature had often landed her in trouble, being sent to bed without pudding when she was in the nursery. It was a trait that lasted through adolescence, despite having a tyrant like Miles for a father.

Bess felt warm, longing for a breeze, however gentle. The summer night was stifling, the prolonged drought raising night temperatures more than usual.

The hastily thrown blanket covered most of the body but Mabel's gaze landed on an exposed bit, a silk cravat with a loud paisley pattern.

"Wait, is that ..."

Before anyone realized what was happening, she tore herself from the Marquess's grip and lunged forward, pulling the blanket off the body.

The scream that followed was almost feral. Bess and Vicky sidled close, watching Mabel's eyes turn wild and helpless in quick succession before she fainted, collapsing on her father's chest.

***

Nigel paced before the fireplace in the great hall, muttering to himself. All the guests who were staying at the manor sat in clusters, wide awake at one in the morning, exhibiting a variety of emotions, sipping tea or brandy. The servants had been about to retire after a hard day when news of the body on the terrace spread like wildfire.

Before Clementine could ring for refreshments, Barnes arrived with several pots of tea and coffee, with platters of sandwiches and fruitcake.

Beatrice had not wasted any time partaking of the food, unaware of Grandma Louise's steely gaze. Bess and Vicky entered hand in hand, along with Dr. Evans. All eyes in the room swivelled towards them.

"Well?" Clementine snapped. "Don't just stand there, girls." She began pouring two cups of tea.

"Vicky prefers coffee," Bess reminded her.

"A shot of brandy wouldn't go amiss," Viscount Cranford told Clementine. "They have had a rude shock." His eyes were full of admiration. "I am surprised you are still standing, girls." Then his face fell and he asked after Mabel. "How is she taking all this?"

"We insisted she go to bed," Bess explained. "Dr. Evans gave her a sedative."

Nigel wanted to know if the police were there yet.

"Why do we need to involve the police, Nigel?" Clementine pursed her mouth. "Buxley does not need another scandal."

"I want to do everything by the book." Nigel was firm. "They will ask a few questions and go away."

"You had an altercation with the dead man," Clementine reminded him. "Are you going to tell them that?"

Louise told them to be quiet and stop squabbling like children. She nodded at the girls to continue.

"Constable Potts has arrived," Bess informed them.

"What happened to Miles, Doctor?" Louise plunged forth with the question on top of their minds. "He was fine at dinner. I suppose a life of dissipation caught up with him?"

After the girls pulled Mabel from the body and carried her inside, two more footmen had arrived with more torches, bathing the body in bright light. Dr. Evans had performed a cursory examination.

"The cause of death is clear, my lady. Miles Carrington was stabbed."

Chapter 6

Breakfast was late the next morning. Clementine had chosen to have hers in bed, so had Imogen. Mabel had been fast asleep when Bess looked in on her. Clara was keeping her company.

Bess, Vicky and Gertrude sat next to each other at the table, facing Sir Dorian, Trevor Carrington and Nigel. None of them had slept much the previous night.

"My poor brother," Trevor sighed, stirring his bowl of porridge. "Father is going to be devastated. He was the favourite."

Since almost everyone in the area knew Lord Shelby was partial to Miles, nobody said anything.

"We are going home to Ridley Hall after breakfast," Sir Dorian announced. "You better come with us, Gertrude."

"Come on, Father, is that necessary?" She took a bite of liberally buttered toast. "Momo needs me here."

Gertrude had virtually lived at Buxley since as far

back as Bess remembered.

"This is her home too, Dorian," Nigel murmured, breaking a biscuit in two and tossing a piece to Polo who sat by his chair. "But your father is right, Bubbles. Why don't you go to Ridley Hall today? You can always come back in a day or two. Bess will pick you up in the motor."

Rather than pacify Gertrude, the suggestion seemed to rile her up.

"I would be more independent if I had my own car," she glared at Sir Dorian. "I do not like having to ask you for the Rolls every time I want to go somewhere."

"We can discuss all that when we get home." Sir Dorian dismissed. "Tell your mother to be ready in an hour. I want to be home in time for luncheon."

It took a mere twenty minutes to reach Ridley Hall by car. Bess wondered why Sir Dorian was so anxious to leave. He answered her question.

"Let me tell you, Nigel. I want nothing to do with this rotten business. I have half a mind to take Imogen with me too."

Lord Buxley flung his hands up in despair.

"You think I chose this? Momo can do what she

wants, Dorian. The women in my family have free will."

Trevor came to his rescue.

"I am sure Miles did not want to die, here or anywhere else. Cut Nigel some slack, Sir Dorian."

Bess scowled at the man and changed the subject.

"Are you going fishing again, Papa? It's a fine day with not a cloud in the sky."

Nigel mumbled he might as well and asked about their plans.

"I am going to show Vicky around."

"This is some welcome, eh?" Nigel asked Vicky. "I am sorry, dear child."

Vicky told him she was fine.

"Give Mrs. Jones a list of what you like to eat," he urged. "And we should get a room ready for you."

Barnes cleared his throat.

"The maids are airing out the chamber next to Lady Bess, my Lord. It should be ready later today."

"Jolly good, jolly good," Nigel approved. "You

think of everything, Barnes."

Bess led Vicky out of the breakfast room, choosing a corridor she hadn't noticed before.

"The great aunts live in the west wing, along with Papa," she explained. "They rarely leave their quarters. Yesterday was an exception."

"These are our father's aunts?" Vicky asked.

"Grandfather's sisters," Bess nodded. "They never married. But don't be fooled by their Victorian manners. They were both trailblazers in their time."

Aunt Hortense was an expert horsewoman and had loved a good hunt. Perpetua had talked her father into starting a school for the village children.

The two ladies were overjoyed when Bess entered the small parlour that connected their bed chambers.

"You came!" they cried in unison.

Dressed in dark lavender, their snowy hair piled in identical buns on top of their heads, a diamond encrusted brooch at their throats, the two aunts were similar in appearance.

"Are you twins too?" Vicky was curious.

"Oh no," Hortense corrected her. "I am older by two years. Richard came before Perpetua but he died when he was five."

She rang a bell and a maid who looked as ancient as them appeared almost immediately.

"Can we have tea, please?"

The woman gave a small curtsy and went out.

"How is your dear mother?" Perpetua asked Vicky. "Hortense and I were very fond of her. Nigel chose well."

Vicky tried to hide her surprise. She had been trying to think of a way to bring up her mother but the aunts had beaten her to it.

"She was a fine woman," Hortense nodded. "Now that Beatrice … she has a black heart. I would stay away from her."

The tea arrived, accompanied by two types of cake. Hortense insisted on pouring.

"Now what's this I hear about you not liking tea?" she asked Vicky. "You are not British unless you enjoy a strong cuppa."

"But she's not, is she?" Bess quipped. "Now if Vicky had grown up at Buxley, things might have been different."

The two aunts looked at each other and a silent message passed between them.

"I know what you're angling for, Bessie, you scamp," Perpetua laughed. "But it's not our story to tell."

"What if I hadn't run into Vicky in France?" she inquired. "Was anyone ever going to tell me I had a twin?"

The aunts grew tense. Perpetua patted her sister's knee and tried to explain.

"We don't know what happened then, girls. But your parents came to an understanding. I think Nigel planned to tell you everything on your twenty first birthday …"

"But you beat him to it," Hortense laughed. "We did warn him. If he hadn't spoken up yesterday, we would have told you ourselves."

The girls stayed until every crumb of cake had been eaten.

"You are not planning to go haring off to London, are you?" Hortense asked as they said goodbye, promising to come back soon. "Your father needs you, girls. Troubled waters lie ahead."

"Can you be any more cryptic?" Bess complained. "Does this have anything to do with Miles Carrington?"

"Why did he have to die here?" Perpetua cried. "If you ask me, tongues are already wagging in the village."

She refused to say anything more.

"What was that about?" Vicky asked when they left the west wing and emerged in the bright sunshine through a side door.

"No idea," Bess shrugged. "You saw Constable Potts, didn't you? Chances are, we will never find out what happened to Miles."

Vicky admitted the local constable had not inspired much confidence. He was probably good at following orders and going by the book but could not be expected to take initiative.

The girls walked to the village, Bess playing tour guide. The Buxley Arms was going to be their first stop that day.

"Wait till you taste the ale, Vicky," she enthused. "It's the best in the area."

"Shouldn't you be drinking claret and champagne, being a high born lady?" Vicky teased. "What will

Aunt Clem say?"

"We are both born with a title, old thing. That doesn't mean we can't live a little. A pint of ale at the pub is the perfect way to connect with the tenants. And what Aunt Clem does not know won't hurt her."

The pub was filling up with the lunch crowd. Bess led them to the bar and greeted the proprietor.

"Good day Mr. Harvey."

Engrossed in polishing a glass, he began to respond, then looked up when he recognized her voice. He almost did a double take when he saw Vicky.

"Blimey, so it's true. Little Lady Victoria has come home."

The butcher's lad had received the big news from the scullery maid that morning and had taken great pleasure in spreading the word in the village.

"You knew about her?" Bess slammed her fist on the bar. "Was I the only one who was kept in the dark?"

Vicky placed a hand on her arm.

"So was I, sweetheart."

Harvey scratched his ear, looking sheepish.

"It wasn't our place, your ladyship. We was under strict orders, like."

Vicky flashed a smile and asked about the ale.

"Why don't you bring us a pint each?"

A rosy cheeked woman of generous proportions came out of the kitchen, followed by a young maid hefting a loaded tray.

"Be careful now, girl," she cautioned. "Don't you go dropping any of that."

"Mrs. Harvey, I presume?" Vicky smiled. "Bess has told me a lot about your cottage pie."

The woman's eyes flew up, noticing the twins for the first time.

"Praise the Lord, Mr. Harvey. Is this who I think it is?" She gave an awkward curtsey. "Your ladyship, how lovely to meet you."

Vicky asked for a slice of the famous cottage pie, flustering the woman further. The maid Flora was dispatched to bring two slices, topped with gravy.

"Lord Buxley bought a round for the whole village when you was born," Mr. Harvey beamed. "He was that proud. What do I need an heir for, Harvey? he says to me. I am blessed with two princesses and no man could ask for more."

Not willing to be left behind, Mrs. Harvey added her two pennies.

"Your mother was the kindest of that lot at the manor. Never put on airs and graces like some people we know."

The crowd swelled and some of the more adventurous men came up to the bar to gawk at the girls, cap in hand. Bess greeted them and asked after their families. They mumbled a few words, bobbed their heads and went back to their seats.

"I think we should go now." Vicky stood up after the pie was eaten and the bread and butter pudding had been tasted.

The scorching sun towered above their heads, making them sweat. Vicky was glad Wilson had insisted they wear hats.

"What next?" she asked Bess. "Although I would rather take a nap in a dark room right about now."

"What about Grandma Louise?" Bess asked. "We might get some answers at the Dower House."

Vicky wasn't too sure. Everywhere they went,

people had welcomed her but they had provided little or no information about anything in her past. It was as if they were under strict orders to say nothing.

"I think we have been patient long enough, Bess. The time has come to ask some tough questions. That's what I am here for, after all."

"You mean go straight to the horse's mouth?" Bess puckered her mouth, quirking an eyebrow. "Papa will have to tell all."

Vicky looked uncertain. She did not want to start her relationship with her father on the wrong foot. But a lot of time had passed since she learned the truth about her birth.

When the girls met in London after the war, Bess had wanted to confront Nigel immediately. Vicky held her back. She wanted to go home to America and talk to her mother face to face, tell her about her decision to study medicine. Although raised to be independent and voice her opinions, she had been groomed to take over the family business. Her mother had been planning her debutante ball when Vicky declared she wanted to travel across the ocean and join the war effort in Europe. Her mother was disappointed but relented when Vicky promised to come home in two years. The timeline had stretched a bit and now it was time to go back and do her duty.

"I want you home at Buxley Manor," Bess had argued. "It's your rightful place, Vicky."

"Let's hold off for now. We can write letters in the meantime."

The Spanish Flu pandemic had further delayed their plans.

"What if he refuses to say anything, Bess?"

"Then we go to America and confront our mother."

Chapter 7

Barnes sat in his office, staring at the footman who stood before him, hopping from one foot to another.

"Think before you speak, John."

"I know what I heard, Mr. Barnes. Them was at each other's throats, they was."

Barnes wished he could fortify himself with some port. The manor had not recovered from the big party, not to mention the unexpected death that had occurred at night. The young ones from London, most of them uninvited guests, had finally departed. Cook was busy preparing lunch, not looking very pleased. The maids had been giggling and gossiping all day, talking about the twins, the party and the body on the terrace. Mrs. Jones had given up trying to reprimand them and was sulking in her office with a headache. To make matters worse, one of the footmen had requested a meeting with him, insisting it couldn't wait.

"Did you actually see this?" Barnes rubbed the spot between his eyes. "Tell me what happened, without any embellishments, please."

"I was walking by the library door, see?" John leaned against the table, towering over the butler. "There was raised voices."

Barnes told the footman he might as well sit.

"Is that all? Did you actually hear what they said? And what were you doing outside the library, John?"

There was no right answer to this question. Barnes and Mrs. Jones knew the footman liked to roam around the house, chatting up the maids. He had to be prodded to perform his duties.

"Lord Buxley told Mr. Carrington he had to mend his ways or he was going to be in trouble one of these days."

"How can you be sure he was talking to Mr. Miles?" Barnes shot back.

"I knows his voice, Mr. Barnes. Mr. Miles guffawed in that hearty manner of his and said don't be a fool Nigel."

Barnes cleared his throat, raising a stern eyebrow. The footman realized his mistake and reddened, rushing over his next words.

"Lord Buxley must have spoken very softly because I didn't hear what he said next. But there was some kind of scuffle. I heard something shatter, Mr. Barnes."

A ceramic vase with daisies painted on its uneven surface had been found in pieces and a suit of armour had toppled over. Barnes had noticed it when he inspected all the rooms before the party and had asked one of the maids to sweep up the debris. Had the garrulous footman learned about this from the maid?

"You better not be making this up, John." He paused, allowing his underling a chance to come clean. "Did you go in to see what happened?"

"Of course not!" John sprang to his feet, scandalized. "I hotfooted it right away, before one of them came out that door."

Barnes wet his lips, yearning for his port again.

"You are not to listen at doors, John. I am going to dock your pay so you don't make the same mistake again."

The footman was unfazed, eager to get something off his chest.

"I say, Mr. Barnes, what if Lord Buxley decided to silence him? He stabbed that Mr. Carrington before he blabbed to the new miss."

Barnes did not mince words.

"You are talking nonsense, man. Why would my lord do anything so crazy."

"That's what I was trying to tell you, Mr. Barnes," John beamed. "Mr. Miles told his lordship they both knew what happened all those years ago. He was going to find Lady Bess and tell her about it."

***

Beatrice toyed with the chicken on her plate, biding her time until dessert. She was visiting Louise at the Dower House. The two women did not rub well together on the best of days. Both were Dowager Countesses but Louise had the upper hand, being the older one.

"Something wrong with your food?" Louise sat back as her man cleared their plates.

"I can't stop thinking of Rose Carrington, Mama," Beatrice clucked. "One more widow joins our ranks."

Louise said nothing. Her daughter-in-law never visited her unless she wanted something.

"Poor Miles!" Beatrice ventured again, hoping to

elicit a comment from the older woman. "Some would say he had it coming."

The footman returned and placed two strawberry tarts before them, topped with fresh cream. Louise took a bite and savoured the dish, making Beatrice squirm.

"Are you saying Miles deserved to die?" she boomed. "Stop beating around the bush and come to the point."

Beatrice backed down. "You must be happy to see Victoria."

"Hmmm. Of course I am. Nigel has wasted enough time. I was prepared to take matters in hand. Had a letter ready to be dispatched to Annie."

"At least the girl's rid of that woman's influence. It will take some time to turn her into a proper young lady."

"That woman is my son's wife, just as you are," Louise warned. "She needs to come and take her rightful place at Buxley Manor."

Beatrice grew alarmed.

"Are you sure about that, Mama? That woman left a trail of broken hearts and bodies behind her. Now her daughter's doing the same."

Louise stood up and headed to the parlour.

"Rubbish! Do you ever think before you speak, my dear?"

Beatrice sat at the edge of her chair, bathed in a sunbeam streaming in from an open window. Flowers bloomed in the garden of the Dower House, a riot of colour on the warm summer day. The footman arrived with the tea tray and left after making sure they had everything.

"Annie didn't exactly have a sterling character, Mama. She had a fling with Miles Carrington."

"Poppycock!" Louise exclaimed. "Annie and Nigel were besotted with each other."

Bea's lips curved in a smile.

"My Philip caught them by the brook and signed his death warrant."

Louise said nothing but her cheeks had grown pink. She had to summon every ounce of restraint to let Beatrice continue.

"That's why Nigel silenced him." She pulled out a handkerchief and dabbed at her dry eyes. "My poor boy! Squashed like a bug in his youth. And the same thing's happening now, of course."

"Do tell," Louise prompted.

"I heard Miles talking to that American girl, asking after Annie. Nigel killed him before he could say more."

Louise stirred her tea, trying to control her emotions.

"So you are saying that my son goes around killing people who displease him?"

"What man likes to be cuckolded, Mama? Nigel will be a laughing stock if people found out his wife was having an affair with his neighbour. If it hadn't been for Philip, I would almost understand."

Louise Gaskins had complete faith in her son. He was an upstanding, moral man who had suffered for a crime he did not commit, thanks to the venom spread by people like Beatrice.

"You should get your story straight, my dear. All these years, you have maintained he killed Philip because he wanted the earldom. Now you are saying it was over some silly affair that probably never happened."

"But Mama …"

"Why don't you go visit your sister in Brighton? And when you come back in the autumn, you might find Primrose Cottage has been let."

***

Harvey poured pint after pint, unable to stem the gossip flowing around him. It had been that way twenty years ago, when young Lord Philip had met a sticky end.

"Mr. Carrington was a good man," a burly man with thick arms and a scraggly red beard peppered with grey nodded. "Look what wonders he worked at Rosehill."

Men around him murmured in assent. Miles was a gentleman but he hadn't been averse to rolling up his sleeves and working side by side in the fields when needed.

"You are saying Lord Buxley isn't?" Harvey cut in. "For shame, Ezra. You forgot what he did when your Ma was sick with the flu."

Ezra seemed chastened for a minute. Then he took another long swallow of his ale and regained his spirit.

"That does not mean he can murder people, Harvey. Where does it end, eh? You and I could be next."

A hush fell over the group. One of the younger

men dared to refute this statement.

"You touched in the head, Ezra? Lord Buxley would not hurt a fly."

Harvey banged a fist on the table, gaining their attention.

"Exactly! Why would my lord kill Mr. Carrington? They been friends for years and the little misses walk around town, arm in arm."

Ezra was not ready to give up easily.

"That Miles musta' seen something all those years ago. I say he had proof of what happened to Lord Philip."

"And why was he quiet all these years?" Harvey demanded. "Why open his mouth now?"

Ezra drained his mug of ale, looking belligerent.

"I ain't got all answers, Harvey. But I knows what I knows."

"Which is nothing!" The young buck chortled and got a slap on the head from another burly man.

An old man had been sitting quietly at the bar, working on a thick mutton stew. He pushed his plate away, wiped his mouth on his sleeve and joined the discussion.

"Don't ya forget one thing, young Harvey. Ain't no smoke without fire."

Ezra pointed a finger at the man, looking redeemed. "Old Jim should know. He's seen a few more summers than the rest of us."

Mrs. Harvey bustled outside, carrying a plate of pudding. She slammed it before Old Jim, looking mutinous.

"That don't make him any smarter, Ezra. What is all this nonsense you is going on about?"

Some of the crowd dissipated, the men returning to their tables. Most of them did not want to get on the wrong side of Mrs. Harvey. She could easily deny them pie and ale.

Ezra stuck to his guns.

"This is what happened last time. Nobody had the gumption to stand up against his lordship so he got away Scot free."

Mrs. Harvey reminded him of his five children under the age of ten and the baby in the cradle. How would he feed them if he was turned out of Buxley?

"That's a threat," Ezra mumbled under his breath, having lost most of his steam. "I ain't staying quiet this time, you mark my words."

***

Vicky and Bess ran into Beatrice at the Dower House.

"Aunt Bea, fancy seeing you here!" Bess exclaimed.

Beatrice sniffed in disapproval and stalked out without a word.

Louise sat in her parlour, her expression stony, a faraway look in her eyes. The tea in her hand had grown cold long ago.

"Why is Aunt Bea in a tizzy, Grandma?" Bess asked when they joined her. "Sorry we're late."

Louise took Vicky's hand and urged her to sit beside her.

"Is she your new favourite?" Bess quipped. "I suppose you won't spare me a glance now, Grandma."

"Hush, Bess." Louise cupped Vicky's face and planted a kiss on her forehead. "It warms my heart to see you back home, child."

Vicky wrapped the old woman in a hug.

"That's the American in me," she joked. "We are nothing if not expressive."

"You remind me of your mother. How is dear Annie? She has been sorely missed."

"She doesn't know I'm here," Vicky confessed.

Bess rang for more tea. She had spent a lot of time with her grandmother and guessed she was barely holding it together.

"What's the matter, Grandma?" she asked. "Did Aunt Bea say something to upset you?"

Louise grew pale, looking her age.

"She never forgave your father for becoming the earl. Bea will use Miles Carrington's death to her advantage."

Bess told her to stop talking in riddles.

"Does she blame Papa for Philip's death?"

"That's it, in a nutshell, my dears. She always has."

"But why?" Bess cried as Vicky frowned, trying to follow the conversation. "And how was I never told about this?"

Chapter 8

Bess and Vicky stormed out of the Dower House, refusing to drink a single drop of tea. Louise had refused to elaborate on her cryptic comments. The girls decided there was only one course of action left to them.

The sun was unforgiving, making them sweat as they began the long trek to the manor.

"I thought English summers were mild," Vicky sighed. "This is as bad as New York, except there is no beach nearby."

Bess told her they were having some exceptionally harsh weather.

"I hope Papa's back home. He tends to lose track of time when he goes fishing."

Barnes greeted them and asked if they needed anything.

"Mrs. Bird made ham and egg sandwiches and a green salad with tomatoes."

The girls decided to fortify themselves before

confronting their father. Bess led Vicky to the breakfast room, hoping it would be empty.

"Most of the guests should be gone by now, since we are late."

Barnes returned with a footman carrying a loaded tray and made sure they had everything they needed.

"What happened to the, err …" Bess stuttered. "Where is Mr. Miles now?"

The coroner had arrived and taken him away. Mabel had not surfaced from her room and Clara was keeping an eye on her. Trips Carrington had gone home, burdened with the difficult task of breaking the news to his sick father.

"Is Papa back yet?" Bess popped a tiny ham sandwich in her mouth and glared at Barnes. "We're going to his study now."

Barnes cleared his throat, looking uncomfortable.

"His lordship does not want to be disturbed."

The girls shared a look and nodded grimly.

"Papa has been quiet long enough," Bess vowed. "We need answers, Barnes, and we are going to get them today."

Barnes secretly admired her. After all, he had carried her around on his shoulders when she was a child and looked the other way when she left the manor in the middle of the night at the age of sixteen, convinced she wanted to play a part in the war. This was the same girl who had not worried about her own life when she nursed the tenants on the estate during the Spanish flu pandemic. If there was anyone who could take matters in hand now, it was Lady Bess.

"As you wish, my lady." He bowed and glided out.

The library seemed deserted but Bess stalked to a sofa facing some bay windows and found her father sprawled across it, snoring lightly in tandem with Polo. She shook his shoulder and stood her ground.

"Papa, wake up."

Nigel opened his eyes and sprang up, looking around him in bewilderment.

"What, eh? What? What?"

"It's just us, Papa."

Bess sat at the edge of the sofa and Vicky pulled herself up to sit on the window ledge. Polo stirred, gave a moan and closed his eyes again.

"Oh good," Nigel smiled, yawning deeply. "What about a spot of tea, eh?"

"Tea can wait." Bess was firm. "You need to answer some questions first."

Their father's eyes darted between the two of them. He still couldn't believe both his girls were right there, living under his roof.

"Vicky, my dear, I'm so happy you're here."

She smiled but said nothing.

"We want to know why," Bess began. "Why did you never tell me my mother was alive, Papa?" Her chest heaved as she took a deep breath. "Do you have any idea what it's like to grow up without a mother?"

"We never said she was dead," Nigel defended himself.

"And what about me?" Vicky burst out. "How could you separate us? Think of the years we wasted, growing up alone, not knowing there was a sister who had the same set of parents?"

"That was the deal, you see." His face fell. "I promised Annie I would not say a word until Bess here was twenty one."

"Were you going to?" Vicky quizzed. "What if I hadn't come here yesterday, would you still have told Bess about me?"

Nigel looked guilty.

"Someone would have," he admitted. "Like my mother or the aunts. They wanted Annie to leave you here."

"Great," Vicky sputtered. "Then we would both have grown up motherless."

Bess gave her a sympathetic look.

"You would have had a father then, old girl."

Their eyes swung toward their father, waiting for him to say something. Nigel stood up and started pacing the room.

"The time has come to tell you a few things, girls. Some of this is not suitable for unwed young ladies but I know you have seen and heard things during the war that I cannot imagine."

Bess told him to get on with it.

"It was the turn of the century and Queen Victoria was on the throne. My brother Percy, the earl, was a lot older than me. His son Philip was my age. We grew up together but there were different expectations from him since he was the heir. I was just the second son, contemplating taking a commission and going to some outpost of the British Army."

"Like India?" Bess prompted.

"Maybe," Nigel nodded. "Clemmie and I had fond memories of the place and I thought I might go back."

"Is that when you met Mom?" Vicky prompted.

Nigel looked irked at being interrupted.

"Annie Rhodes met Momo at some ball in London and was invited here for a house party." He gave a deep sigh. "She was a vision, girls. I fell in love with her. But I knew she was a dollar princess, here to snag a title."

"And you were just a second son," Bess clucked. "Did you give up before you started, Papa?"

Nigel turned red.

"I don't know why but Annie seemed to like me. We were thrown together a lot, of course, but there were many other young bucks hovering around her."

"Like Miles Carrington?" Bess narrowed her eyes.

Nigel didn't respond.

"To cut a long story short, Annie and I got married and moved into the manor. Percy was getting Primrose Cottage renovated for us but he died of apoplexy and Philip became the earl."

"Was he married at that time?" Vicky asked, trying to keep all the names straight in her head. "To Momo, right?"

Philip and Imogen married a couple of months after the twins were born. Beatrice moved to Primrose Cottage and Nigel considered moving to America.

"Seriously?" Bess raised her eyebrows. "You were prepared to leave Buxley?"

"I didn't have many options, girls. The Rhodes family had a lot of businesses and a cushy position was created for me. Then all those plans fell apart."

There was a hush around the room as the girls processed this.

"Philip had an accident," Bess whispered. "Was there no hope for him, Papa?"

Philip Gaskins had been thrown off his horse during a hunt. He hit his head on a rock and died instantly.

"I went from being plain Nigel Gaskins to the Earl of Buxley, a mantle I was ill prepared for."

The girls had wondered about it.

"Mom became Lady Buxley," Vicky nodded. "Was she not happy with the title? I thought she wanted that."

"The Rhodes family was happy," Lord Buxley told them. "They had buckets of money and now their daughter had pedigree. We had no idea about the storm that was going to rage around us."

Vicky realized the man who was her father had grown paler as he recited his tale. She urged him to take a seat.

"I think we should ring for tea now, Bess."

There was a knock on the door before she could respond and Barnes came in, followed by two footmen carrying trays of sandwiches, biscuits and cakes, and a big pot of tea.

"You're a life saver, Barney," Bess cried. "My throat is parched and a drop of Darjeeling is just what I need right now."

Barnes maintained his inscrutable expression, silently ordering the footmen about with his hawk like gaze. His demeanour slipped a bit when Vicky giggled but he righted himself just in time and followed the footmen out of the room.

Bess loaded cucumber sandwiches on a plate and handed it to her father. He swallowed a couple without saying a word, watching her slather the scones with clotted cream and blackberry jam.

"Why did Mom leave?" Vicky prompted after they had fortified themselves with enough tea and food.

"There was talk, girls. I still don't know where it began. Maybe it was Beatrice. There were whispers and murmurs in the village. The police questioned me but found nothing."

"For what?" Bess squirmed.

"They thought I got Philip out of the way. Why would I do that? We were in the nursery together, had the same nanny, went to Eton and Oxford … he was more of a brother to me than Percy."

The girls could not hide their shock.

"Was there any evidence? Could anyone prove you committed this heinous act, Papa?"

Nigel's eyes were sad.

"The court of public opinion trumps everything, girls. People pointed fingers at us everywhere.

Annie had a hard time. She was always treated as an outsider. Now they began saying her influence had made me stumble."

Vicky wasn't buying it that easily.

"You were lord of the manor. I thought that counted for something here."

Nigel looked beaten.

"There were other things I'd rather not mention. Living here became impossible for your mother. I don't blame her."

Annie wanted him to move to America, just like they had planned. But he had responsibilities as the new earl.

"Of course you did," Bess sided with him. "All our tenants, the village, they all depend on you for their livelihood."

"I suppose I could have handed things over to a steward," Nigel mused. "What can I say, I was young and righteous. I had dreams of living up to my ancestors."

"So you decided to split up," Vicky summed up. "How did you choose between us, Dad?"

"What was the plan?" Bess was riled up. "Was she

ever going to come back?"

"Nothing was decided," Lord Buxley told them. "I thought Annie would come home after some time. Twenty years passed in the blink of an eye. I suppose we just drifted apart after some time."

Bess poured herself another cup of tea, cursing under her breath to find it cold.

"I have wronged you, girls." Nigel stared at the formal gardens in the distance. "Will you ever forgive me?"

"Are you sure you are telling us everything?" Vicky didn't look convinced.

"More or less."

"I think I have had enough shocks for one day," Bess declared.

Nigel went to the window and stared out.

"The same thing is happening again, girls. The gossip mill is churning. Our tenants are wondering if I murdered Miles Carrington."

"That's a load of crap," Vicky exclaimed. "Don't these people have anything better to do?"

Bess was too shocked to respond. Hadn't she

hobnobbed with the locals in the pub just a few hours ago?

Nigel clasped his hands behind his back.

"Constable Potts has his limitations."

"You mean he's an ass," Bess snorted. "I can't say I have much faith in the local police."

"That's exactly why I am calling in Scotland Yard," Nigel declared. "Sir Edward Harding promised to send one of his best detectives."

"You mean Uncle Ned?" Bess asked. "Oh right, he's a superintendent at Scotland Yard." She turned to Vicky. "Papa and Uncle Ned were at Eton."

"Are you sure you are not opening Pandora's Box?" Vicky was sceptical. "Every family has skeletons in their cupboard."

Nigel pursed his lips, pulling himself straighter.

"I have nothing to hide, my dears. Let us hope the truth shall set me free. I am tired of living under a cloud."

Chapter 9

Vicky sat in the breakfast room, staring at a plate of kedgeree. The concept of eating fish first thing in the morning was completely alien to her. As were most things she found at Buxley Manor. Bess was trying hard to make her feel at home but she was struggling. Her mother's family was one of the richest in America so she had never lacked for anything. She believed she had grown up in the lap of luxury but it did not compare to what she found at Buxley. The gigantic manor, the expansive grounds that stretched as far as the eye could see, the hordes of servants, it was going to take getting used to.

The most disturbing were the questions that sprang up every day. She had come to England, hoping to get some answers around why her parents had split up. But things were a lot more serious than that.

"Aren't you hungry?" Bess asked, shoving a forkful of kedgeree in her mouth with a flourish. "Your mood will improve once your stomach is full."

"Maybe some toast." Vicky picked one from the rack a footman set before her and started to butter it. "How can you eat this rice? It's yellow and it stinks."

"Don't let Aunt Clem hear you say that. Kedgeree is a Buxley Manor mainstay. We may not have plum pudding on Christmas but there will be kedgeree for breakfast every day. Our grandfather started the tradition."

"There is so much I don't know. I am being bombarded with new information from all sides, Bessie. How do I remember everything?"

"You don't have to, silly."

Vicky took a bite of the evenly browned toast and sipped her coffee.

"I have been thinking about what our father said. Actually, I was up all night trying to make sense of things."

"You called him Dad yesterday," Bess quipped. "Did it feel natural?" She wondered if she would be as comfortable talking to her mother, when she met her.

Vicky didn't hide her impatience.

"Pay attention, won't you? Clearly, our father needs our help. We have to come up with a plan."

Bess scooped up the last bit of kedgeree and started on the toast.

"You mean exonerate him of the old crime, prove he had nothing to do with Miles Carrington's death and reunite him with our mother."

Vicky stared at her twin, her mouth hanging open in shock. Had Bess read her mind or was she mocking her?

"In a nutshell, yes."

"You've lost your marbles, old girl."

Vicky considered voicing what had been plaguing her all night.

"Do you believe in him? Our Pops? Can you wholeheartedly say he is innocent, Bess?"

"I do. We stand by our own here, sis. Loyalty and all that, you know." She flung a half eaten piece of toast down, suddenly losing her appetite. "Ask anyone. Papa is a gentle soul. How do you think he survived living among so many forceful women? He avoids confrontation at all costs."

A footman cleared the table, his expression inscrutable, but Vicky knew he must be listening to every word they said.

"How about going for a walk?" she suggested. "Show me some of the gardens."

"The morning constitutional," Bess exclaimed in dramatic fashion. "Topping."

The girls stepped out into the sunny morning. Vicky shaded her eyes with her hand and pointed at the lake in the distance.

"Let's go there."

"I will show you how to punt," Bess nodded. "Papa taught me when I was six."

They walked through neatly trimmed hedges and flower beds bursting with a profusion of sweet peas and lilies.

"Where can we get more information about what happened in 1901?" Vicky asked. "I think we should talk to at least three people."

Bess realized Vicky wasn't going to back down.

"We should find out if the police were called in. The servants know everything, of course. Barney, Mrs. Jones and Mrs. Bird have all been at Buxley for ages. We can talk to them."

"And the aunts?"

"Aunt Hortense and Aunt Perpetua, of course. Let's not forget Grandma Louise."

"What about Beatrice?"

Bess made a face.

"I have tried to be neutral when telling you about everyone here, Vicky, so I don't bias you against anyone. But I have to say this. I have always sensed that Aunt Bea did not like me. She called me a hoyden when I was a young miss and was always quick to find fault."

Vicky's eyebrows scrunched together in a frown.

"You mean Aunt Clementine, don't you? I thought she was a tough nut."

Bess corrected her. "Aunt Clem's a dragon, but she's sweet. She just likes things done a certain way. After what Papa told us yesterday, I am convinced I was right. Ghastly Aunt Beatrice doesn't just hate my guts, she hates me. And now she won't spare you either."

"Keep your enemies closer, remember?" Vicky bit her lip. "It should be interesting to hear what she has to say. Doesn't hurt to get a differing opinion."

"Whatever you say," Bess shrugged. "So we have the police, the servants, the aunts and Grandma …

how do we proceed now?"

Vicky sat down on a bench placed under the shade of a tree.

"Remember Nurse Margo's missing ring? We managed to find it, didn't we?"

Bess smiled at the memory. The war had just ended and the girls were billeted, waiting to go home. A senior nurse had just become engaged to one of her patients, a captain in the army who took a bullet in his arm in a skirmish. There was a big party with lots of dancing and things got wild. It wasn't until next morning that Nurse Margo realized her engagement ring was gone.

"How did we do that?"

"We talked to people, cross checked facts, weeded out the chaff …"

"And came to a logical conclusion," Bess beamed. "Golly, that seems so long ago, Vicky."

"What I mean is, we are smart enough. We eliminate what is not possible and what's left has to be the answer."

"Follow the logic." Bess pulled her lower lip and frowned. "I say, let's do it. And we can have a marvellous time while we are at it."

Vicky laughed, shaking her head with mirth. "Does life always have to be a party?"

"Why not?" Bess winked. "Haven't the last few years been bad enough? I want to erase every memory of bloody corpses and mangled bodies from the brain. I still hear the canons boom when I go to bed at night."

The girls grew sombre at the shared memory. They had different ways of dealing with the trauma of war. Bess put on a stiff upper lip and pretended she did not have a care in the world. Vicky had become more serious, determined to study medicine and provide care for needy women from poor backgrounds.

"Shall we go and meet Grandma Louise?" Vicky fanned her face with her hand, wishing she had remembered to wear a hat.

The day was getting oppressive as the sun rose in the sky. There was no sign of a breeze and thin cracks were visible in the grounds, parched from the lack of rain.

"She might shoot down the whole idea," Bess warned.

Vicky gave a shrug. She barely knew her grandmother and was prepared to face opposition. They walked back to the main house for the car and drove to the Dower House. Louise sat in the parlour, apparently waiting for them.

"Took you long enough," she grumbled. "What have you decided?"

Bess and Vicky shared a glance, stupefied.

"Nigel telephoned me," Louise clarified. "Tell me, are you going to condemn your sire or stand by him?"

Bess bristled at the question.

"Don't you know me at all, Grandma?"

Vicky explained what they were thinking.

"You are right about Beatrice. She will not help your father. Clementine is loyal but she's so full of herself, I doubt she notices anything else."

"Aunt Clem was not living at the manor when Philip died," Bess pointed out.

Louise agreed she had a point.

"What about Momo?" Vicky asked.

"She can barely make up her mind about anything. Has no backbone, that one." Louise shook her head. "Same goes for Bubbles. Flits around like a butterfly. She is a forty year old party girl with no purpose in life."

Bess started to laugh.

"Bubbles is a lady and a spinster to boot. What would you have her do, Grandma? Join the suffragettes? How very modern."

"Don't be cheeky, Bessie. If only she would stop dithering!"

Vicky declared she was hungry.

"Are you giving us lunch, Grandmother?"

Louise told them she had planned to have lunch at the manor. Mrs. Bird was making braised lamb, her favourite.

"Hortense and Perpetua will be joining us, girls. We can have a bite to eat and recruit them over tea."

Back at the manor, the great aunts Hortense and Perpetua sat with Clementine, counting the minutes.

"We don't come down for lunch every day," Hortense grumbled when the twins and Louise swept in. "Clementine promised lamb."

"And Mrs. Bird is making rhubarb pie," Perpetua

chimed in.

"We need to talk," Vicky told her as they went in.

"Later," Bess whispered, hoping Clementine hadn't heard. "We don't talk shop until tea is served."

The lamb and the pie were duly appreciated.

"Has anyone seen Papa?" Bess wondered.

"Hiding in the library," Clementine frowned, staring at Louise. "Maybe you should talk to him, Mama."

"He's not a child in the nursery," Louise dismissed. "Give him some time and he will be right as rain."

Clementine reminded her about what had happened the last time. Vicky's eyes darted between them, wondering how her grandmother would counter that. But Louise said nothing.

"We will have tea in your rooms, Hortense." Louise ordained, looking at Bess and Vicky. "Come on, girls."

Clementine complained it was inconvenient. She was meeting Mrs. Jones to inventory the furnishings.

"We can manage without you, my dear," Louise

chuckled, setting her at ease.

The group reached the west wing without further incident.

"What are you up to, Louise?" Perpetua asked after they had rung for tea.

Bess and Vicky took turns, telling them about the grand plan.

"You read our mind," Hortense beamed. "That clodhopper Potts is useless."

"Our father is calling in Scotland Yard," Vicky reminded them.

"Regardless, we will do our bit," Louise declared. "Are you getting cold feet?"

Bess assured her otherwise.

"We almost forgot, Grandma! We ran into Constable Potts on the way to the Dower house."

"And what did that nincompoop have to say?" Hortense piped up.

Vicky's eyes grew wide.

"Guess what the police found next to the dead body?"

"A playing card." Bess forged ahead without waiting for a reply. "Queen of Hearts, to be precise."

"What does it mean?" Hortense and Perpetua chorused, cutting Louise off.

"The killer is sending us a message," she replied. "Miles died because he broke someone's heart."

Chapter 10

Detective Inspector James Gardner was not known for showing emotion. Driving his 1919 Hispano Suiza H6 was one of the few pleasures of his life. The country roads the car zoomed past were mostly deserted, lined with trees and wildflowers he rarely saw in the city.

He was not pleased when the Super pulled him off a case he had been working on for months, sending him to rusticate in the country. Pandering to lazy aristocrats and holding their hand was a task he was not fond of. But he could not disobey a direct order from Sir Edward.

The fresh air was a welcome change from the grime of London. He had been advised to treat this sojourn as an unofficial holiday. No case file was handed over. If the press was to be believed, 'Bulldog' Gardner could smell a crime before it happened. Sir Edward was sure he would get to the bottom of things soon. His only brief was to avoid ruffling any feathers.

"You expect me to look the other way if your friend is guilty, Sir?" He did not mince words.

"If Nigel Gaskins is guilty, I'm Jack the Ripper." Sir Harding tapped his pipe, his steely gaze fixed on James. "Just solve the crime, my boy. A word of warning, though. Don't let the natives influence you."

The summer sun was high in the sky and James was parched. He considered looking for a pub to quench his thirst. The car went around a bend, almost ploughing into a chubby helmeted figure on a bicycle.

"Constable Potts?" James hit the brakes and came to a stop. "DI Gardner."

The bobby almost fell off the bicycle in his haste. He gave a clumsy salute, his brow mottled with drops of sweat.

"Yes Sir. Welcome to Buxley, Sir."

James bit off a curt reply, taking the man's measure in an instant. He could not expect much from him. Potts gave him directions to the local police station which also doubled as his living quarters. Twenty minutes later, James sat in a small room barely enough to hold an ancient scuffed table and two chairs.

"What can you tell me about the crime, Constable?" he began, yearning for a drink.

"There were this big party at the manor, like. Lots of them wild young ones from the city arrived in a bus. And toffs from the surrounding area. It were a right to-do, the likes we haven't seen since the war."

"Never mind all that," James interrupted. "Tell me about the victim."

Constable Potts gave a long winded description of Miles Carrington, his family and his life story. James guessed most of it was local gossip and all of it was not necessarily true.

"Was he a popular man?"

"Yes and no, Sir. He cut a dashing figure but also liked to get his own way. And one more thing …" Potts hesitated.

"Out with it," James ordered. "Don't leave anything out. I will decide if it is significant."

"Mr. Miles Carrington were a gambler, Sir. They say he had a way with cards. Never lost at the tables. At least, nobody's ever heard of him having any debts." Potts rubbed his nose. "Was well set up. Even better than Lord Shelby."

James had to ask a few more questions to gather that the peer the constable referred to was Miles Carrington's father.

"Tell me about the body, Potts."

"Never went near it. Doctor Evans was present and already checked his pulse and what not. Someone at the manor had thrown a blanket over it." His rotund frame shuddered at the memory.

James bit off a curse. He would have to talk to this doctor first.

"You mean you did not try to learn how the man died?"

"Stabbed, I reckon." Potts shrugged. "That's what the doctor said." He brightened, puffing up with pride. "None of them saw the playing card lying next to the man's head."

James leaned forward eagerly, encouraging the constable to continue.

"It were a Queen of Hearts," he chortled. "One a' them old playing cards. My grandpa told me about 'em.'

"Where is it?"

Potts rummaged in a drawer of the desk and began pulling out a bunch of items. A pencil stub came out first, followed by bits of paper, a ball of string, some old letters, followed by the aforementioned card.

James could barely hold his temper.

"What in blazes is that?" He pointed at the pile. "Explain yourself, Constable Potts."

"This be the evidence drawer, Sir."

"Good God, man, have you never heard of a bag?" James exploded. "And what about gloves?"

"What do you mean, Sir?" Potts was unruffled. "I wiped my hands on my trousers before picking up the card."

James groaned in despair. He pulled out a paper bag from his pocket, picked up the card with his gloved hands and deposited it in the bag. He didn't have much hope but he would get it checked for fingerprints.

"Where was the dead man's wife when he died?" he asked with a sigh.

"All the ladies was in the parlour, having tea."

"And the daughter?"

"On the terrace with the other young ones, I reckon." Potts averted his eyes. "They was watching the fireworks."

James decided talking to the victim's family would

be his first order of business. He looked around the room, hoping to spot a kettle.

"Any chance of a drop of tea, Constable?"

The door banged open just then and a florid woman entered, hefting a tray loaded with cups and plates and a kettle covered in a woollen tea cosy made up of five different colours. Her girth rivalled her husband's and her wide smile revealed two missing teeth.

"This be the missus, Sir." Potts beamed with pride. "Makes the best currant cake in the village."

Mrs. Potts stayed long enough to pour the tea and thrust a plate loaded with a generous slice of cake toward him. James readily obliged her by taking a bite and provided fulsome praise. The woman promised to bake a pie for him on the morrow.

"I reckon you will be in the village for a while, your lordship."

"Just Inspector will do, Mrs. Potts."

James devoted the next few minutes to replenishing himself. After two cups of strong, milky tea and several slices of the cake, he turned toward earthen matters.

"Let me have the guest list, Potts."

"That be everyone at the manor and the young ones what came from the city, Sir."

"Right. Now give me the list of all their names. I presume you took down their addresses too."

The constable stared back, his mouth open. James waited for him to say something.

"Please tell me you interviewed all the guests, Constable?"

Potts gulped and shook his head.

"Never had a murder in Buxley, Sir. I reckoned someone would be sent from the station at Chipping Woodbury."

James took a deep breath, schooling himself to be patient.

"But are all the people from the party still at the manor, Potts?"

"Not the young ones, Sir. The two buses left for town the next morning."

Had the murderer already slipped away? James groaned at the futility of his mission. He quelled the urge to sit in his car and go back to London. But he could not let the Super down. He would have to stick around and at least make an attempt to solve the murder. There was no point in blaming Potts. Clearly, the man was in over his head.

"Do you have an inn I can stay at?" he sighed.

"The Buxley Arms has a room or two," Potts replied. "Just head into the village square, Sir."

James thanked him and stepped out, hoping the landlord of the pub would put him up. So much for keeping a low profile. He got into the car and followed the directions Potts had given him, parking in front of a building that had been around for a hundred years or more. Two men in farmers' garb gave him curious looks as they went in.

A tall man in a poorly fitting tweed suit came out and greeted him with a friendly wave.

"I say, what brings you to Buxley?"

"This and that." James held out his hand, introducing himself. "James Gardner. Are you a local, then?"

"Gordon Phipps." The younger man laughed. "Sort of. I live at Rosehill. It's an estate a few miles from here, near Oakview. That's Lord Shelby's land."

James asked if he was related to him.

"Hardly," Gordon laughed. "I work for his son. Or used to, anyway." He paused, as if debating what to say next. "You will find out soon enough if you stick around."

James wished him a good day and strode into the pub. It was dark and cool inside. The landlord stood behind the wooden bar, wiping it down with a cloth that had seen better days.

"What can I get ye?"

"A pint of ale, please." James climbed up on a stool and looked around. "Constable Potts said you have rooms to let."

"Only if you pay for the whole week." The landlord placed a tankard before him. "I will have to ask the missus."

James pulled some coins out of his pocket and placed them on the bar.

"Can you do meals?"

Harvey frowned at him, polishing a glass with the same rag.

"How does you know Potts? We don't eat fancy. The missus can do sandwiches or pies and nothing wrong with 'em either. Lady Bess likes our cottage pie, she does. Why, she were here just yesterday with Lady Victoria, her that's come from America. Two peas in a pod, they are and why not? Born minutes apart, wasn't they? Look a bit like …"

"Stop yapping, Harvey." A woman, presumably his wife, came out, wiping her hands on a crisp apron. "Don't talk the poor man's 'ead off."

The terms were discussed and Mrs. Harvey ushered him up a flight of slick stone stairs to a room under the eaves. A young maid came up with his suitcase and set it near a dresser.

"This is nice." James looked around. "I won't trouble you much, Mrs. Harvey."

"Least we can do for a fine policeman such as yourself." Mrs. Harvey proved to be sharper than her husband and the constable. "Lord Buxley needs all the help he can get."

So the pub owner and his wife were loyal to their lord. James surmised the rest of the village was against him. Sir Edward had sent him there for a reason. Was there any underlying resentment or was Lord Buxley just the victim of malicious gossip?

"What kind of a lord is he, Mrs. Harvey? Does he raise the rents often, for instance? Or have a roving eye, perhaps?"

"Hush!" Mrs. Harvey stopped him midsentence. "The people of Buxley have never had any reason to complain, Sir. His lordship is a baa-lamb. 'ardly gets a word in, what with all them ladies up at the manor. And he dotes on Lady Bess, he does. Brought her up on his own, didn't he? She's grown up to be a fine lass, not afraid of anything. Went and fought in the war, and her barely sixteen."

James let her words roll over him, planning his next move. Once he met the victim's family, he would go to the manor and introduce himself, making it clear he was there to do a job. The murderer would be caught and brought to justice, no matter who he was.

Chapter 11

Breakfast was in full swing at Buxley Manor the next morning. Viscount Cranford was the only guest at the table. The Carringtons had returned home after lunch the previous afternoon. So none of them had been present when DI Gardner arrived to introduce himself.

Vicky had chosen to sit far away from Bess.

"Can't stomach the smell of fish in the morning," she shrugged, managing to irk Clementine.

"You are not British until you enjoy a kippered herring for breakfast, or smoked haddock."

"Are you saying she is not a Gaskins because she does not like kedgeree?" Lord Buxley boomed. "Leave the poor girl alone, Clemmie."

Vicky tapped her spoon on her soft boiled egg, flashing a look of gratitude toward her father. Maybe she could talk Mrs. Bird into making flapjacks.

Barnes appeared to announce that Bess was wanted on the telephone. She sprang up to go to the hall and returned five minutes later.

"That was Bubbles, crying for help. She's going mad over there and wants me to motor down and bring her back."

Momo looked up from her plate.

"Papa can be so hard to please. He must be making some dreadful plan to keep her busy. Will you go and rescue her, Bess?"

"I have to show Vicky around anyway," Bess replied. "It's a fine day for a drive in the country."

Lord Buxley looked disappointed. "I was hoping you girls could join me. We are choosing the final eleven today."

The annual cricket match between Buxley and Ridley was fast approaching. Every year, men in both the villages worked themselves into a frenzy until the big day. Ridley had won for five years in a row before the war and there had been no match in the interim years.

"New decade, new beginning." Lord Buxley's eyes gleamed. "Maybe you can spy for us, eh, girls? See what our opponents in Ridley are up to."

Bess promised to keep her eyes and ears open. The girls stepped out and waited for someone to bring the car around. Vicky offered to drive but Bess would have none of it.

"Ask Papa to get you a new car, maybe a Hispano?"

"I could have my Duesenberg shipped here." Vicky was thoughtful as they set off across the expansive grounds toward the village.

Bess pressed her foot down on the accelerator and veered to avoid a pothole.

"Do you have to drive so fast?" Vicky complained. "We are not at war anymore, you know."

"Old habits die hard."

They reached the village of Ridley and drove through a set of tall iron gates that guarded Sir Dorian's estate. Gertrude rushed down the steps before they had barely come to a stop in front of the house.

"I'm so glad to see you. Let's go before anyone spots us."

Bess was having none of it.

"I say, bad form, Bubbles. How about offering us a spot of tea? Vicky has never been here, you know."

"Well, alright." Gertrude deflated. "Mother will want to see you."

The Ridleys' butler Hawks was short and bald, with a flat nose, shiny head and a generous protruding belly. He wheezed as he led them down a hall into the drawing room. Lady Ridley sat there with a piece of embroidery in her hand. Her eyes widened in alarm when she saw Bess.

"Is it Momo? What has happened to my darling?"

"Don't be silly, Mother." Gertrude frowned at Lady Ridley. "Bess has come to pick me up."

"My poor daughter!" A lace handkerchief materialized from the folds of her dress and the older woman dabbed her dry eyes. "Living in that monstrous place. Why, she might be murdered next."

Gertrude told her mother to stop being dramatic and dispatched Hawks to get some tea.

Vicky told them about the detective from Scotland Yard.

"He has quite a reputation, Lady Ridley. I believe he will get to the bottom of things soon."

"And if he doesn't, we will." Bess cut her off. "Grandma's helping us, so are the Great Aunts."

"The Victorian Brigade on the rampage," Gertrude laughed. "What fun, Bess."

Bristling at the insult, Bess told her about the card that had been found near Miles.

"Tell us what it means then," she challenged.

Hawks ushered in a maid pushing a tea trolley. The cook had sent a lemon cake along with some fresh buns. Lady Ridley began pouring the tea. Vicky thanked her but declined.

"Can you get some coffee for Lady Victoria, Hawks?" Bess asked. "She's not a tea drinker."

Lady Ridley looked scandalized but Gertrude spoke up.

"You should go to Europe, Vicky. The Italians make a lot of fuss over coffee. So do the French, I think."

Bess cut a big slice of lemon cake and offered it to Vicky.

"The Queen of Hearts, Bubbles?" she prompted. "What do you think it means?"

Gertrude took a sip of tea before she ventured her opinion.

"I think it points to Gordon Phipps. Surely you noticed how he was eyeing Mabel? And she blushed every time he looked at her. I say there is something between them."

Bess was not convinced.

"Mabel is crazy about anything wearing pants. Didn't you notice how she clung to the Marquess?"

"You are both right, girls."

They turned around as Sir Dorian entered the room, accompanied by a man who was his younger version. Cedric Ridley, his son and heir, was in his late twenties, closer in age to Bess.

"Gordon Phipps is in love with Mabel," he declared. "All the chaps know about it."

"Are you sure, Cedric?" Gertrude frowned. "Did Miles know?"

Cedric nodded, accepting a cup of tea from his mother. "He did not approve."

Bess railed at him for missing her party. He had been in London with his friends and had stayed behind instead of coming to Buxley.

"I'm sorry I missed all the fun," he chortled. "A murder trumps a scavenger hunt any day."

Vicky praised the lemon cake, wondering if she was actually going to get any coffee. The door opened and Hawks came in, carrying a silver coffee pot on a tray.

"Have you met my twin?" Bess dug an elbow in Cedric's side. "Or were you lying to me too, like the rest of them?"

Cedric assured her he had also been kept in the dark.

"Whoever said a group of people cannot keep a secret?" He shook his head and patted Vicky on the shoulder. "Welcome to the fold, young Victoria. This place can use some fresh blood."

Sir Dorian told him to hurry up. They were late for a meeting in the village.

"For the cricket match?" Bess winked. "Buxley has a strong team this year so you better watch out."

Vicky let her twin banter with Cedric for a few minutes.

"Let's get back to Gordon," she spoke up. "What do you think happened, Cedric?"

"Any fool can tell Miles Carrington would never have approved of the match. So Gordon killed the old man, of course. Now his coast is clear."

"And what about the Queen of Hearts?" Gertrude needled.

Cedric thought it was a sign or a warning. Gordon wanted them to know he would do anything to win his lady love.

Bess laughed till crumbs of cake flew out of her mouth.

"That sounds dumb. He might as well surrender himself to the police."

Vicky thought she was right. The police could lift fingerprints from the card, helping them narrow down the victim.

"You must have heard of the Thomas Jennings trial in Chicago?" she asked the assembled company.

Sir Dorian cleared his throat and looked at a clock on the wall.

"Cedric, my boy, we need to leave now."

He glowered at his daughter, scowled at Bess and ignored Vicky before stalking out. Cedric gave a shrug and followed him.

"Shall we go now?" Gertrude asked brightly, well acquainted with her father's disapproval. "Aunt Clem will throw a fit if we are late for lunch."

Bess came up with the idea as they drove out of Ridley.

"I say we go to Rosehill and talk to Gordon ourselves."

Vicky approved but Gertrude vetoed it, giving a wide yawn. She told the girls they could do anything after they dropped her off at Buxley Manor.

"You're such a bore, Bubbles!" Bess pouted. "Grandma Louise has more energy than you do."

"Then take her with you," Gertrude whined, pleading a headache.

She rallied around once they reached the manor, where Momo welcomed her with open arms.

"Weren't you here yesterday?" Clementine grunted and headed to the solarium.

After a lunch of asparagus soup and ham sandwiches followed by a dessert of strawberry fool, Bess and Vicky set off for Rosehill. It was somewhere between Buxley and Ridley but slightly toward the west at the edge of a small valley.

"We are late, Vicky." Bess pulled up behind a familiar Hispano Suiza, hoping the man from Scotland Yard had not spooked Gordon.

The butler led them to a small room which served as Gordon's office. DI Gardner was nowhere to be seen.

"Hello ladies." Gordon stood up to greet them, looking like his usual self. "To what do I owe the pleasure?"

"Where is he?" Bess looked around.

"If you mean the good Inspector from Scotland Yard, he is down in the kitchen, talking to the staff."

"Oh," Vicky let out. "We thought …"

Gordon offered them tea and leaned against a window that looked out over a walled garden.

"He did interview me."

Bess asked how he was doing.

"What happens to your job now, Gordon? Miles is not around to give you a reference."

"Mr. Trevor has asked me to stay on for now. In fact, he hinted at giving me more responsibilities."

Vicky asked after Mabel.

"Hasn't surfaced yet, poor girl," he replied. "Still in

shock."

"At least she has you," Bess consoled. "She is so lucky to have found love at such a young age."

Gordon turned pink.

"I say, Bess. It's not ... things are not like that between us."

"Are you sure?" Vicky probed. "Many of us noticed the looks that passed between you two. Young love is hard to hide, Gordon. And Mabel will be of age soon. So what's the problem?"

Gordon's gaze darkened.

"Her father didn't think I was good enough. Not high born."

Bess told him the world was changing. That seemed to incite him further.

"Miles is gone now though," Vicky needled. "You are free to marry Mabel."

Gordon told them to come to the point.

"Stop beating around the bush, Bess. I will tell you the same thing I told that Inspector. I did not kill Miles Carrington. The whole idea is absurd."

"Where were you when we found him?" Vicky asked. "In the card room with the other men?"

Gordon told them he had been dancing with Clara. They were watching the fireworks with the other guests when Vicky stumbled on the body.

"Was Miles in trouble?" Bess asked. "Do you have any idea who might have done this?"

"He managed to antagonize a lot of people," Gordon told them. "Like Lord Buxley, for instance. I think they had some history." He popped a cigarette in his mouth and looked around for a lighter. "You don't mind?"

"The Gaskins and Carrington families have been friends for generations. Papa was with Miles at Eton." Bess smiled. "You never said where you went to school?"

"Eton," Gordon replied. "I was a scholarship student, of course."

"How awfully clever of you," Bess crooned, her hard eyes belying her tone. "What are you doing here then, hiding in a small village in the Cotswolds? You should be in London."

Gordon admitted he had big plans. He was just getting his feet wet, learning the ropes.

Vicky realized Bess was mad because Gordon had pointed a finger at their father. She wondered if he had a hand in spreading the nasty rumours in the village.

"So you have no idea who killed your employer?" She folded her arms and stared at him. "Nothing peculiar or out of the ordinary springs to mind?"

Gordon finally located the lighter and clicked it open.

"He did have a row with that lawyer friend of yours, Bess. Osborne. They were going at it like cats and dogs after breakfast."

Chapter 12

Barnes greeted the twins back at the manor.

"The Dowager is waiting for you with Lady Hortense and Lady Perpetua, my ladies."

They thanked him and headed toward the west wing. Bess wondered what the old dears had unearthed.

"About time!" Grandma Louise greeted them. "I hope you were doing something related to our little project, girls."

Hortense and Perpetua nodded in unison. Bess planted a kiss on their cheeks and flopped down in an armchair, looking around for something to drink.

"Tea will be served in a few minutes," Hortense assured her. "We already rang for it."

Vicky told them about their trip to Rosehill. She admitted they had not learned much. Louise waved a paper in the air.

"I made a list of things we have to do. Did you

know that Inspector talked to the staff yesterday? Barnes gave us an account of everything he wanted to know."

"Why should we copy what he did?" Bess argued. "We have brains, don't we?"

The aunts looked at each other and smiled.

"Pride goes before a fall, Bessie. Haven't we taught you that?"

They thought there was no harm in going over the Inspector's actions. After all, he had been trained for the job and had a reputation. Louise agreed with them.

"They call him Bulldog for a reason."

The twins burst into laughter.

"What?" Bess chortled. "Where did you hear that, Grandma?"

Vicky told her twin to shut up and urged the older women to continue.

"He went out on that terrace," Hortense took up the story. "Walked the length and breadth of it apparently and asked questions about who discovered Miles and where. Talked to the staff too."

"We have not done that yet." Louise pointed out. "I propose we do the same. Each of us can question a few of them, those we come across every day and glean some information from them."

Bess had to admit her grandmother was right.

"Did you know there was a scream?" Hortense asked. "That is what caused all the gentlemen to rush out."

This was news to the twins.

"We can talk to Papa about it," Bess nodded.

"And the other men," Vicky prompted. "We should consider everyone's version."

Grandma Louise decided they should join the others for tea. Barnes would serve it under the large oak tree in the park as usual. She urged Hortense and Perpetua to join her.

"We are fine here, Louise." Hortense wrung her hands and looked at her sister. "It is too warm outside."

"Nonsense!" Louise leaned on her cane and stood up. "Wear a hat. Get a parasol. Some fresh air will be good for you."

The twins left the older ladies and headed to the

library, hoping to get hold of their father. Lord Buxley sat at his desk, his head buried in a ledger. His eyes lit up when he saw them.

"Harvey's nephew is back in the village. And his leg is as good as new now."

"Is he in the final eleven?" Bess asked, knowing her father would not rest until he brought her up to date. "I hear he is a fine batsman."

"He will be opening for us," Lord Buxley beamed. "He stays put, you know. Slow but steady. Now I need to talk to young Phipps."

"You mean Gordon?" Vicky asked. "But he doesn't live in the village."

Rosehill lay between Buxley and Ridley so both sides were trying to recruit Gordon.

"Miles was a good bowler," Lord Buxley sighed. "Big loss for our side."

"That's what brings us here, Papa," Bess began. "We never talked about that night. Can you tell us what the gentlemen did after dinner? Don't leave anything out."

"Dash it, Bess. It's all a muddle. I'm still trying to wrap my head around what happened."

Vicky told him to close his eyes and take a few deep breaths.

"You don't have to remember everything right now," she soothed. "Just begin at the point where the ladies left for tea."

Lord Buxley closed his eyes and leaned back in his chair. He relaxed visibly after a minute.

"Pipes and cigars were lit and Barnes offered brandy and port. You know I don't smoke. Honestly, I was fuming inside, really mad at Miles. How dare he disparage my girls?"

Bess thought this was a sentiment her father should keep to himself. The police would read a motive in it.

"When did you come here?" Vicky prompted.

Lord Buxley closed his eyes again and continued his tale. The men had not lingered over the port much. Someone, he didn't remember who, suggested they head to the library and play a hand or two.

"That's the norm after these dinners," he explained. "The men like to deal the cards. Some of them are serious gamblers. Your Uncle Percy was one."

They lost track of time after a while, engrossed in the cards. Miles was winning at first. Then the tide turned and Viscount Cranford got a good hand.

Lord Buxley sat up with a jerk.

"That's when we heard the scream. It was a rummy thing. We sprang up as one and rushed outside."

Bess thought back to the hordes in the ballroom. Many couples had sneaked out and were cavorting in the gardens.

"Did you find the damsel in distress?" Vicky probed.

The terrace had been dark. Music from the ballroom filtered out and there was a buzz of conversation audible. But there was no one in sight.

"Are you sure it was a woman, Papa?" Bess asked.

"Hard to say, my dear. Some of the young ones ventured forth into the gardens and looked around. Eventually, they came back and we all went inside."

But had everyone really come back, Vicky wondered.

"Did Miles return with you?" she asked, still not sure how to address him.

Lord Buxley looked perplexed. "I suppose. But now that you mention it, I am not sure."

"Surely one of you would have noticed a player's absence?" Bess mused.

"But that's the thing, Bess. We discussed the scream and the game was abandoned. Dorian thought one of the crazy young people was playing a prank. Like the ones the London newspapers write about."

"You mean Bright Young People, Papa," Bess corrected him. "And we cannot rule that out. There were scores of them at the party, full of champagne and cocktails. Exactly the sort who would start that kind of rannygazoo."

Vicky realized they had completely overlooked something.

"What of the time you were dancing with us in the ballroom? Was it before or after the scream?"

Lord Buxley was not sure.

"How many people were here in the library anyway?" Bess scratched her nose and looked at the clock. It was ten minutes past four and she was hungry.

"Miles, Trips, Peter, that secretary fellow, Cecil …

that's about it, I think. Maybe Ian? And Dorian."

"Cecil?" Vicky had not heard of him before. "Was he at dinner?"

Bess told her she was yet to meet Cecil Chilton, the local vicar. He had been called away by some ailing parishioner and must have arrived after they finished eating.

"He's Great Aunt Cordelia's son," she explained. "They live at the vicarage, of course. We must visit them."

"Is she related to Great Aunts Hortense and Perpetua?" Vicky asked.

"They are all my father's sisters," Lord Buxley supplied. "Cecil has a sharp memory. You might learn something new from him, girls."

Bess proposed heading outside for tea. Lord Buxley agreed wholeheartedly. He walked out of a side door to the terrace and down a flight of steps to the garden. A paved path lined with rose bushes led them to a gurgling fountain displaying a stone cherub. Vicky mulled over what she had learned in the past hour as she followed her father to the giant oak where most of the family was assembled.

Had the scream been a diversion, created to draw Miles out? That would mean the killer had an accomplice. Or the killer had been the one to scream which meant none of the people in the library were involved in the murder. Then she thought of the chaos in the ballroom. It was also likely that one of the guests had been having some fun.

"Let's not forget the fireworks," Bess said, intruding in her thoughts. "Plenty of girls squealed in excitement."

Vicky surmised Miles had already been dead when the fireworks started. Talking to their father was not enough, she decided. They needed to interview everyone who was in the library that night. Maybe one of them would remember something the others missed.

"Who do you want to talk to next?" she asked Bess. "We have our work cut out."

"We can go to Oakview tomorrow and talk to Trips. Maybe drive into Chipping Woodbury after that and tackle Peter."

"What about the servants?" Vicky asked. "Do you know each one of them?"

Bess told her she was familiar with most but Barnes had hired people from the village for the party. He would have a list but the more people they talked to, the more the gossip would spread.

"We cannot be sure they will be loyal to us."

"I thought our family owns the village," Vicky frowned. "That should count for something."

"They gossip among themselves, though. And everyone likes to voice an opinion. The more contrary, the better."

They reached the others and sat down, watching Barnes walk toward them at a stately pace, followed by a bunch of footmen carrying trays of food.

"What have you scamps been up to, Elizabeth?" Clementine asked, beads of perspiration dotting her upper lip.

"This and that." Bess shrugged. "I hope you ordered coffee for Vicky."

"Barnes will make sure of it," Clementine grumbled. "Although I don't approve."

Gertrude told her she was wound as tight as a spring.

"You act more like a General every day, Aunt Clem. This is not a battlefield, you know."

"On the contrary," Clementine argued. "Every day should be treated as a battle and planned with military precision. How else are the girls going to find a good man? I don't want them to be bitter old spinsters like you."

"Hardly bitter," Gertrude mocked. "And I am young at heart."

Bess told them to calm down because she was not interested in finding a husband.

"I am going to make something of myself first. The world will recognize Lady Elizabeth Gaskins in her own right, not as somebody's wife." She looked at Vicky.

"And I am going to be a doctor so there is hardly any time to socialize or meet men."

Clementine flung her hands up in despair. "I give up."

Viscount Cranford had been listening in. He threw back his head and guffawed, then started coughing.

"Bravo Bess!" He whispered after he caught his breath. "You do your mother proud."

Lord Buxley looked like he would burst with pride.

"How about joining us for practice, eh, Bess?" he cajoled. "We have our eleven and two more but we still need some extras."

"That's very progressive of you, Papa. But I will stick to croquet and shuttlecock. Cricket is a game I prefer to watch from the pavilion, fortified with some champagne and cakes."

Vicky pushed herself forward. She had played baseball as a child.

"I would like to give it a try."

"Capital!" Lord Buxley beamed. "First practice is at seven sharp tomorrow morning."

Barnes and his posse finally reached them. There was a flurry of activity as tea was poured and cucumber sandwiches and cakes were dispensed. Vicky was surprised when one of the footmen handed her a steaming cup of coffee, fixed just the way she liked it, black.

"How do you remember my mother after all these years?" Bess asked Viscount Cranford, taking a sip of her tea.

"She is one of a kind." He broke a sandwich in two. "I hope she and your father can reconcile now that Miles is dead, the bugger."

Chapter 13

Replete after working through several trays of sandwiches and cakes, the assembled company drifted. Clementine went back to the house at a fast clip, no doubt ready to tackle the next thing on her agenda. Imogen and Gertrude went for a long walk. Bess considered taking a nap. She had seen Vicky tag along with their father, heading toward the stables. Maybe he wanted to introduce her to his favourite horses. It was high time they spent some time together.

"More tea, my lady?" Barnes intruded her thoughts.

"No, thank you, Barnes. Tell me, what is Mrs. Bird up to right now?"

Barnes raised one eyebrow and smiled.

"Dying to ask you a lot of questions, no doubt."

Bess stood up and brushed the crumbs off her skirt. She could kill two birds with one stone.

Ever since she was a child, Bess had found solace in the kitchen. Buxley Manor had an abundance of motherly influence, some quick to reprimand, others ready to coddle her. But the kitchen provided a warmth she found lacking elsewhere. Mrs. Bird's ample bosom and round figure had provided the warm hugs and kisses the aristocracy were stingy with. The kitchen at Buxley was her refuge, the place where she could shut off the noise and hear herself think. There was no judgement below stairs.

Mrs. Bird beamed from ear to ear and opened her arms wide when Bess entered the kitchen. She flew into them and closed her eyes, breathing in the scents of butter and vanilla mixed with thyme.

"I wondered when you would look in here, Lady Bess."

A couple of scullery maids watched, their mouths hanging open. Mrs. Bird shooed them out, warning them to stay away for an hour. She set out flour and butter on the table that served as a working area and handed Bess a freshly starched apron.

"How is she holding up?" Mrs. Bird asked. "Lady Victoria?"

"Seems fine. Why didn't you ever tell me?"

"It was not my place, my lady." Mrs. Bird was contrite. "How is your dear mother? We were very fond of her. She always had a kind word for everyone. Never drank tea, ate bacon and fried eggs for breakfast and simply loved my jam roly poly."

Bess measured out the flour and added it to a basin.

"Just like Vicky, then."

"Have you talked to her, dear?" Mrs. Bird cut the butter into tiny squares and handed them to Bess.

"Not yet." She began working the butter in the flour with the tips of her fingers, making a well in the centre. "What am I going to say to her? I am the daughter you abandoned twenty years ago?"

"We all have our trials." Mrs. Bird sighed. "She cried her eyes out when she said goodbye. Said she depended on us to make sure you were taken care of."

Bess began kneading the dough, asking questions about her mother, smiling when she learned of her quirks. It was clear the servants had adored her.

"The food at the party was excellent, Mrs. Bird." Beth rolled the dough and began cutting scones out of it. "Especially the roast duck and berry sauce we had for dinner. I never got a chance to thank you properly."

"Couldn't do any less for your special day." Mrs. Bird pulled a screaming kettle off the stove and added tea. "Now you sit yourself down and have a nice cup of tea, my lady. I have been saving some ginger biscuits for you."

Bess let herself be pampered. The shadows were beginning to lengthen outside and she would have to go up and dress for dinner soon.

"Have the maids recovered from the shock?" She thanked Mrs. Bird for the tea and took a bracing sip. "Still feels a bit unreal."

"If you want my opinion, he was asking for it." Mrs. Bird heaved herself up on a stool.

Bess asked if Miles Carrington had really been that bad.

"A bit stuffy but he was a hard worker, unlike many of his class. They say Rosehill was a ruin when he bought it, not like the flourishing estate it is now."

Mrs. Bird began to respond but clammed up.

"Some girls from the village helped me in the kitchen," she began. "None of us ever go upstairs so we had no idea what was going on. We thought all the noise was just young people having fun. Then Mr. Barnes sent a footman down to ask for tea. Plenty of it and quick, John said. And then he told us Mr. Carrington was dead as a post. Two girls fainted on the spot. One of them hit her head on the floor and had a nasty bruise."

Bess asked if they were better now. "Dr. Evans was here that night. He could have patched her up."

"I am guessing he was busy tending to Mr. Miles. And the vicar too, although why he missed dinner I can't say. Marcy's Ma saw him at a pub in Chipping Woodbury that evening, talking to some woman."

Bess told her he had been visiting an ailing parishioner.

"She must be mistaken."

"Not recognize our own vicar!" Mrs. Bird exclaimed. "The only time that woman has missed church is when she's confined to her bed, giving birth to yet another young one."

***

Vicky followed Nigel to the stables. Polo ran in front of them, heralding their arrival with energetic barks. The head groom rushed out to greet them, cap in hand.

"Meet my other daughter, Shields. We need a good mount for her."

The groom asked if she had ridden before.

"Not a lot," Vicky admitted. "And frankly, I am not sure I want to start now."

"Nonsense, my dear," Nigel argued. "You can't live in a country manor and not ride. Why, there are some pretty good rides through the parkland and over the hills. We have several hundred acres you can explore. And there will be hunts in the autumn. We put Bess on a horse when she was three and she was a natural."

"I am not her," Vicky bristled, trying to control her emotions.

She did not want to be compared to her twin. Bess was in her element at Buxley while she felt like an unwanted outsider. Vicky was ignorant of every aspect of life in the country but she did not want to advertise it.

"My dear child … I didn't mean … err … of course not." Nigel appeared chagrined. "I just thought it was something you might enjoy."

"I guess I can try." Vicky gave in.

The groom pretended he hadn't heard a word. Vicky wondered how the people working at Buxley could be so aloof. Back home in America, their household staff was a lot more vocal. They could be depended upon to provide an opinion in every argument.

They strolled through a big cavernous space, passing several stalls occupied by a variety of horses. Some neighed a welcome while others thudded against the stall door, eager to get out.

Shields stopped in front of a stall before they reached the other end and beckoned Vicky.

"This is Cinderella. She's gentle as a lamb. We can start you off with her, my lady."

Vicky picked up a carrot from a bin and offered it to the mare. Black with a white ribbon across her forehead, the horse nuzzled her hand and chewed placidly.

"She looks like she's smiling," Vicky grinned. "I guess I can give it a shot."

Nigel nodded vigorously and thanked the groom.

"Bess will set you up with the right clothes. Shields will make sure you have the right saddle. Early morning tomorrow sound good?"

Vicky nodded grudgingly, hoping she wouldn't have an audience.

They walked a few paces and headed down a tiny path almost concealed by some shrubs. Vicky gasped when they went around a bend, staring around her at a riot of blue and purple delphiniums scattered around a pond. Butterflies fluttered in the air, swooping down to drink the sweet nectar from the prolific blooms. Lilies grew at the edge of the water and two swans floated on the surface.

"What is this place?" she exclaimed.

"Eden." Nigel smiled, a faraway look in his eyes. "Your mother's favourite place at Buxley."

Annie had hated the pristine formal gardens on the estate, especially the topiaries.

"It's like I have no room to breathe, Nigel."

She had been plain old Annie when she arrived, the friendly American who fell in love with the younger son of the family. Being Lady Buxley imposed an unwanted set of responsibilities on her.

"Did you think Mom was a wimp?"

"She was awfully young, my dear. Younger than you are now. She was easily led."

Vicky frowned. Was her father implying something?

They sat on a stone bench facing the water.

"But you blame her."

Nigel did not respond, causing her to flare up.

"She is the strongest person I know. And she gave up a lot for me. Do you think you can poison my mind against her?"

Vicky watched her father turn ashen. She had an axe to grind with him.

"My dear, you are a credit to your mother." Nigel wrung his hands in despair. "How has she been? Does she ever talk of her time at Buxley?"

Vicky admitted Annie had never mentioned it.

"I have always been Vicky Rhodes. Bess told me I was British, an earl's daughter to boot. Frankly, I don't know what I am supposed to do about it."

She hadn't gone to a fancy finishing school. But then, neither had Bess. The war had seen to that.

"Be yourself. I am so happy you are finally here. You can depend on us."

Vicky broached the subject that had been nagging her.

"Viscount Cranford hinted Mom and Miles were close. What did he mean?"

"They were friends." Nigel offered a simple

explanation.

Vicky had sensed the Viscount wanted to insinuate more but maybe she was mistaken.

"The other night, at dinner, Miles wasn't very polite when he talked about Mom."

Nigel looked pained.

"We were a tight group. Philip and Momo, your mother and I, Bubbles, Miles, Trips ... we were inseparable that summer. "

Vicky felt his body relax.

"It was tradition to kick off the hunting season at Buxley. Everything was going so well until Philip's accident."

"That's when things began to fall apart," she murmured.

"Miles could have stood up for me. We had been together all day, you see. I was scarcely out of his sight." Nigel's voice rose. "That's how the rumours started."

Vicky wanted to be sure what he was referring to.

"You mean he threw you to the wolves? But why? What did he have to gain?"

Nigel gave a shrug.

"Revenge."

Revenge for what, Vicky wondered, more confused than before.

Chapter 14

The Buxley Arms was filled to the rafters with the evening crowd. Farm laborers and men who spent the day doing back breaking work had assembled for their daily pint. The regulars lined the bar, in a pleasant daze, looking around for someone gullible enough to buy them another.

One man sat under a beam of light in the centre of the pub, at the best table it offered. He was already in his cups and Harvey, the proprietor was relieved he was a happy drunk. Lord Buxley frequented the Arms many a times, especially when he had a hankering for Mrs. Harvey's cottage pie, so Harvey was used to pandering to the toffs, especially the Gaskins family. Viscount Cranford he was not sure about.

The jungle patrol had let it be known that Lord Buxley's dear friend was sick. He might not see Christmas! His face was ashen and he had a nasty cough that made it difficult to breathe, but the deep blue eyes under his bushy brows had a life of their own. He sat by himself, his hands wrapped around a pewter tankard, smiling and nodding to a tune only he could hear.

Harvey set a plate heaped with pasties before him.

"The missus thought you could use a bite, my lord."

Ian invited him to share a pint. Harvey glanced at the bar, sent a silent signal to Mrs. Harvey who was guarding it with hands on her hips and sat down with a sigh. He had been on his feet for several hours. Mrs. Harvey would not grumble much if he said he was just doing the Viscount's bidding.

"Justice has been served, my man." Ian banged the tankard on the ancient wood table. "We are all going to get our reckoning, what?"

Harvey didn't attempt to understand. If he taxed his brain to comprehend the ramblings of every drunk who came into his establishment, he would hardly remember his own name.

"You know best, my lord."

"Miles had it coming, I say." Ian's face broke into a wide grin. "That miserable son of a gun. We are well rid of him, what?"

That got Harvey's attention.

"Are you talking about Mr. Carrington? Him that was found stabbed to death at the manor?"

"None other. And a worse scoundrel I have never met."

Harvey sensed a story, one he could regale his customers with for years.

"Had you known him well, my lord?"

"You can say that, bar man." Ian dissolved into a fit of coughing. "Couldn't have planned it better myself."

A crowd was beginning to assemble around the table. It was the scene Peter Osborne came across when he entered the pub for a quick pint. He had been up at the manor with Lord Buxley, going over some legal matters. One look at the Viscount and he decided to hang back to keep an eye on him.

The maid Flora answered his summons and brought his drink, along with lamb stew and a hunk of fresh bread and butter. Peter was aware of how precarious the Viscount's health was. It was prudent to be on hand so he could offer any assistance. The thick lenses of his spectacles fogged as he blew on the hot stew and took a bite. Mrs. Harvey reminded him of the cook his family had when he was growing up. Hearty stews and puddings had been his favourite and the lamb stew transported him to a time when he was a young lad, secure in the cocoon of his happy family with not a care in the world.

"The butcher's boy said he were found on the terrace with his throat slit." A scraggly beard with black teeth leered. "Musta' been a sight."

"So he must have gone out," Harvey mumbled.

"It was the scream, you see," Ian explained. "No gentleman can ignore a damsel in distress."

The men in the library rushed outside and looked around, trying to spot who cried for help. But their calls had not yielded a response.

"Couldn't have planned it better myself," Ian laughed and started panting, trying to catch a breath.

The man behind his table thumped him on the back, trying to be helpful. Ian rallied and banged his hand on the table, noticing the circle of men towering over him.

"A round for everyone, bar man."

There was a deafening roar as everyone began cheering. Harvey abandoned his seat with alacrity, eager to serve the drinks before the Viscount changed his mind. He knew some of the assembled company would sneak an extra pint or two, since they were not bound by the same honour code as the lords. And there was nothing wrong in it. The Viscount could well afford it, considering he was at death's door anyway.

Very few people noticed a man dressed in a lightweight summer suit walk in and grab the seat Harvey had occupied a few minutes ago. He looked around with a vague smile, curious to learn more about the uproar in the pub.

"Fancy lord here's buying everyone a pint," the man with the black teeth explained. "You come just in time, mate."

James took the tankard someone pressed on him and took a large gulp to assuage some of his thirst.

"Thank you, kind Sir." He raised it in the air and tipped his head at Ian. "Are you celebrating something?"

"That bloke what got his throat slit at the manor." The man nearest offered. "Was a rotten scoundrel."

Ian thumped the table with his fist again and roared. "Another round!" He managed a squeak but the many sharp ears around him got the gist and echoed the message loud and clear, chanting until Harvey arrived and confirmed he had heard.

"Are you sure, my lord?"

"Of course, man." Ian waved him off. "I haven't been this happy in a long time."

"Who is the lucky lady?" James asked. "We will drink to her health."

The crowd murmured its assent.

Ian blinked and the light in his eyes went out, replaced by a deep sorrow.

"You have it wrong, mister. I am celebrating the death of the worst scum that ever inhabited this earth. Miles Carrington. I simply loathed him."

"And this man is dead?" James prompted. "How?"

"Couldn't have planned it better myself," Ian boasted again. "What can I say, my heart is full. We are well rid of him. Justice, my dear Sir, has been served."

Harvey had stopped counting the drinks by this time. He set a few bottles of whiskey on the bar and began pulling pint after pint. Many of the men had succumbed to the need to be horizontal, finding chairs, tables or the dusty stone floor in some instances. Only some iron constitutions were still standing.

Peter Osborne had polished off the delicious lamb stew and was digging a spoon into Mrs. Harvey's bread and butter pudding, studded with sultanas and topped with warm, creamy custard.

"Why did you hate this man so much?" James started on his second pint, eager to hear a good story. "What did he ever do to you?"

Ian finally picked up a pasty from the plate before him and took a bite. He had indulged more than he was used to and his chest was beginning to burn. His eyes narrowed as he considered the series of injustices Miles had been responsible for over the years. What he did to Marion was unforgivable. Marion, his sweet Marion. Innocent as a baa lamb.

"He was a handsome devil, Miles. And he could charm anyone with his silver tongue. I was older but more composed, being the heir, you see. We thought Miles would take up a commission and leave for some far flung outpost of the empire. But he acquired Rosehill and decided to be a country gentleman. Who would've thought, huh?"

"You mean he was not the sort to run an estate?"

"Takes time. The kind of patience Miles didn't have. The ladies loved him, of course, with his dashing manner and flamboyant behaviour. Every girl was fair game for him, rich or poor, married or otherwise. But he went after Marion."

The Viscount rubbed his chest and coughed into

his handkerchief, managing to dab his eyes at the same time.

"Did he, err, do right by this girl?" The newcomer leaned forward, his hands on the table.

The Viscount told him things had seemed alright at first. Miles professed his deep love for the girl and married her. They had two daughters but a third one died in childbirth. It was a boy. The doctor told them they could not have any more children.

"That was unacceptable to the rascal." The viscount was getting riled up. "He needed an heir and he was going to get him one way or the other."

"You mean he was already bedding some other woman?" James sneered. "It's very common among you lords, isn't it?"

Ian was ready to drop. His voice had grown weaker as the tale unfolded. He raised a hand and looked around, hoping to spot a familiar face. Harvey came rushing to his aid.

"Is everything alright, my lord?"

"Do you have a telephone?" he rasped. "Get a message to the manor. Tell them to send a car for me."

Harvey guessed his illustrious customer was at the

end of his tether. He sprang into action and went behind the bar, urging Mrs. Harvey to catch hold of their boy and tell him to cycle to the manor at top speed.

Ian's eyes closed and he almost drifted into a deep sleep, jerking awake at the last instant. He stared at the man before him, wondering who he was.

"Where was I?" he asked. "Oh, right. I suppose Miles could have had his way with any woman but he did not want a bastard. So he killed Marion."

"What?" James sputtered, spraying Ian with his drink. "You cannot be serious."

Ian stuck to his ground. Miles had taken a life, done away with Marion so he could marry again and have a legitimate heir.

"It was my fault," he wept. "If only I had stepped up and declared my feelings sooner. She was the love of my life, you know. A gentle soul who never had an unkind thought. Sometimes I think Miles did it just to spite me."

"Why would he do that?"

"Rivalry!" Ian shrugged. "He was my friend but he always hankered after what the other man had. In this case, Marion. He knew how much I admired her. She would have been perfect as my

Viscountess."

"What do they say? Revenge is a dish best served cold. You were biding your time, waiting for a chance to get even all these years."

Ian leaned on his cane and tried to stand up. Nothing would bring Marion back.

"He was high handed with Mabel too," he added. "Would never have let her marry that secretary."

James stood up and folded his hands, staring Ian down. His friendly manner had turned steely.

"Do you admit you stabbed Miles Carrington?"

"Good Lord!" Ian's eyes grew wide. "Why would I do that?"

James pointed out he had just admitted having a strong motive to murder the man.

"Who are you, Sir?" Ian's legs wobbled and he sat down with a thud. "Not from around here, I can tell. How dare you make these wild allegations?"

"Detective Inspector James Gardner, Scotland Yard."

A murmur travelled through the circle of people around the table and a hush fell.

Peter Osborne had been whiling the time with a game of patience, wondering when the Viscount would be ready to go. He gathered his cards together and slid them in his pocket, stepping out of the pub, unnoticed.

Chapter 15

"How well do you know this Trips?" Vicky slapped on a pair of dark glasses to get rid of the sun's glare.

The girls had breakfasted with the family and set off to check on the Carringtons. Clementine warned them to mind what they said, handing over a basket Mrs. Bird had prepared.

"I'm sure they are not starving, Aunt Clem." Bess thought the struggling farmers needed their largesse more than landowners like the Carringtons.

"There's calf's foot jelly for Lord Shelby," Clementine admonished. "And strawberry jam and a pie Mrs. Bird baked. You do know he's not long for this world, Bess?"

Bess bit back a retort. Lord Shelby had been on his deathbed since the Armistice. Was he really sick? She had wondered many a time.

The car passed through the village of Buxley and started climbing a small hillock. They rode through an impressive entrance, across an avenue of oaks that stretched for several hundred meters and ended in acres of lush parkland.

"You are not paying attention," Vicky grumbled.

"I hear you loud and clear." Bess gave a deep yawn and yanked the wheel to bypass a squirrel who had run into her path. "Trips has been around all my life. I always thought he whined a lot but now I am beginning to think he may have been justified."

Vicky asked why and Bess told her the story of the two brothers.

"Lord Shelby had a bit of a roving eye in his youth. At least that's what Grandma Louise says. Maybe that's why Miles was his favourite."

"And Trips is straitlaced?"

"He's a namby pamby, Vicky. Lord Shelby isn't the only one who runs all over him."

Vicky pitied the man. She thought he had kind eyes.

"Don't you go feeling sorry for him," Bess warned. "We need to be tough when we question him."

Vicky wanted to go back to Buxley and sit on the bench in her mother's garden.

"What do you think about Eden?"

Bess crinkled her eyes and looked at her. "Are you talking about the garden in the Bible?"

"No, the one at Buxley."

Bess slammed the brakes and the car shuddered to a stop in the middle of the road.

"What in the blazes do you mean?"

Vicky told her about the wild garden Nigel had taken her to.

"Our mother planned it, apparently. It's so beautiful, Bess. And there's a pond with two swans. Monte Cristo and Lady Liberty. Mom will be surprised to know they are still alive."

Bess curled her fists and tried to tamp down the rage that bubbled up inside her. A vague memory surfaced. Her nurse had taken her to the pond a few times to feed the swans. She had bent over too far once and tumbled into the water. Nanny pulled her out immediately but she had been soaked to the skin. Aunt Clem had decided it was too dangerous so they never went there again.

"Buxley spans a thousand acres, more or less. Hard to know every inch of it, old girl."

Vicky patted her arm, blaming herself for being inconsiderate.

Bess started the car and neither of them said a word until they reached the house. The butler ushered them in and took them to a parlour where most of the clan was assembled. Clara squealed with delight when she saw them and jumped up to envelop Bess in a hug.

"You're just in time for tea. I am bored out of my mind, Bess. Mother arrived yesterday with a list of do's and don'ts. I have to wear this ghastly black dress which doesn't even fit."

Bess realized the family was in mourning. Clara looked like a sausage in a crepe dress she had outgrown years ago.

"Maybe we shouldn't have come."

"Nonsense!" Trips assured her. "You are family, my dear. We could use a bit of cheering up."

Bess took the cup of tea Mrs. Carrington offered and inquired after the Baron.

"He's aged ten years," Trips replied, munching on a thick slice of fruit cake. "Miles was his favourite and the only one he spoke to nowadays."

Vicky thought the whole county must know how much Lord Shelby favoured Miles over Trips.

Bess ate fruit cake, drank tea and made small talk.

The cricket match came up as it always did this time of the year.

"Miles was an all rounder," Trips clucked. "The Buxley side is weak now that he's gone. Poor chap had been working on his spin the past month."

Clara suggested going for a walk, her mouth set in a mutinous pout, daring her mother to intervene. The future baroness ignored her and soon the girls were out in the sunshine, ambling down a damp path lined with hollyhocks.

"She's insufferable!"

Bess and Vicky didn't need to ask who Clara was referring to.

"Wear black indeed! Are we living in the Victorian Age? Why, you wore a black dress for your birthday!"

"Right." Bess quirked an eyebrow. "It's actually quite the fashion."

"Oh Bess!" Clara sighed. "Your birthday party was the best! And the ball was just magical. All those posh girls from the city … I hope they didn't think I was a country bumpkin."

Bess asked how many men she had danced with.

"Not a lot of the city folks," Clara admitted. "Mabel introduced me to that Marquess but he had eyes only for her. I was stuck with Gordon."

Bess and Vicky shared a swift glance, glad Clara had brought him up herself.

"You don't mean he's the only guy you danced with?" Vicky asked. "I hope he didn't step on your toes."

"Gordon's alright," Clara shrugged. "A bit frumpy and not quite from our circle but he went to the right schools, I suppose. He knew quite a lot of the guests."

Bess needed a better answer.

"At least he was with you when they found Miles. Must have been a shock."

Clara told her he had been fetching champagne.

"I warned him he would miss the fireworks," she prattled, "but he insisted. Thankfully, I had no idea what was going on until he returned. Then I heard Mabel scream."

Bess told her about their upcoming jaunt to London.

"Bubbles insists. She wants to go flat hunting."

"I don't think Mother will allow me to go." Clara fidgeted, declaring she was going inside to change. "I am itching all over."

Bess looked around for Trips when they went inside, saying she had a message for him.

"He'll be in the library," Clara shrugged, beseeching them to take her to London. "I can sneak out of here somehow."

"We'll see," Bess promised, heading to the library.

Trips sat behind a large desk by the window, barely visible behind a tome of ledgers.

"Anybody home?" Bess crooned. "Papa wants to know how you are holding up."

"Oh, it's you, Bess." Trips gave her a sheepish smile. "And Vicky, is it? A bit of a kerfuffle this, what?"

The girls offered to help him any way they could.

"I can barely make sense of these." He pointed at the ledgers. "But you can take a stab at them if you like." He bit his tongue. "Wrong choice of words. I am not the brightest bulb in the box at the best of times. Miles and I might have had our differences, but I loved him, you know. He was my baby brother."

Vicky asked him about the funeral. Trips told them it would take place in the next few days.

"That Inspector called this morning. Dr. Evans has finished the post mortem. It's nothing unexpected. Miles was killed with a sharp knife or dagger. There is an inquest tomorrow but it is merely a formality."

"You met DI Gardner?" Bess inquired.

"I didn't have a choice." Trips laughed. "Was here to interrogate me. I am surprised he did not ask me to go to the station."

Neither twin had to pretend about their interest. Bess tried to be delicate while framing her next question but it was not necessary. Trips volunteered the information himself.

"Wanted to know my whereabouts during the evening," he told the girls. "Poor man's just doing his job but he couldn't be more ridiculous. I was right there, playing cards with the rest of them."

Bess decided she would ask her father to confirm that.

"Was taken aback when he learned I was in line for the title," Trips continued. "What could I possibly gain from my brother's death?"

"Did he tell you if he suspects anyone?" Vicky

nudged. "You have every right to ask how far he has come with his investigation."

Trips told them nothing would bring Miles back.

"People know Rosehill flourished at his hand but the truth is, Oakview couldn't be profitable without him either. And Gordon helped. That boy did all the legwork Miles didn't have time for."

Bess remembered how brusque Miles had been with Gordon.

"Did they get along well?"

"Well enough in the beginning," Trips shrugged. "But the boy overstepped. Miles caught him alone with Mabel and it was clear he did not approve."

Miles had warned Gordon to back off.

"Young blood!" Trips chuckled. "I'm surprised he didn't elope with Mabel."

Bess thought that was a bit bold for a hired hand.

"I don't think Gordon has the gumption to do something like that."

"Miles wasn't taking any chances, my dear. He fired Gordon. Told him to clear out in a week."

This was news to the girls. Gordon Phipps had a strong motive to kill Miles. Had he been hotblooded enough though? He was free to marry Mabel now that Miles wasn't around to object. Bess was sure Mabel came with a sizable fortune that couldn't hurt.

"Where will he go?" Vicky asked, feeling sorry for him.

New York and Newport had a hierarchy but class differences were not so rampant in America. A well educated, hard working man had plenty of opportunities to better himself.

Trips told them they didn't need to worry.

"Asked him to stay on, of course. I can barely keep up with Oakview. Need help managing both estates."

"But what about Mabel?" Bess was curious. "Does this mean you approve of her interest in Gordon?"

Trips wasn't worried.

"She's just stretching her wings. Clara told me she's terribly into some Marquess she met at your party, Bess. As for Gordon, I know how to keep him in line."

There was a knock on the door and the butler came

in.

"It's time, Mr. Trevor."

Trips shut the ledger he was perusing with a bang and stood up.

"Duty calls, girls. Time for Papa's lunch. Miles joined him every day. Unfortunately, I'm a poor replacement."

Bess knew Trips wasn't joking. Lord Shelby's indifference must be hard to bear. She felt sorry for him.

They accompanied him to the hallway and said goodbye.

"Who do you think did it?" Bess asked at the last minute, expecting him to shrug and walk off.

Trips gave a big pause, then managed to surprise her.

"My money's on Ian. Viscount Cranford? Miles stole Marion from him."

"Stole?" Vicky frowned.

"Just a figure of speech, my dear." Trips smiled. "Miles took great pleasure in snatching things from people. The more coveted, the better."

Had he snatched her mom from her father, Vicky wondered.

"Marion? Mabel's mother?" Bess quizzed. "What was her connection to the Viscount?"

Trips told them how Ian had been in love with her.

"He never forgave Miles. And now that he's dying, he has nothing to lose."

Chapter 16

Cecil Chilton had spent the morning working on his sermon in vain. He finally gave up the effort, admitting he could not concentrate. The clock in the parlour down the hall began chiming the hour of eleven. It was time for tea.

The study door opened and Cordelia Chilton bustled in, followed by a maid bearing the tea tray.

"Set it over there," she directed. "And mind you don't spill a single drop."

The maid was new, one in a succession of girls from the village who Cordelia had undertaken to train. She gave a light curtsy and went out.

Cecil stood up, stretched and pulled at the collar around his neck. Sometimes it felt more like a noose.

"This blasted heat," he swore under his breath.

"How many times have I told you, Cecil? You are supposed to be a role model for your parishioners, the picture of propriety."

"There's no one here but us, Mother."

He accepted the cup of tea she handed him and took a long sip. Cook had sent scones with clotted cream and strawberry jam. Cecil put liberal amounts of both on one and proceeded to eat.

"I worry about you." Cordelia nibbled on a biscuit, her brow set in a frown. "Someone is bound to find out sooner or later. What happens then? Have you thought about that?"

Cecil reminded her he was firmly ensconced at Buxley.

"Nigel will never ask us to leave, Mother. Surely you trust him that much."

"He's not the one I'm worried about. It's your reputation."

Cecil bit his lip, trying to curb the bile that rose in his throat. He had suffered from nightmares for months, thinking about the ridicule he would face if his past was revealed.

"If push comes to shove, I will confess everything."

Cordelia thought her son was being dramatic. People could be so cruel. They would become fodder for gossip. Her own family might judge her, and then where would they be?

"I thought we are trying to avoid that."

Cecil turned his back on her and stared out of the window. Purple wisteria bloomed in profusion over a trellis. Pink and yellow roses lined the path leading to the graveyard. There was a sense of peace here. He preferred the simple life he led, so different from the days of his youth. People had expectations from a vicar. He had fit himself in the mould years ago and now his time was accounted for. There was little room to stray or be tempted by shiny objects. Other than the occasional visits to the manor, his life was bleak and devoid of luxury.

"My life of dissipation has caught up with me, Mother."

"Again with the drama." Cordelia shook her head. "You should never have listened to Miles."

The silence stretched between them until Cecil flared up.

"What choice did I have? The man showed up at my door, needled me with endless insinuations. What did I ever do to him?"

"Some old grudge?" Cordelia speculated. "Miles had a reputation for being nasty. I don't think he needed a reason to badger someone."

Cecil thought it had been pure harassment with an unknown motive. With Miles gone, he would never know what had driven him.

"Remember what he did to Nigel?" Cordelia brought up the past. "The way he carried on with Annie was just scandalous. I don't blame her, of course. The poor girl was just being friendly. But Miles knew how it would be perceived. He might have been raised to be a gentleman but he wasn't one."

Cecil wished his mother would stop talking about Miles Carrington. The man had been a menace when he was alive. Was he going to taunt him from beyond the grave too?

"We need a good spinner for our side. And our boys need to handle the swing better. It's high time we taught those upstarts from Ridley a lesson."

"Your life's on the line and you talk about cricket? Are you trying to be facetious, dear?"

Cecil told her he was changing the subject.

"Miles is a closed chapter. Promise me you won't bring him up again, Mother."

Like her Gaskins ancestors, Cordelia was headstrong at best and stubborn as a mule at worst.

"On one condition … tell me what happened that day? Don't skip a single detail."

Cecil surmised she was talking about the day of the party. After a lot of deliberation, he had finally decided to confront his nemesis. Miles had been hinting at some dark secret for months, one that would finish Cecil off. He never actually said what it was, leaving Cecil to agonize over the numerous possibilities.

"He was going to meet me at a pub that evening, as you know."

"The Buxley Arms?"

"No, another pub somewhere else. That's beside the point."

Cordelia nodded, encouraging him to continue.

"There's not much to tell. He never showed up."

Cecil had waited an hour beyond the appointed time, going over and over what he would ask Miles, trying to remember some of the shenanigans of his youth. There had been drunken parties he didn't remember, some nights in the slammer, that time he had purloined a girl's bracelet and pawned it for cash, some secretary he had a fling with. Actually, there had been two or three secretaries but they had been willing, girls eager to embrace the modern ways of the new century. He had never forced his attentions on anyone, he was sure. At least not while he was in his senses. Miles wasn't a part of his usual crowd but there had been times when Cecil tagged along with Philip and his posse, Nigel and Trips and Miles. Try as he might, Cecil could not remember doing anything dishonourable on purpose.

"Why were you late?" Cordelia asked, not convinced. "You missed dinner, a lavish one too."

Cecil had been looking forward to it. He had disappointed his niece. Bess was so cross with him, she hadn't spoken to him at all that night. She had not even brought Vicky to the vicarage yet, sending a silent signal.

"I was held up. A woman wanted my advice and I could not refuse."

"What woman?" Cordelia's eyebrows shot up. "Was it someone you know? And why won't you tell me where all this took place?"

Cecil realized his mother wouldn't let go until she had the whole story. The woman was a stranger to him but she was clearly distressed. She must have seen his collar and grabbed it like a lifeline.

"I don't know who she was but I couldn't refuse to help her. It took me the better part of an hour to listen to her woes and offer my opinion."

Cordelia had buried her eldest son, never admitting she had no expectations from Cecil. When he was young, she had resigned herself to be disgraced by him. Then he became a man of the cloth. He was bound by an oath but she could not be sure he was not lying to her.

"You realized you were going to be late?"

Cecil flung his hands in the air.

"I couldn't ignore a weeping woman who needed me, Mother. And I had a faint hope Miles would make it."

"He sent you there on a wild goose chase. I doubt he ever intended to meet with you."

Cecil had come to the same conclusion.

"Do you think the ball will swing much in August?"

Cordelia refused to comment, choosing to leave the room.

Cecil turned his attention toward his sermon, trying to concentrate. He gave up after a few minutes. His mind turned to the night of the party and the shock of finding Miles dead. Stabbed, Dr. Evans had said.

Had one of Nigel's guests done it, or Nigel himself? Cecil knew how much the Gaskins family had suffered over the years. But Nigel was a gentle soul. He hoped the police would find the culprit. Otherwise, all those present would forever stay under suspicion.

Several of the assembled men had a motive to kill Miles. But who had been audacious enough to actually do the deed? Viscount Cranford had blamed Miles for Marion's death but did he have the strength to subdue another man when he could barely breathe?

He saw a man walk past the window, wearing a well cut suit, screaming authority. There was a knock in the distance and Cecil braced himself for the inevitable questions.

Cordelia came in, followed by the stranger.

"Scotland Yard, I presume?" Cecil clasped his hands behind his back and met his gaze.

"Detective Inspector James Gardner. I would like to ask you a few questions."

Cordelia might have lingered but the Inspector suggested she leave.

"How can I help you?" Cecil swallowed a lump, trying to sound cordial.

The first few questions were easy enough. Cecil's mind was whirring, trying to anticipate what was coming.

"So you missed the meal but joined the men in the library."

Cecil gave a nod.

"Did you hear the scream too?"

Cecil leaned against a rolltop desk, puzzled.

"I'm not sure what you are talking about, Inspector. I wasn't there for long. Someone started a card game and I slipped out and made my way to the parlour."

There was a pause while the Inspector mulled over this.

"You preferred to join the ladies?"

"I was hankering for a cup of tea. Mrs. Bird sent up some sandwiches, knowing I missed dinner."

"Did you go back to the library that night?"

Cecil shook his head.

"What was your opinion of Miles Carrington? Would you say he was a good man?"

"Every man is equal in the eyes of God," Cecil replied. "Are you just fishing, Inspector? Or did you have a specific question?"

"Who wanted him dead?"

Cecil considered diplomacy.

"One can't help but hear gossip in a village. Miles was not happy with his secretary."
"Because he was courting Miss Mabel?"

Cecil shrugged.

"There is this rivalry between the brothers …"

"I hear Trevor Carrington is helpless and ineffectual. He reaped the benefits of his brother's hard work." DI Gardner folded his hands and leaned back in the Hepplewhite chair. "What about Lord Buxley?"

"Nigel wouldn't hurt a fly."

"Apparently, Miles insulted Lord Buxley's daughter at dinner. They had words in an alcove in the hall, on their way to library."

Cecil's eyes sparkled with interest at this new

information.

"Ian, Viscount Cranford …"

DI Gardner smiled, thinking of the scene in the pub.

"I doubt he would celebrate with the whole village if he was the killer."

Cecil shrugged his shoulders and shook his head.

"That's all I can think of, Inspector. Are you shaking the tree, waiting for the apples to fall?"

The Inspector let a smile slip.

"What about your relationship with him? He was spotted going in or out of the vicarage several times in the past few months."

"People see me for various reasons," Cecil replied.

"He wasn't one of your parishioners, though."

Cecil was tired of the cat and mouse game.

"Why would I kill Miles, tell me? What could I possibly gain from his death?"

DI Gardner stood up and flicked a speck of dust off his shoulder. He pinned the vicar with a sharp look.

"I don't know yet, Reverend. But you can be sure I'll find out."

Chapter 17

"Did we have to get up so early?" Bess grumbled as Vicky and Bubbles piled into the car to leave for the railway station.

The girls were going up to London for the day to look at flats. Sir Dorian was firmly against the idea so he had not been informed. As far as anyone at Buxley knew, it was a shopping trip to replenish their summer wardrobes and show Vicky around.

"We meet the agent at 9 AM sharp." Bubbles could not hide her excitement. "I plan to see as many properties as possible today but I won't decide anything."

They had tried to persuade Momo to join them but she stuck to her ground, claiming she didn't want any part of it.

Vicky clutched a brown paper bag Barnes had handed her, filled with sandwiches and cake Mrs. Bird had provided for the journey.

"Why not something civilized like a basket, Barnes?" Bubbles frowned.

"You don't want to lug it all over the city, Miss Gertrude."

Dew drops clung to shrubs and the flowers were just opening their petals, bathed in the early morning sun. A few cumulus clouds dotted the deep blue sky and the forecast was favourable, promising another scorching day.

They reached the station at Chipping Woodbury minutes before the guard gave the signal and the train began to move. The girls scrambled up the steps of the first class compartment and pulled Bubbles in.

Bess wasted no time in finding their seats. Bubbles bagged the window opposite Vicky and they dissolved into laughter.

"Long live Mrs. Bird." Bess pulled egg and bacon sandwiches from the bag and handed them out.

"So tell me, Vicky," Bubbles said after they had polished off the food. "What do you think of Buxley? Is it terribly rustic compared to New York?"

"Rustic or not, it's her home," Bess cut in. "She's hardly seen anything yet, Bubbles. We are yet to go punting in the lake or camping out at the folly. Miles Carrington has seen to that."

Bubbles declared they were not to talk of anything unpleasant.

"We are going to have fun, girls. Don't start the day off with any morbid talk."

Bess thought Bubbles had a one track mind.

"He was your age, wasn't he? You must have known him better than us."

Bubbles acted outraged. "Please! He was older. Closer to Philip's and Nigel's age than mine. They were great chums. Went off to Eton the same year and even shared dorms, if I remember correctly."

"Is it true what they say?" Vicky spoke up. "Did he have an affair with our mother?"

"Philip?" Gertrude was vague on purpose.

"No, Bubbles!" Bess rolled her eyes. "Miles Carrington. We heard some rumours at the pub."

Gertrude looked at the countryside flying past the window. There was a lot of brown interspersed with green that year, thanks to the harsh weather.

"Your parents married for love, girls. Nigel didn't have a penny to his name. He might have played second fiddle to Philip all his life but Annie cared tuppence."

Bess thought that was an evasive answer.

"You can be frank." Vicky sighed. "Our parents may have been in love once but something broke them apart."

"Something or someone," Bess interrupted. "And I want to know if that someone was Miles."

"What if it was?" Gertrude huffed. "He's gone from our lives now."

The twins did not like the answer. That meant Nigel could have a motive to kill Miles.

Bess thought of the man she had only thought of as Mabel's father. He had always looked askance at her, calling out her hoydenish ways, unlike Trips who showered her with affection.

"Who do you think killed Miles?" she asked. "And why?"

Gertrude thought it could have been anyone.

"Miles liked to have fun at the other man's expense. And he didn't always move in the best crowd. He was an inveterate gambler and he would go anywhere in search of a card game. Places toffs like us never see in their lifetime."

Bess thought something didn't add up.

"How would such a person get access to the manor? Most of our servants have been with us for decades. And Barnes never takes on any new staff without checking references."

Vicky reminded her of the catering company from London.

"Do you think the killer might have been disguised as one of their staff?"

Bess folded her arms, twisting her mouth.

"If that's the case, we are doomed. They will never find him. Or her."

Gertrude gave her a sardonic smile.

"What?" Bess exploded. "If he frequented disreputable places, chances are there is a spurned woman or two out for his blood."

An attendant walked by with the tea trolley, providing a welcome diversion. Bess dozed off after that and Vicky buried her nose in a book. Before they knew it, the train was rolling into Paddington Station. A taxi took them to the estate agent Gertrude was going to meet. He sized them up quickly and began showing plans of the properties available.

Gertrude waved a hand in the air, impatient to get

going.

"I would rather see these places with my own eyes, if you don't mind."

The agent cleared his throat, looking uncomfortable.

"If Madam could give an indication of her budget …"

"Oh please!" Gertrude gave him a withering look. "Don't be vulgar. I am a baronet's daughter. Money is no object."

Vicky stifled a smile but Bess didn't hold herself back.

"That means she won't be any wiser if you tack on a few hundred pounds on the actual price. It's your lucky day, Mister."

The agent's mouth hung open and drops of sweat dotted his brow. He pulled out a handkerchief and pressed it against his temples, hastening to assure them he would give them a fair deal.

They headed to Mayfair where most of the flats were situated. Gertrude dismissed the first two as too small.

"I don't relish traversing three flights of stairs every

time," she complained. "And how on earth am I supposed to make do with only three bedrooms? What if I have guests?"

The last one on the list finally made her smile. A passenger lift whisked them up to the fifth floor, offering five bedrooms and three receiving rooms, two bathrooms and separate staff quarters.

"Draw up the paperwork." Gertrude nodded at the agent, handing him her card. "It's time for champagne, girls. The Savoy's calling our name."

Another cab took them to the famous hotel on the Strand. Vicky admitted she had never been there before.

"Mom loves this place," she told Bess. "She used to sit at a window table and watch the bustle on the street outside."

Gertrude told her they were in for a treat.

The maître de greeted them with a deep bow and led them to their table. Champagne was ordered, along with canapes to tide them over until their chops were ready.

"You are welcome to visit me in the city any time, girls. One of the bedrooms in that tiny flat has your name on it. Now if only I could persuade Momo."

Bess spotted a lot of familiar faces as she sipped her champagne. A group of girls she vaguely knew were darting glances at their table, trying to be inobtrusive but managing to be the exact opposite. Although Bess could not hear what they were saying, she could easily guess.

"I think we are famous."

Vicky gave a shrug. In her experience, a group of girls could always be counted on to gossip, however mundane the topic. And murder trumped everything.

"Just ignore them," Gertrude advised. "They will forget all about you the minute any eligible young men enter the room."

Truer words had never been spoken.

A couple of shrieks emanated from the table when a trio of men came in, dressed to the nines in dapper suits and cravats. One of them twirled a cane in the air, a benevolent smile plastered on his face. He saw them a moment before Bess realized who it was.

"What ho, ladies." He bowed and nodded, staring at the fourth chair which was empty. "Dare I hope Mabel is here with you?"

"You remember the Marquess of Turnbridge,

Vicky?" Bess asked her sister.

"Oh please!" The man sat down and picked up a canape. "Call me Curtis. We go back a long way, eh, Bess?"

A waiter arrived and poured champagne for the Marquess. Gertrude told him she was going to be a resident of the city soon.

"Oh bravo, Bubbles!" Curtis clapped his hands. "Do you promise to be my dance partner?" He started telling them about an exclusive club that had just sprung up. "They have the best jazz band, straight from America. But I have yet to find a young woman who can keep up with me."

Gertrude slapped him on the shoulder, unable to hide a blush.

"I'm old enough to be your mother, you rogue!"

"Surely you jest, my lady?" Curtis placed a hand on his heart and acted outraged.

Vicky smiled at their banter, mentally drafting a letter to her mother. It was time Annie knew her daughter was living at Buxley Manor. Vicky was fascinated by her hitherto unknown family, especially the great aunts and her Grandma Louise. She already felt an affinity toward them. But Nigel was the one she was most curious about. So many things about him were an enigma.

Curtis lingered after the usual pleasantries had been exchanged, prompting Gertrude to ask if he would like a lamb chop. Instead of taking the hint, he ordered a cocktail and told the waiter to keep them coming.

"I say, have any of you been to see Mabel?" He drained half his Gin Rickey in a single gulp. "The poor girl! Imagine the shock of coming across a dead body, then discovering it's none other than your own pater. I mean, I don't go hobnobbing with the Duke on a regular basis, but I would lose it if I came across him like that. I mean, dash it, it's too much, what?"

He finished his drink and started on another, speedily supplied by the waiter who sensed a big tip coming his way.

Bess popped a poached oyster in her mouth, knowing he wasn't done.

"You're very taken with young Mabel then." Gertrude took the bull by the horns. "Are you planning to see her again?"

Curtis assured her he wanted to.

"She makes the heart sing." He flashed a sheepish grin. "But I'm not sure she's interested."

"You are giving up that easily?" Gertrude teased. "Young men were a lot more tenacious in my day."

"Oh, Bubbles! I've been trying to write a poem for her but I'm stuck. Should I quote Byron or Shakespeare?" He gave Bess a pleading look. "What are her hobbies?"

Bess told him she liked to ride, then debated telling him about Gordon.

Curtis picked up his third cocktail, growing morose before their eyes.

"I may be too late, of course. One of the chaps told me she had a thing for Phipps."

"You know Gordon?" Bess didn't hide her surprise.

"He was at Eton." Curtis waved a hand in the air. "We know the same people. You know how it is."

Bess wanted to ask if he had spoken to Gordon at the party but he beat her to it.

"I tried to talk to him that night, you know. Just to make sure he was fine with me spending time with Mabel. I mean, I didn't want to encroach, what?"

Bess and Vicky were on tenterhooks, wondering what he would say next.

"Bumped into him as I was going to get champagne."

"Was this before we found Miles?" Vicky asked.

Curtis drained his drink and stood up, swaying for a second.

"A few minutes before the fireworks. He walked in from the terrace, somewhat red in the face. I half expected a girl to come in after him."

Chapter 18

The girls had been exhausted when they got home from London the previous night. Momo was waiting for them, eager for an update.

"I was thinking of going straight to bed," Bess groaned. "Why didn't you come with us, Momo?"

"Exactly!" Gertrude backed her up. "Serve you right if we all ask for a supper tray and keep you hanging."

Barnes cleared his throat and whispered something to Bess.

"On second thoughts, I think I will wash and come down. Come on, Vicky!"

As it turned out, Mrs. Bird had made Railway Mutton Curry, knowing Bess would be tired from the journey.

"Birdie's a brick," she told Vicky as the twins scampered up the stairs. "She knows how to pamper me."

Vicky knew her sister loved her curry and wild

horses wouldn't drag her away from a spicy meal. Bess coaxed her to try some every time. Vicky concluded it wasn't bad, not as fiery as she had expected.

"Bravo, my dear. You're catching on." Nigel had beamed in approval.

They congregated in Momo's sitting room after the meal and told her about their day over cups of tea and petit fours.

"You must come next time," Gertrude urged. "There is a world out there, waiting for you."

It was past midnight when the twins bid the other two goodnight and headed up. Bess stayed up for a long time and then overslept. Breakfast had been cleared when she went down and there was no kedgeree.

A footman set a rack of toast before her at a nod from Barnes.

"I beg your pardon, my lady." He was suitably apologetic. "Shall I ask Mrs. Jones to come and see you?"

Bess tapped her egg open with a spoon and relented.

"Never mind, Barnes. Have you seen Vicky?"

"In the library with Lord Buxley," he replied.

Eager to join them, Bess rushed through her meal and headed over, requesting Barnes to send some tea to the library. Polo ran over and placed his paws on her knees, greeting her with a wide smile.

Nigel wore a proud expression as he pointed out all the first editions to Vicky.

"This section here is for American authors. I ordered them for your mother so she wouldn't feel homesick."

Bess had read all of them, wondering what her mother was like as she flipped through the pages. Had Vicky ever read Dickens or Byron?

"What ho!" she sang with all the bonhomie she could muster. "Are you neglecting me in favour of your oldest child, Papa?"

Nigel dismissed her with a laugh.

"What nonsense you utter sometimes, Bessie."

Vicky asked about their plans for the day, wondering when they might visit the vicarage.

"I say," Nigel interrupted. "Can you girls run down to Chipping Woodbury? I need some papers delivered to our solicitors."

"Can't Peter come here?" Bess collapsed in a faded leather chair and stretched her feet before her, scratching Polo's ears. "Honestly, I think I need a nap."

Vicky offered to drive but Bess shot her down with a horrified look.

"You stick to the healing, sis," she sighed. "Leave the mundane tasks to me."

Nigel started talking about the cricket match, roping them in to watch a practice session the next morning. Vicky had never seen anyone play the game and agreed readily. Bess asked if he wanted to come with them but Nigel declined. His face turned grave for the first time that morning, reminding the girls of the tough target they had set for themselves.

After informing Mrs. Jones to not expect them for lunch, the girls set off.

"This gives us a chance to talk to Peter." Bess stifled a yawn as she steered the car around a ditch. "Papa's done us a favour."

Vicky tried to remember him from the night of the party.

"He barely said a word."

"Don't be fooled by his quiet persona. Peter is very clever and an excellent solicitor. Papa has placed a lot of trust in him."

Kettering and Osborne was set in a nondescript house in the centre of the bustling market square. Peter looked surprised to see them but greeted them warmly.

"Hardly got a chance to chat, Bess. How are you liking being twenty one?"

"I haven't thought about it much," Bess replied honestly. "You know Vicky, right?"

Introductions were made again and Peter expressed surprise at their situation.

"I had no idea."

"You are in the minority," Bess smirked. "Along with us. Turns out most of the senior servants knew, as did the great aunts, Grandma Louise and so on. Even Momo knew, dash it."

Peter sympathized with them.

"Do you feel duped? How are you coping with it?"

"Deprived, more like." Vicky spoke up. "We had some time to get used to it. But it was a big shock when we found out."

Bess handed over the papers they had brought and mentioned Miles, watching Peter's face for any sign of emotion.

"Vicky and I were planning to make a big splash on our birthday but he stole our thunder."

He clucked and shook his head, sighing over how shocking the whole episode had been.

"Who do you suspect, Peter?" Bess pushed. "You might hide behind those thick glasses but I know how observant you are."

"I barely knew the man, girls. He was a lot older, more your father's age than mine."

Vicky asked about motive.

"You must have heard people talk. Why was he killed, do you think?"

Peter fiddled with an ink pot, reluctant to answer.

"He was a rich man, wasn't he? I think that must have been the reason he lost his life." He stared in the distance, mulling over something in his mind. "If I were to guess …" He shook his head. "No, I'd rather not say."

"Come on," Bess groaned. "Be a sport. It's just us. We won't go telling tales on you."

Peter smiled, looking younger than his thick glasses and grey hair allowed him to.

"I know you are a good egg, young Bess. Well, since you insist … his brother, Trevor."

"Trips?" Bess burst out. "What absolute rot!" She noted Peter's crestfallen look and relented. "I mean, are you sure? Trips is a brick."

Peter told them it was logical. Word on the street was that Miles not only had money, he retained full control over his father's properties.

"Trevor might inherit but he cannot keep the estate going," Peter explained. "All that will change now."

They talked about where Peter had been when the body was discovered. Then the girls took their leave.

"I wish I could offer you a spot of tea." Peter was apologetic. "But I just walk down to the tea room next door."

Bess told him it was alright. It was late and they were expected back home for lunch. "Toodle-pip."

They squeezed into the car and drove half a mile away from the market square.

"Where are we going?" Vicky wanted to know.

"To sample the best onion gravy in the Cotswolds, served over local sausages and the creamiest potatoes you ever dug a fork into."

Vicky decided to keep an open mind.

They stepped into a two storied structure called The Laughing Mongrel, built of a faded yellow stone, with stacks of chimneys rising up from a slanting roof. Ivy ran up one side and Vicky spied the hint of a garden at the back. The interior was dark and cool and the girls were happy to get out of the sun. Exposed beams lined the ceiling and a particular smell that was at once savoury, sweet and a bit sour filled the air.

Bess greeted the barmaid like an old friend.

"The usual please, Lottie."

"With extra gravy." The girl gave an awkward curtsy. "Yes'm. Your ladyship." She darted a glance at Vicky and bent at the knee again. "Err, your ladyship."

Vicky watched amused as the pub owner bustled over to greet them, wiping his hands on a dirty apron.

"How are you, Mr. Jones?" Bess greeted, informing Vicky the man was the youngest brother of their housekeeper Mrs. Jones.

"Haven't seen you since Christmas, my lady. The missus will be glad yer here." He bowed before Vicky. "Spitting image," he murmured. "Welcome to the Laughing Mongrel, my lady."

The maid brought two tankards of ale for them. Vicky hesitated before taking a sip, letting the deep flavour of caramel and malt roll over her tongue. It wasn't unpleasant.

The sausages arrived, smothered in a rich, dark gravy. Lottie placed a small jug filled to the brim with more gravy next to Bess.

Bess dug in and went into raptures. Vicky had to admit the food was good.

"The pork is from our home farm," Bess told her. "Buxley pigs are the best. "

"Are these the same you play with?" Vicky was aghast.

There were aspects of rural life she found hard to understand.

"A pig is bacon, all said and done." Bess told her. "No point in getting emotional. "

Vicky thought a lifetime wouldn't be enough to understand the British.

"You are one of us, darling." Bess read her thoughts again.

The pub owner's wife came out, carrying an apple crumble oozing with sticky caramel. The scent of cinnamon and nutmeg perfumed the air with a heady aroma.

"Look at you two. The vicar didn't say anything when he were here."

"Cecil was here?" Bess dug a bit of sausage into the creamy potatoes and dipped them in gravy. "When?"

The woman looked at her husband, seeking his confirmation.

"Last week? Before last Sunday it were because we missed church on account of our Lottie twisting her ankle."

She turned to the girl.

"Go get the vicar's muffler, dear."

Bess laughed out loud.

"Muffler? What was Cecil doing wearing a muffler in this heat?"

Vicky couldn't hide her frown.

"That's a woollen scarf," Bess explained.

Lottie came out with the garment in question.

"We thought the same," the proprietor nodded. "But it's not our place to question the vicar." He stood up straighter, his eyes widening a bit. "Are you sure it were not that woman's he was with?"

Lottie confirmed she had spotted the vicar wearing it. It was wrapped around his ears and neck so she had not recognized him at first. He had chosen a table in the darkest corner.

"We try to give him our best table otherwise," the proprietor insisted. "The missis has a theory." He nudged his wife. "Tell her."

She gave them a knowing look.

"Is the vicar walking out with someone then? High time there was wee ones at the vicarage."

Bess confessed she had no idea but she vowed to find out.

"I can give him the scarf."

"Not the type of woman the vicar would go out with," Lottie grimaced.

A troop of local farmers came in, demanding their

pints. Lottie and family finally left the girls alone.

"Why haven't I met this Cecil yet? And why did he miss our birthday dinner?" Vicky asked on the drive back.

She rubbed her stomach, feeling queasy as Bess took a sharp turn.

"Sorry, old girl. Well, Cecil was supposed to be there but he was late. That's a rum thing because Cecil is fond of a good table. Aunt Cordelia was there, of course."

Vicky wanted to know exactly how they were related and Bess explained.

"Don't you remember? Cordelia is Papa's aunt, so Cecil is his cousin but he is anything but avuncular. More like an indulgent older brother." She swerved to the side to let a farm cart pass. "Tell you what. Why don't we stop at the vicarage? We can ask him about this secret rendezvous."

Vicky shrugged. She had nowhere else to go.

Chapter 19

Vicky held on to her hat as they crested a hill and plunged into a small valley. The warmth of the sun seeped into her skin, making her drowsy.

"Can't we go back to the manor and take a nap?" she pleaded. "I'm stuffed and falling asleep as we speak."

Bess wondered what they ate in America.

"Our mother is not poor, is she?"

"Anything but," Vicky snorted. "The Rhodes family is well known on the east coast and we had a French chef along with an American cook while I was growing up."

They talked about the differences in their upbringing. Surprisingly, neither parent had placed any restrictions on the girls, allowing them full freedom. They were both trailblazers in their own right, achieving things most women were forbidden to do.

Bess longed for a cup of tea. Vicky wrinkled her nose, calling her a glutton. A hissing sound interrupted their banter and the car veered sharply to the edge of the road, threatening to land in a ditch.

"I say!" Bess swore as Vicky clutched the edge of the door, steeling herself for an impact that never happened. "We have a puncture."

"English, please!" Vicky growled. "Can't you drive carefully for once?"

Bess had managed to stop the car by the side of the road. She jumped out to check the damage, flashing Vicky a beatific smile.

"Can't help it. I will change the tire in two shakes of a lamb's tail, my dear."

Vicky climbed out more decorously and groaned when she looked at the offensive wheel. They were in a verdant dale, in the middle of the glorious English countryside and they were all alone.

"Are you going to make me walk in this heat?" She sighed. "I don't see a garage in sight."

"You don't need one because I am going to fix this myself."

Vicky didn't doubt her but when the roar of another motor sounded in the distance, she shielded a hand over her forehead and squinted in the sunlight. A car crested over the hill they had just crossed. It was a Hispano Suiza and her rumble filled their ears.

Bess was busy setting up the jack and didn't look up.

The car rolled to a stop beside them.

"Hello ladies," a familiar voice greeted. "May I be of service?"

The detective was met with unexpected opposition, Bess informing him she was more than capable of changing the spare.

"I was an ambulance driver in the war," she boasted. "I have done this under worse conditions."

Vicky backed her up.

"Guns that sound like they are going off next to you, shells exploding all around ..." Bess gave the detective a withering look. "I don't think you will understand."

The detective's mouth hardened.

"So true. I was not privileged to serve at the front."

Bess looked at the strapping six foot man before

her and wondered why he had shirked his duty. The leathery skin on the side of his face raised questions.

DI Gardner was seething inside. He faced the same condemnation every time people realized he had not gone to war. They were unaware of the number of times he had placed his life in peril without being at the battlefront. His superiors had convinced him he was indispensable at home.

"You are needed here," the superintendent had declared in no uncertain terms. "There is more than one way to serve your country."

James took it to heart and excelled during the air raids, rescuing people from torched buildings, carrying the injured to safety. A burning beam had crashed over him once, scorching one side of his face. His hand went up to his cheek involuntarily, rubbing the charred skin.

"Are you sure I cannot help?" he tried again. "If not, I will be on my way."

Bess realized they had a good opportunity to find out how far he had progressed.

"You can help by exonerating our father. Tell us you don't suspect him, Inspector."

James read the steely determination in her eyes and

knew she was serious.

"I'm afraid I can't do that, my lady. This is an ongoing investigation and we follow a certain process."

Bess flung her hands up in despair.

"There are so many people who had a strong motive to kill Miles. My Papa had none. None!"

James folded his hands and leaned against the bonnet of the Hispano.

"Enlighten me."

"Gordon Phipps, for one. He was in love with Mabel and Miles didn't bless the union. Now he is free to marry her, with Miles out of the way."

James remained inscrutable, prompting Bess to go on.

"Have you checked his alibi? Where was he when Miles was being killed?"

"You can be sure we are looking into it."

Bess thought it was an evasive answer. Vicky agreed with her.

"Did he tell you he was with Clara?" she asked

James. "I hope you didn't believe him because he lied."

"He wasn't with her all the time," Bess sneered. "Did you know that, Inspector?"

James bit back a retort, feeling weary.

"It's Detective Inspector, my lady. And …"

"Did you know Gordon was on the terrace, just before the fireworks?" Vicky interrupted. "You will agree that is very suspicious."

Bess wasn't going to be left behind.

"Clearly, he had a motive and he was right there on the terrace, Detective Inspector. What do you think of that?"

James realized the girls had managed to discover something the police did not know. But he didn't want to encourage them.

"Gordon Phipps is among the people we are checking up on. We will find the culprit in due course. Meanwhile, I suggest you stop interfering in police business."

Bess did not like to be dismissed.

"He is not from around here, you know? Gordon.

What do we know about his past? He might be a criminal hiding out here in the Cotswolds."

"I will thank you not to teach me my job." James climbed into the Hispano, making a mental note to himself to speed up the background check on Phipps. "Don't you have a ball or something to attend?"

The Hispano roared past them, leaving Bess fuming.

"How dare he! Who does he think he is?"

Vicky tried not to laugh.

"Are you going to fix the car, Bess, or should we start walking?"

They were on their way a few minutes later, soaked in sweat from the unforgiving heat. Bess sported a smudge of grease on her cheek.

"Grandma Louise says ladies are not supposed to sweat."

"That is impossible," Vicky replied, always ready with scientific facts. "Sweat is the body's natural cooling mechanism and is essential for maintaining the optimum body temperature."

Bess slapped her forehead, exclaiming in disgust.

"We are supposed to meet the great aunts at three. What time is it, Vicky?"

They barely made it. Bess insisted they go up to their rooms first to wash up and put on clean dresses.

"It just won't do, looking like this when we go meet them," she told Vicky. "You don't want a lecture on how young ladies should behave, do you?"

They ran to the west wing, rushing past Barnes and two footmen.

Louise greeted them with a twinkle in her eye.

"What mischief have you been up to, Bess?"

Aunt Hortense and Aunt Perpetua tittered, amused as the girls tried to catch their breath.

"We have talked to a lot of people," Bess began. "But I admit I am a bit stumped. What about you, Vicky?"

She agreed they needed to organize everything they knew and draw some conclusions.

The older ladies were quiet as Bess relayed what they had learned. She left out the part about Cecil because she wanted to tackle him first.

"Trips is not capable of malice," Grandma Louise declared. "I absolutely refuse to believe he would hurt Miles. Now if Trips had been the victim, I would have no qualms in thinking Miles was responsible."

The great aunts agreed with her.

Peter Osborne was dismissed as a nobody.

"Your father is trying to elevate him, my dears. My guess is he made some promise to the young man's father."

Bess was curious.

"Is that why Peter spent so many summers here? I thought Aunt Clem's boys invited him."

Vicky brought up their father.

"Why do the police think my father is involved? Based on what Bubbles said, he and Miles were great friends when they were young."

Bess gave her a sly look, marvelling at her diplomacy. Neither Louise nor the great aunts gave a pertinent reply.

"Philip, Miles, Nigel, Trips ..." Grandma Louise sighed. "They were always together, even before they went off to Eton."

Aunt Hortense mentioned the Viscount.

"We know Ian hated Miles with a passion. But I think we can take him off the list. The man can barely walk a few paces without wheezing. He does not have the strength to slash a man's throat."

Aunt Perpetua sucked in a breath and stared at her sister.

"My dear, a little delicacy wouldn't be amiss."

Grandma Louise ordered them to stop bickering and focus on the matter at hand.

"So you think this Gordon Phipps did it?" she asked the twins. "But where is the proof?"

Bess ran a hand through her short hair. She was sure they needed to look into the man's past.

"Do you know anything about the family, Grandma?" she asked. "He came from somewhere in the north. Yorkshire, I think."

Louise offered to write to an old friend who had an estate near York.

"They stay there in the summer so there is a chance she might know some people in the area. But is he one of ours, this Phipps? I have never heard of the name before."

Bess reminded them he was well educated.

"He must at least know the right people."

"That settles it," Aunt Hortense summed up. "Louise, you write to your friend. We can move on to the next item on the agenda."

"Which is?" Louise quirked an eyebrow. "Not that nonsense about some silly moniker?"

Bess and Aunt Perpetua supported Hortense. They needed a name to operate under.

"We might be famous!" Her eyes gleamed. "What if we are in the newspaper, Louise? People are not interested in reading about a bunch of old ladies gossiping over their knitting but give them a catchy name and we could be the talk of the county."

Louise thought they were deluded.

"I don't want to see my name in some trashy tabloid. It's not proper."

"What are you talking about, Grandma?" Bess interrupted.

Aunt Perpetua explained what she was thinking.

"We are like a crime solving club, aren't we? Of course we need a name."

"Oh!" Bess looked at Vicky. "We already have one. You can make it official."

The three older ladies grimaced when they heard what Gertrude had come up with.

"That's insulting!" Louise burst out. "We don't want to remind the world how old we are, Bess. A lady never reveals her age."

The twins suppressed grins. Anyone looking at the great aunts and Grandma Louise could easily guess they were born in the previous century.

"The name has to be short and catchy," Aunt Hortense stated. "Something memorable that will just roll off the tongue."

Aunt Perpetua banged her fist on the stool next to her.

"We shall be the Nightingales."

There was a brief silence as the rest of them mulled over it.

"I like it," Aunt Hortense declared. "Louise?"

"It does have a certain ring to it," Grandma nodded. "Girls?"

Bess wanted to know the significance of the name.

"Why, after Florence Nightingale, of course!" Aunt Perpetua quipped. "She wasn't a detective like Sherlock Holmes but she was a strong woman, a trailblazer, just like you two, my dears." Her eyes softened as she gazed at Vicky. "Our Victoria was a nurse in the war, wasn't she? This is a way to applaud her bravery."

"So was Bess," Vicky argued. "She might have been hired as an ambulance driver but the first aid she administered to the wounded saved many a life."

"We can agree you are both strong women," Grandma Louise beamed. "Well ahead of the times."

The older ladies looked at each other and nodded.

"Nightingales it is, then."

Chapter 20

Vicky's head reeled with an overload of information. She had woken early to watch the cricket practice, eager to spend some time with Nigel. Bess stuck to her resolve to sleep in, claiming she could not bear to exert herself before breakfast.

Eleven players were spread around a pitch on the south end of Buxley land. It was where all the matches were played, Nigel told her. The ball wasn't behaving well, making it almost impossible to bat.

"I don't know what that means," she admitted.

"Never mind, my dear. Why don't you just sit in the pavilion and enjoy the spectacle?"

This was a makeshift tent with some chairs and a table or two. Polo had claimed a sunny spot, his neck swivelling left to right as he watched the game. A tea service had been set up for the players, along with a tray of scones. Vicky was surprised when a footman arrived and poured her a cup of coffee. She supposed she had Barnes to thank for that.

The ball was thrown by a few men while a man standing beside a set of stumps swung a bat and hurled it in different directions. A man at the opposite end made wild gestures with his arms, raising them in the air or waving them around when the fancy took him.

"That means he's got six runs," Nigel whispered in her ear once. "And that finger in the air means he's out. Clean bowled, by gosh."

Peter Osborne was one of the men with the bat and was quite popular. Time passed slowly and Vicky found herself dozing off despite consuming two cups of coffee. Finally, the session came to an end and the men walked back to the pavilion, pulling off gloves, eager to quench their thirst.

Nigel complimented everyone and warned them to be on time the next day.

"This is going to be the year we beat Ridley, boys. We need to buck up."

He handed over his bat, gloves and pads to a footman and climbed into the waiting car, whistling for his dog. Vicky joined him, once again awed by the number of people who were always on hand to fetch and carry for the family.

"Did you enjoy yourself?" Nigel asked with a wink, informing the chauffer to take them back to the house. "A spot of breakfast will set you right."

"It was a novel experience."

Five minutes later, the car stopped in front of the house and Barnes came out to greet them. Nigel jumped down after Vicky and cleared his throat. She turned around and met his eyes, wondering what he wanted.

"Something wrong?"

"Does Annie know you are here?"

Vicky took a deep breath before shaking her head.

"I wrote a letter, telling he where I am. But I haven't mailed it yet."

Nigel told her Barnes would send someone to the post office whenever she was ready. They walked down the hall without another word and headed to the dining room.

Gertrude and Imogen sat next to each other, buttering toast. Bess was scarfing down a plate of kedgeree while Aunt Clem glared at her with a disapproving eye.

"Good morning Pops!" she flashed a smile at

Nigel. "And sweet sister of mine. How was the cricket?"

"Jolly good, jolly good." Nigel tried to look terse but failed miserably. "You were expected, my pet."

Bess dabbed her mouth with a napkin.

"I am like Alice, Papa. You know there are things I simply cannot handle before breakfast. Cricket is top on the list."

Vicky tapped her soft boiled egg, letting the conversation roll over her. She could almost predict what each of them would say.

Aunt Clem wanted to know if they were home for lunch.

"We are going to the vicarage," Bess informed her. "I doubt Aunt Cordelia will invite us to stay. She's more likely to come back here with us."

Nigel told her they had enough to feed an army. Hadn't they actually done it during the war, when the manor had become a convalescent house for the wounded?

"Tell Aunt Cordelia I would love to see her for lunch," he issued. "Why make her angle for an invitation?"

Bess poured herself another cup of tea while Vicky ate. Half an hour later, they stepped out in the bright day, ready for their mission. Both wore colourful summer frocks in the latest fashion with wide brimmed hats to protect them from the sun.

The vicarage was set at one edge of Buxley land and was a ten minute drive.

"Don't be nervous, old bean," Bess soothed. "Cecil is alright, even though he must be as old as Papa. He always looked the other way when I snuck sweets under the table."

"He wasn't at our birthday dinner," Vicky sighed. "So why do we need to question him?"

Bess agreed with her.

"This has nothing to do with Miles. Aunt Cordelia is cross I took you to meet the other great aunts first."

"Oh, do they have some kind of rivalry going?"

Bess laughed. "Hortense and Cordelia were inseparable in their youth, apparently. Then Cordelia married and got involved in her own household, with no time for her sisters. Perpetua and Hortense stayed single and inevitably grew closer to each other over the years."

Vicky wanted to know if Cecil was Cordelia's only child.

"He is now. Her life hasn't been easy, poor thing. The eldest son died from some tropical virus in the colonies. The one who was actually going to be our vicar was killed in the Boer War. That's when Cecil stepped in and took orders. And she had a girl a few years younger than us. The Spanish flu got her."

Vicky gasped, sorry for the many tragedies the Chiltons had faced.

"Thank you for telling me now. I might have inquired about her family."

The vicarage looked older than the manor. Beds of larkspur interspersed with yellow roses lined the path to the entrance. A maid answered the door and led them to a small parlour where Cordelia sat near the window, embroidering a cushion. Her lips twisted in a sneer when she saw them. Vicky realized she was nothing like Hortense or Perpetua.

"So you finally found time to visit."

"Hello Aunt Cordelia," Bess sang, refusing to cower. "You know Vicky, don't you?"

Vicky flashed a smile, unsure what to say. Bess had said nothing about the woman's sour disposition.

Cecil came in and saved the day. He slapped Bess on the back and beamed at Vicky.

"I say, this is spiffing. What are you girls doing here?"

Cecil appeared overjoyed to meet Vicky. He was the exact opposite of his mother and Vicky wondered how he managed to be so cheerful, living in her company.

"It's good to see you back home where you belong. Now what's this I hear about you becoming a doctor?"

"I like helping people," she replied. "Nursing is fine but I think I can do more for the disadvantaged classes with a medical degree."

"That's very noble," he praised. "Nigel will be proud of you. "

"It's unnatural," Aunt Cordelia grimaced. "My dear, you may not have been brought up to be an earl's daughter but you are one. And don't you forget that."

"Come on Mama, isn't it our duty to help the less privileged? What would you have her do? Marry some fat idiot who lives off his inheritance?"

Cordelia folded her hands and fumed but said

nothing.

"You should have seen the big fuss at our birthday dinner. Miles called Vicky all sorts of names. But Papa stuck up to her."

"Are you talking bad about the dead now? I declare, Elizabeth. You get worse every day."

Cecil apologized for missing their dinner.

"Sorry I got held up, Bess. I would have starved if Mrs. Bird hadn't sent up some sandwiches."

"So where were you?" Bess asked with an impish grin. "What was so important that you missed my 21st birthday celebration?"

Cecil turned red.

"Well, I got waylaid by a parishioner, don't you know? Couldn't get out of it. Have to assist a person in trouble, being a man of the cloth and all."

Bess told him to hold on a second and stepped out. She was back two minutes later, brandishing the scarf from the pub.

"You left this at the Laughing Mongrel. We know all about your ailing parishioner."

"What are you insinuating?" Cordelia's frown

deepened.

"Tell us about your lady friend, Cecil," Bess urged. "Does she live in Chipping Woodbury? When are we going to meet her?"

Cecil's eyebrows shot up in alarm and his eyes flew to meet his mother's.

"I say, Bess. What? What? I'm not sure what you mean."

"Aunt Cordelia will be happy to see you settle down. So will we."

Cecil refused to say anything on the subject.

"I have a sermon to prepare so I will take your leave now."

Not one to be brushed off, Bess confronted him.

"What are you hiding? And why were you wearing a scarf in this heat? Mrs. Jones at the pub said you had it wrapped around your ears and throat, as if you were trying to hide who you were." She added the last bit on her own.

"I say, Bess, this is not cricket. What?"

Bess turned to Cordelia.

"Did you force him to wear that scarf, Aunt Cordelia? You do know it's the middle of summer?"

"Now, Bess. I cut myself while shaving. Not something a chap tells a girl, least of all, his niece."

Vicky thought he was lying but she held herself back. Bess did not.

"Say I believe you. Who was that woman? Lottie said she wasn't our sort."

Cecil looked about to burst. Vicky tried to pacify him.

"Look, I don't know much about your past or present. And I really don't mind if you are in love with some maid." She shrugged her shoulders. "Times are changing, you know. Class distinctions are not going to matter much."

Cordelia gave a most unladylike snort.

Vicky ignored her and plunged ahead. "Pardon Bess for getting carried away. But we are just trying to help our father. That Inspector believes he is involved in Mr. Carrington's murder."

"But that doesn't make any sense." Cecil expelled a breath. "Nigel would never hurt anyone. I am willing to testify in court if need be. And now, girls,

I really have to go."

There was no point in lingering at the vicarage after that. Cordelia gave the girls a nasty look and Bess decided she did not deserve an invitation to lunch.

They drove back to the manor, trying to process what had happened. Bess stopped the car under a willow tree and got out. The river shimmered in the distance.

"Cecil is not a liar. He's a vicar, for heaven's sake. But I am willing to bet my car he was hiding something."

Vicky agreed with her, her eyes darting to and fro as Bess paced in front of the car.

"Can you please stop? You are making me giddy."

Bess obliged her by leaning against the tree. Cecil had a strong alibi since he had been with the ladies, having tea. She was not sure if he had visited the men in the library or not.

"Does he have a motive to kill Miles?"

Vicky's eyebrows shot up.

"Why do you say that? Didn't someone say they were friends? I think there are too many facts running around in my head, Bess. I am getting mixed up. I don't know these people like you do."

Bess corrected her.

"Papa, Philip, Miles and Trips were friends. But maybe Cecil was one of them too. He's about their age." She climbed back into the car. "You know what? Let's ask Papa."

Chapter 21

Clementine saw them return and accosted them in the hall.

"Where's Aunt Cordelia? And Cecil?"

Bess told her they were busy.

"What's for lunch, Aunt Clem? I could use some sustenance right about now."

The family had gathered in the dining room but Nigel was nowhere to be seen.

"Where's Papa? We really need to talk to him."

Clementine looked at Barnes who informed them he had asked for a tray in the library. She did not hide her displeasure.

"How long have you tried to whip everyone in shape?" Gertrude asked with a smile. "This isn't a military camp, Aunt Clem."

"But it is my home," Clementine shot back. "The home of my ancestors." She stressed the 'my', clearly implying Gertrude was an intruder. "I have had to assume the responsibilities of the lady of the house, due to certain unfortunate circumstances."

"We are very thankful, Aunt Clem," Bess interrupted before the two launched into a full blown argument. "And you are doing a jolly good job."

Mrs. Bird had made mushroom voul-au-vents and onion tarts, in honour of the Chiltons. There was a fresh summer salad, ham pie, gratin of cauliflower and bread and butter pudding with raspberry jam for dessert. It was served buffet style so everyone could pick and choose what they wanted.

Vicky sampled everything. She was beginning to develop a taste for Mrs. Bird's cooking.

Clementine ordered Barnes to send some of the tarts to the vicarage. He told her a footman had already been dispatched with a basket of the food.

The twins headed to the library after enjoying a second helping of the pudding.

"I don't think we will find him there, Vicky."

Bess was right. The library was almost deserted with no sign of Nigel but the girls were in for a surprise.

"Gordon!" Bess exclaimed. "What are you doing

here?"

He sprang up when he saw them and clasped his hands before him.

"I say! Your butler asked me to wait in here. Didn't want to disturb your lunch, what?"

Bess had a dozen questions she wanted to ask but Vicky placed a hand on her arm, silently asking her to stay calm.

"What brings you here, Mr. Phipps?" She sat on a sofa by the fireplace and urged him to sit. "Have you met Lord Buxley?"

Gordon collapsed in a chair before her, tapping his foot as he shook his head.

"I am here to meet you!"

Bess took a seat next to Vicky, perplexed.

"You have our attention, but you are not one of my favourite people right now, Gordon. Let me be very clear. This whole Miles business is hard on my Papa. The police think he might be implicated." She held up a hand, warding him off when he opened his mouth to respond. "You are the one who's lying. We know that because we have been talking to people."

Gordon turned ashen.

"You don't think I had anything to do with Mr. Carrington's death? My God, does Mabel also believe that?"

Bess thought he had played into their hands by mentioning Mabel.

"He thought you were not worthy of his daughter. That must have rankled."

"Yes, he did. But I was expecting that. My father is a doctor, not a peer of the realm. We are not posh people."

Vicky wondered why he had been flirting with Mabel if he was aware of his meagre background.

"It started as a flirtation," he admitted. "But I fell in love. Mabel is beautiful inside out and I want to spend the rest of my life with her."

Bess and Vicky believed he sounded serious. Did Mabel feel the same?

"You told everyone you were with Clara that night but you weren't. Not all the time."

Gordon admitted he had left her to get drinks.

"What were you doing on the terrace?" Vicky

leaned forward, trying to read his expression.

Bess thought he had enough time to stab Miles and come back to the party before the body was discovered.

Gordon shook his head vehemently, his eyes wild.

"That Scotland Yard chap asked me the same thing. I just wanted to scope out the place, look for the perfect spot to watch the fireworks."

He hadn't been there for more than two minutes. Bess wanted to know if he had seen anyone out there.

"Did you see anyone in the garden? Or hear something?"

Gordon told them it was quite dark outside, especially after the brightly lit ballroom. He had come back in before his eyes adjusted.

Bess was getting impatient.

"Why are you here? You need a favour, don't you? What is it? A recommendation from Papa?"

Gordon took a deep breath. Vicky sensed he was about to level with them.

"I am not entirely innocent." He rushed to

elaborate he wasn't talking about Miles. "My past will catch up with me soon and I wanted to come clean before everyone knows my secret."

Bess thought he was being melodramatic. Vicky had no inkling of what was coming.

"Surely you haven't killed someone else?"

To their immense surprise, Gordon's eyes filled up. "I am not proud of it."

He told them he had been trying hard to turn over a new leaf in the past year. Bess would never have guessed what he said next.

Educated in all the right schools, Gordon had gone back home after university to work for the local lord. He soon made himself indispensable, making the decrepit old estate turn a profit through his hard work. Then disaster struck. The lord had invited a bunch of Londoners for a summer party. After a week of picnics, excursions and dinners, the guests were getting bored. Gordon ran into one of them on a back staircase, misbehaving with a maid.

"She was barely fourteen, poor thing," he breathed. "What can I say? I tried to be polite but the man wouldn't budge so I punched him."

There was a scuffle and the man had fallen down the stairs.

"He almost died." Gordon sighed, looking contrite. "Obviously, I surrendered myself to the police."

The twins sat back, their mouths hanging open.

"Golly! It was not your fault!" Bess exclaimed. "Surely the police saw that?"

The lord had wanted to avoid scandal at all costs. Gordon was told he was free, as long as he left the county. He had managed to get a job with Miles, thanks to an old school friend.

"I am not sure if I have a police record but people talk. If that police detective contacts anyone up north, he is bound to find out."

Bess thought he had nothing to worry about since he had not been indicted.

"Mabel is the one I am thinking of," Gordon confessed. "I know she idolizes you, Bess. You are a role model for her, everything she aspires to be."

He wanted them on his side if push came to shove.

"Why don't you get ahead of all this?" Bess mused. "Talk to Detective Gardner now."

Vicky agreed with her.

"I am thinking one step ahead." Gordon sounded

eager. "You know that card the police found near Mr. Carrington's body?"

"What? The Queen of Hearts?" Bess had forgotten about it. "We think it points to a jilted lover. Was Miles involved with a married woman?"

Gordon shrugged, indicating he had no idea.

"That card is sure to lead us to the real killer," he gushed. "That is why, I took it upon myself to find out more about it."

Bess was disappointed.

"It's a playing card like any other."

Gordon didn't back down.

"Is it? I have been asking around, Bess. There's a bloke in Gloucester who knows a lot about vintage playing cards. I have a meeting with him tomorrow."

The twins wished him luck.

"Talk to DI Gardner," Vicky stressed. "He seems fair."

"After I run down this lead," Gordon promised.

Bess paced around the library for a few minutes,

growing restless by the second.

"I think I can guess where Papa is. You ready to go out in the sun, Vicky?"

They encountered Aunt Clem in the hallway.

"Tea at four sharp," she warned. "Don't be late. And bring Nigel back with you. After all this time, let's hope he at least caught something for our dinner."

The girls donned hats and stepped out.

"She has eyes like a hawk," Vicky murmured, prompting Bess to giggle.

"It was more fun sneaking out on her."

The sun had begun its descent to the horizon. They walked down a path Vicky had never seen before. She wondered how long it would take her to be really familiar with the grounds.

"We should go to the folly." Bess pointed toward a tall Grecian temple in the distance, set on a small hill. "The view from there is just priceless."

The sun warmed their backs as they set a course for Nigel's favourite fishing spot. Patches of wildflowers sprung up between the grass, making the landscape colourful yet soothing.

"There he is!" Bess pointed to the top of a hat in the distance. "I don't know how he does it, Vicky. Sit out here for hours on end."

They reached the lone figure by the stream after a good hike and were both out of breath.

"I say!" Nigel was happy to see them. "How are you, girls? Have I missed tea?"

Polo gave a joyful bark at the prospect of a treat.

Bess told him they would have to hurry.

"Aunt Clem's in a mood because we didn't bring Cordelia back for lunch. And you were gone too."

Nigel handed two brace of trout to the girls, slung his fishing rod on his shoulder and set a brisk pace back to the manor, peppering the girls with questions.

"What mischief have you been up to, Bess?" he teased.

Vicky told him about the visit to the vicarage.

"I know Aunt Cordelia counts her pennies," Bess complained, "but are they really very poor, Papa?"

Nigel frowned.

"What? How could I possibly know the answer to that?"

Bess told him how they hadn't even been offered a cup of tea.

"Did you say anything to annoy her?" Nigel sighed. "Aunt Cordelia is set in the old ways. You are never going to turn her into a suffragette." He found it funny and laughed at his own joke.

"As if I would try!" Bess was indignant. "But I say, I took Vicky there for the first time …"

She didn't finish her sentence, Vicky quelling her with a shake of the head.

"You did confront her son, Bess."

"Cecil?" Nigel stopped in his tracks. "Our vicar? My dear Bess, he dotes on you. He's spoiled you rotten ever since you were a child."

Bess poured out the whole story.

"What, what, what?" Nigel's eyes popped out. "Cecil met some strange woman at The Laughing Mongrel? Impossible!"

"The Joneses were sure, Papa."

Nigel reasoned if Cecil wanted to meet a woman,

he would do so at the vicarage or at the Buxley Arms.

"Why go to Chipping Woodbury?"

"Precisely!" Bess waved a hand in the air. "He tried to deny it, then stomped off when he realized he had been caught."

Nigel gave a yawn. They had traversed a good distance and were in sight of the manor. Barnes stood below the big tree, officiating over the footmen. A procession of ladies stepped out of the house and headed in the direction of the tree, led by Clementine.

"He's about your age, isn't he, Pops?" Bess asked. "Cecil?"

Nigel was walking faster, determined to reach the tree before Clementine.

"More or less," he replied.

"He must have been part of your gang." Vicky took up the questioning, walking slightly ahead of Nigel. "Miles, Trips and Philip, was it?"

"Cecil?" Nigel reached the tree and flopped down in a chair, completely out of breath. Polo collapsed beside him, panting. "I shouldn't say this, but Cecil was a bit wild in his youth. Nobody expected him to be a vicar, you see?"

Bess reached them, her eyes gleaming with excitement as Nigel went on.

"He ran with a fast set, drinking, gambling, err, and other things."

"Women?" Bess prompted, glancing at Vicky.

Barnes set a tray of sandwiches before them and poured a cup of tea. Nigel picked up a cucumber sandwich and paused, greeting his sister with aplomb.

"Good afternoon, Clem. You are late."

Chapter 22

Most of the women in the Gaskins family were gathered at Primrose Cottage, the abode of the second Dowager Countess. Beatrice rove her eye over the assembled company, making sure she had their attention.

"We are behind schedule. I am glad all of you could finally make the time to meet."

Sarcasm and acrimony were the mainstay of most things she said. The assembled company was well aware of that. Louise gave a brief laugh and told her to get on with it.

"As you know, the annual Buxley summer fete is always held in the third week of August. It's tradition."

"Why don't you get on with it, dear?" Hortense prompted. "All of us know about the fete and we have been doing the same thing every year for the past two decades. Perpetua and I will manage the tea stand, Clementine will handle the pie contest, Louise will judge the bonny baby contest, Nigel will judge all the agricultural ones, the vicar …"

Beatrice stopped her with a glare.

"I am in charge this year so don't mind if I wish to run things my way, Aunt Hortense."

Louise told her to stop being pompous. Beatrice frowned more and began to propose her new ideas.

"The villagers should not be part of the planning committee."

"What?" Louise erupted. "You know there is at least one person from the village per committee. It makes them feel wanted and helps bridge the distance between the manor and the tenants."

Beatrice responded with a smirk.

"I say we need to maintain some distance between us and them. We are the landlords and they work for us. Their duty is to do what we ask them to without raising any questions."

Bess had been yawning her head off, barely listening to the buzz around her. Vicky sat next to her, looking wide eyed, no doubt overwhelmed by the abundance of strong personalities around her.

"What century are you living in, Aunt Bea?" Bess leaned forward in her seat, stifling another yawn. "I propose we let the villagers head each committee, let them do things their way. We can just watch over them and guide them as needed."

"That's the most ridiculous thing I heard in my life," Beatrice sputtered. "Too outlandish, even for you, Bess."

Louise and Hortense had put their heads together. Perpetua spoke up, defending Bess.

"I think Bess here has an excellent idea. We need to show our tenants we care about their future. This will help them develop leadership abilities and grow confident."

"Confident to do what?" Beatrice shrieked. "Drive us out of Buxley?"

Everyone started talking at once. Louise accused Beatrice of losing her mind. Hortense and Perpetua offered to call Dr. Evans to have her checked out. Clementine looked speechless.

Bess tugged Vicky's hand and glanced at the door. They tiptoed toward it and slipped out, trying to hold back their giggles. Bess started laughing as they walked down the path, away from the cottage.

"What was all that?" Vicky asked. "Does that happen every year?"

Bess shook her head. "Aunt Bea wants the upper hand in everything and she hates mingling with the villagers. There would be no cricket match or fete if we let her have her way."

Having grown up in America, Vicky was used to a more informal class structure. New York society could be unforgiving but her own mother had always been friendly and gentle with the people working for her.

"Papa isn't like that," Bess told her. "Nor is Grandma Louise. Our villagers are a happy lot, Vicky. They know they can come to us with any problem."

They found themselves close to the vicarage. Cecil was outside, pulling weeds in the garden. He waved when he saw them.

"Hello girls! Why aren't you at the fete planning meeting?"

Vicky gave a shrug and looked at Bess. She wasn't comfortable sharing her opinions with anyone.

"Aunt Bea!" Bess flung her hands in the air. "Need I say more?"

Cecil offered them a cup of tea. Bess grabbed the opportunity to bend his ear.

They entered the lone parlour in the vicarage and waited while Cecil rang for tea. A maid arrived five minutes later, bearing a large fruit cake and some thin slices of bread and butter.

"Nothing like the manor, I am afraid," Cecil grinned. "But we have not starved yet."

Bess looked around her, noting some details for the first time. The furniture was of good quality but was chipped in one or two places. Bess realized she had seen some similar pieces at the manor. The upholstery was a bit faded. Was Aunt Cordelia stingy or were the Chiltons barely making ends meet?

Vicky complimented the fruit cake and took a second slice. Bess brought up something that had been bothering her all morning.

"Did you know Viscount Cranford is staying at Primrose Cottage?" she asked Cecil. "When he packed up his things and left the manor, I assumed he was going home."

Cecil gave her a curious look.

"Are you saying it's improper?"

Bess chuckled. "Oh please! He's old! And Aunt Bea is derelict. Who's going to know, anyway?"

Cecil told her Ian Lowe and Beatrice were old friends.

"They are polar opposites, actually. Don't know how they get along so well."

Bess repeated her question. "But what's he doing here in Buxley? And why leave the comfort of the manor?"

Cecil gave a shrug, pursing his lips.

"There you go again, Bess. How should I know? All I can tell you is he came here last evening, desperate to consult me."

"About what?" Bess shot back.

Cecil would not say anything more. Bess realized he wouldn't budge. The girls bid him a good day and left the vicarage, trudging along a shaded path that would take them to the manor.

"Why are you so worried about what the Viscount said to Cecil?" Vicky asked after Bess had kicked the umpteenth stone in their path.

"Cecil is the vicar. People confess their sins to him. What if Viscount Cranford wanted to get something off his chest?"

Vicky couldn't remember where he had been when the body was discovered on the terrace.

"He was resting in his room." Bess bore a

triumphant look. "At least that is what he told the police."

"I'm not a doctor yet but I can tell you he doesn't have long."

"So he has nothing to lose. He's dying anyway."

Vicky didn't believe the Viscount had enough strength to inflict a fatal wound upon a vibrant, healthy man like Miles.

Barnes greeted them back at the manor.

"Shall I send the car to pick up the ladies?" he inquired, looking over their shoulder.

Bess told him they would be a while and asked after Nigel.

"He is touring the old cottages with the steward, but he should be back for lunch anytime."

Nigel was pleased to have them to himself. They caught up over lunch, savouring lamb chops and boiled potatoes with steamed carrots. Dessert was strawberry fool, made with fresh berries from the farm.

"How is Annie?" Nigel asked Vicky after they had adjourned to the library.

Everyone chose their favourite spot. Polo opted to sit close to Vicky.

The twins could see how nervous their father was but they took it as a positive sign. Was it possible Nigel still cared for his estranged wife?

A sharp knock on the door interrupted them. Barnes entered, looking piqued yet concerned.

"I hate to be the bearer of bad news, my lord. Detective Inspector Gardner is here and he requests an immediate audience."

The light mood in the room evaporated in an instant. Barnes ushered the Inspector in and closed the door.

"Good afternoon," Nigel greeted James. "All good?"

Bess noted the grave expression on the detective's face and braced herself.

"You have absolutely no proof my Papa hurt Miles," she cried. "He's innocent."

"Lady Bess …" James began but Vicky cut him off.

"Have you talked to Gordon Phipps?"

James held up a hand, motioning them to be quiet.

"Phipps is dead. His body was discovered earlier today. We believe it was an accident."

There was a stunned silence. Nigel had turned white. Vicky looked puzzled while Bess lost her temper.

"But how is that possible?" she exploded. "He was here two days ago and he had a theory about how Miles died."

Barnes arrived with snifters of brandy and offered them to everyone. James declined but the others picked theirs up mechanically. Nigel threw his back in one gulp and looked around him, bewildered.

"I am sorry for the poor boy, Inspector," he began. "But how does his death concern us?"

Bess placed her hands on her hips, eyes wide in consternation.

"You are not going to blame this on Papa."

James assured them he had no such intention. Gordon Phipps had been discovered at the edge of the river Windrush, at a spot somewhere between Buxley and Rosehill. Judging by the fishing pole found on the scene, he had been trying to catch some trout. He must have slipped and fallen into the water.

"You are saying he drowned?" Vicky asked. "Who conducted the post mortem?"

Dr. Evans had been called and his preliminary findings indicated that Phipps drowned.

"You will be glad to know we are ready to close the investigation, Lord Buxley."

Nigel's face broke into a smile.

"Capital! Old Ned was right. You didn't waste much time getting to the bottom of this muddle."

Bess asked him to clarify what he meant.

"Are you saying Gordon killed Miles? That would be convenient, since he is not here to defend himself."

James released a long breath.

"I am not required to explain myself to you, Lady Bess. But you may have pointed me in the right direction."

Out came the story of Gordon's sordid past. He had clobbered a man until he almost died.

"Five crushed ribs, a broken leg and multiple bruises," James told them. "The poor man lost one eye and will walk with a limp forever."

The police up north had been very clear. Gordon Phipps was a menace to society and was capable of killing.

"I suppose it is fortuitous that he died before inflicting any more harm."

"No, no, no …" Bess interrupted. "We know all that. Gordon was protecting a young maid. He told us all about it, Inspector."

"That was his defence, but the girl in question denied being molested. He was no knight in shining armour, I am sorry to say, my lady."

Vicky told him Gordon was sorry Miles was dead. He was in love with Mabel and had been trying hard to win her father's favour.

James scratched his chin, his eyes narrowing in thought.

"Funny you say that, my lady. One of the constables wondered if the chap committed suicide. He must have attacked Carrington in a fit of fury and then repented his actions."

Bess had been observing her father. He sat back in his favourite chair, sipping brandy, a beatific smile on his face. The frown that had marred his brow since Miles died was missing.

"Thank you for letting us know, Inspector. We are grateful. Right, Papa?"

Nigel snapped out of his reverie.

"What, what? Oh yes! Yes, yes. Jolly good. Are you going to stay in the area, Inspector? The home team could use a strapping fellow like you on the cricket ground. That looks like a good bowling arm."

James actually smiled.

"I have been known to take a wicket or two. But I must take your leave, my Lord. I will be returning to London once I finish the paperwork."

Vicky waited until Barnes led the Inspector out. She pulled Bess towards herself and whispered, her tone urgent.

"But what about the Queen of Hearts?"

Chapter 23

Bess and Vicky had been summoned to the west wing. Hortense, Perpetua and Louise were lying sprawled in plush armchairs, their eyes closed, their feet propped up on stools and ottomans. All three had a cold compress on their heads.

"Never again!" Hortense groaned.

"Beastly!" It was all Perpetua could manage.

Louise grumbled about letting herself be manipulated every time.

Vicky glanced at Bess, a question in her eyes.

"It's the summer fete, Vicky. Or Aunt Bea, to be precise."

"Rather." Perpetua shot another pithy reply.

Louise squirmed in her chair and dabbed her eyes with the cold cloth.

"How do we let that woman affect us every time?"

"She can't help but spill the vitriol that's running in

her veins," Hortense smirked. "Aren't you glad the summer fete is the only thing she is in charge of?"

The ladies griped and whimpered in a similar vein for some time.

Bess collapsed in a chair and slung her legs over one arm. She clapped her hands to get everyone's attention.

"We come bearing the most awful news."

"What could be worse than spending hours in the company of Beatrice?" Louise grumbled.

Vicky hoped the women would sit up and take notice.

"A man is dead," she snapped, then regretted it. "I'm sorry, I didn't mean to be rude."

The ladies sat up, exhibiting shock and surprise in different ways.

"Someone we know?" Louise arched an eyebrow. "Not anyone here, I hope."

Bess told them about the visit from Inspector Gardner.

"Why did that Scotland Yard fellow come here?" Hortense questioned. "Not as if we knew the poor boy well."

"He worked for Miles Carrington, dear," Perpetua reminded her.

"Exactly my point," Hortense huffed. "I can understand the police going to Rosehill to notify the Carringtons. What do we have to do with his death?"

Bess narrated everything the DI had told them.

"Let me get this straight," Louise frowned. "The police have concluded that this Phipps boy killed Miles and then died himself. Seems a bit convenient, if you ask me."

"That Scotland Yard fellow looks eager to wrap it all up and tie it with a big bow," Perpetua nodded.

The ladies trained their eyes on the twins, an intent look on their faces.

"What?" Bess sat up.

"My dear, you have never been able to hide anything from me," Louise chuckled. "You don't believe it is that cut and dried, do you?"

Bess looked at Vicky.

"Our father is pleased," she told the ladies. "If the

police close the case, he is free of any blame."

Louise gave a deep sigh. Hortense and Perpetua looked saddened.

"We never ascertained what happened to Philip," Louise began. "But there were whispers. Even after twenty years, people have not stopped pointing fingers at Nigel. The police never had any evidence against him."

Vicky hoped Bess would elaborate. She did not want to appear dense.

"The law is one thing," Hortense explained. "But public opinion matters. The only way Nigel can relax is if the people believe he is innocent."

"Wait a minute, Aunt Hortense, Grandma …" Bess looked around. "Are we still talking about Gordon Phipps?"

Louise admitted they were going around in circles.

"Let me come to the point. You girls don't believe Gordon Phipps murdered Miles. Is that right?"

Hortense and Perpetua wanted to know why.

"We met him just a few days ago," Vicky replied. "He is in love with Mabel and he was willing to do anything to get her father's blessing."

"He may have found another way to get around that problem," Perpetua cackled.

Hortense disagreed. Like the twins, she believed that a man in love would try to please his lady. He might go out of his way to ingratiate himself with her father but he would never hurt him.

"As odious as Miles was?" Louise was thoughtful. "I would be sorely tempted."

There was a general consensus that hurting Miles would not have played to Gordon's advantage. Bess asked them to consider Gordon was innocent of killing Miles. His death had either been an accident or he was the victim of foul play.

"Why do you say that?" Hortense asked.

The ladies had abandoned all efforts at trying to relax.

"Regardless," Louise began. "The real killer is still out there, in that case. And what do you mean, he was a victim, Bess? Are you saying someone deliberately killed this boy?"

Vicky told them it was not impossible. Gordon's theory about the Queen of Hearts was brought up. He had been on a mission when the twins met him.

Louise thought it was outlandish.

"What if that card just fell out of someone's pocket?" she looked around. "The men were playing cards in the library and they all went out on the terrace at some point."

Bess wasn't sure about that but she decided to hold her opinion. She felt she needed to sit in some quiet corner and go over everything from the beginning. Vicky gave her a slight nod. She agreed.

Perpetua declared she was parched and rang the bell.

"Isn't it time for tea yet? I could eat something substantial."

A maid arrived and was dispatched to bring tea for all of them. Barnes arrived ten minutes later.

"Tea will be served momentarily, my lady. I presume you will all proceed to the lawn?"

Louise had a rebellious glint in her eye.

"Actually, Barnes, we are all a bit indisposed. We will have our tea right here."

Vicky marvelled at the alarm on the butler's face.

"But …" he sputtered. "Lady Clementine has ordered …" he thought better of what he was going to say next.

Louise told him Clementine would survive her plans going awry for one meal.

"Ask Mrs. Bird to be generous," she quipped. "We are all famished."

Vicky had been sitting on the edge of a chair. Louise told her to relax.

"Are you still walking on eggshells around us?"

Before she could reply, Clementine swept into the room, her mouth set in a firm line.

"You look like someone who just sucked a sour lemon." Hortense gave a snort. "Come to round us up?"

Clementine ignored her and stood before Louise, arms folded, feet planted apart.

"You have thrown the staff in a tizzy, Mama. Why can't you come and have tea in the garden?"

Louise sat up straight in her chair, looking every inch the Dowager.

"Mind what you say next, Clem. You might be able to order Nigel around but we are not going to cower before you."

"Not afraid," Perpetua croaked, then bit her lip.

Clementine reminded them that tea was always served outside at 4 PM sharp, barring inclement weather. The servants were used to a certain routine and there was no point in disturbing it.

"Oh, Aunt Clem, they don't mind," Bess interrupted, flashing a cheeky grin. "Mrs. Jones will handle everything without a hitch."

The great aunts wondered if they were talking about a royal visit.

"It's tea," they chorused. "And we will partake it here today. Off you go, Clementine."

"Chop, chop!" Louise added.

Vicky's laugh was spontaneous. Clementine pinned her with a glare and stalked out of the room.

"Takes after Percy," Louise murmured. "Their father was spontaneous, always ready for a laugh. Nigel's more like him."

"Papa? Spontaneous?" Bess stared at her grandmother.

There was a knock on the door and Barnes came in again.

"Miss Mabel Carrington," he announced, his tone appropriately grim.

Bess leapt up from her chair and embraced her friend. It was the first time she was coming face to face with her since her father's death.

"My dear Mabel, my deepest condolences at your loss. How absolutely horrible for you."

The ladies offered their regrets one by one and inquired about the entire Carrington family. Mabel's response was cursory, almost curt. Bess took one look at her red eyes and shaking fingers and realized she was very close to breaking down.

"Sit here." She led Mabel to a sofa and urged her to rest. "Tell us what's on your mind."

"Whatever is happening with the tea?" Hortense groaned. "Do you think Clementine can order the servants not to serve us?"

The door opened again and a procession of maids came in, pushing a trolley laden with tea. A collective sigh of relief travelled through the room.

Louise offered to pour. She added two lumps of sugar to a cup and passed it to Mabel.

"Drink this first, child. Then we can hear what you have to say."

Bess noted the flash of apprehension on Mabel's face. They could not hope for privacy before the aunts.

"Or, we can let you ladies enjoy tea in peace and go somewhere else."

"My sixth sense tells me this is a job for the Nightingales." Hortense looked up from loading her plate. "But battles are not won on an empty stomach, girls. Eat up."

The girls knew when they were beaten. Plates were loaded with cucumber, egg and ham sandwiches. Scones were slathered with clotted cream and topped with strawberry preserves. Silence reigned as the ladies devoted all their energy to doing justice to the meal.

"Mrs. Bird never disappoints," Bess declared. "That chocolate cake must be for you, Vicky."

Mabel picked at the food but drank three cups of tea. Vicky realized she was at the end of her tether.

"You will need to be strong."

Louise finally took pity on her.

"Now, dear, tell us what's the matter. "

It's Gordon!" Mabel burst into tears. "I am a bad person, Bess."

The women in the room were perplexed.

"What on earth, Mabel?" Bess exploded. "Get that bally idea out of your head."

"I didn't mean to lead him on," Mabel sobbed. "He was so nice to me, it was easy to get carried away. You know how Papa was ... and Mama, well, she never cared to stand up to him."

Vicky was the only one who was unfamiliar with the dynamics of the Carrington household. Bess had taken on the role of Mabel's protector at an early age. It hadn't endeared her to Miles.

"We know, darling." She gave an encouraging nod.

When Gordon declared his love, Mabel went along, not wanting to hurt him. She liked him well enough and she hadn't really thought ahead. Part of her knew Miles would never approve of the match, giving her an easy way out should she want it. Then she met the Marquess at the party.

"He's so dashing," she blushed. "Curtis is a man I can imagine spending the rest of my life with."

It was clear the attraction was mutual although neither of them had said anything to each other. Bess wondered what the problem was since Gordon had so conveniently cleared the way for them.

"He didn't fish, Bess." Mabel's eyes grew wide. "In fact, he hated fishing. He told me he was too energetic to just stand by a stream, waiting for them to bite."

Vicky caught on first.

"You think he was too athletic to lose his footing and fall in the river."

Mabel's pulse quickened with excitement.

"I am saying he would never have the patience to just stand there by the water. And no, he wasn't the type to brood."

Bess opened her mouth but Mabel warded her off.

"What's more, the Windrush is very shallow and the spot where he fell was barely four feet deep. It must have come up to his waist at best."

Vicky told her it would be enough to drown in if a man lost his footing. But Mabel would not listen.

"I believe Gordon has been wronged, Bess. And I want to find out why and by whom. I think I owe him that much."

The older ladies had been following the conversation closely. Hortense was the first to bang her fist on a table.

"You may have something there."

"What do the police say?" Bess already knew the answer.

"They think I am hysterical," Mabel sniffed. "That's why I came to you, Bess. You simply must help."

Louise patted Mabel's arm, her eyes flashing with excitement.

"Don't you worry, dear. We are going to get to the bottom of this."

Chapter 24

Vicky was up early the next day. She had promised Nigel she would accompany him to the cricket practice. Although she could not make head or tail of the different rules Nigel explained, she liked starting the day in his company. And she was surprised at how hard he was trying to get to know her. He was genuinely trying to make up for the past.

"What's a slip again?" she laughed as Nigel shook his head in disgust. "Why don't you just call him a man?"

They headed back to the manor, having worked up a good appetite. Vicky had sampled more of Mrs. Bird's creations in addition to eggs and toast. Maybe she would develop a taste for kedgeree one day.

Louise reigned over the breakfast table, finding fault with Clementine. Imogen looked like she was ready to bolt but Bess and Gertrude were enjoying the spectacle

"Good morning, Grandma Louise." Vicky greeted

her with a hug.

Louise cleared her throat, looking bewildered. The British did not go around embracing people at breakfast.

"What are you doing today, Momo?" Bess asked, plunging a fork in her kedgeree.

Lady Ridley had put her foot down, ordering her daughters to have lunch with her at the Hall. Gertrude was not looking too pleased about it.

"Why don't you come with us?" she asked Vicky and Bess. "Take the spotlight away from me?"

Louise interrupted before Bess could think of an answer.

"They are having lunch with me. And don't you dare talk them out of it."

Imogen and Gertrude left after two cups of tea and Clementine bustled off to discuss the menus with Mrs. Jones.

"Finally!" Louise stood up and allowed a footman to pull her chair back. "Let's go, girls. Hortense must be ready to throw a fit."

"Say what?" Nigel looked up from his paper. "You leading my girls into trouble, Mama?"

Louise ignored him. Bess and Vicky sprang up and the trio set off toward the west wing. The sun was up and time was wasting.

Mabel had stuck around long after tea the previous afternoon, leaving only when Bess promised they would leave no stone unturned in finding out what had happened to Gordon. The ladies had dispersed, their minds flooded with entirely too much information. They agreed to tackle the problem with fresh minds after a hearty breakfast the next morning.

Hortense and Perpetua sat ramrod straight in their chairs, their eyes bright and eager to tackle the day.

"You are late!" Hortense glared. "Did Clementine hold you up?"

Sunlight streamed through a window, bathing a plush armchair in its bright light. Louise settled into it and the twins sat side by side on an upright sofa.

"Shall we begin?" Bess looked around, making sure she had their attention. "I think we should start by assuming that Miles and Gordon were killed by the same person."

The ladies nodded. They had already debated over this the previous day.

"So we start at the night of the party," Vicky spoke.

"First we look at the people in the library because they were in the immediate vicinity."

"One of them has to be lying," Perpetua ventured. "Or maybe more."

They started with Gordon. He had lied about being with Clara all the time and Curtis Pierpont had seen him coming from the terrace.

"I think we can safely assume he was innocent though," Bess offered. "He told us he had been in trouble with the police. Why would he admit to that if he was guilty?"

Louise had a thought.

"What if the obvious is true, Bess? Gordon did kill Miles. He told you about his past so you would not suspect him. But someone else saw him and that person avenged Miles's death by pushing Gordon in the river."

Hortense gave a hearty laugh.

"Frankly, my dears, that's hard to digest. I can see more than one person wanting to hurt Miles but I doubt there is a man on earth who would go out of his way to do something for Miles Carrington. Especially a dead Miles Carrington."

They moved on to Trevor.

"Trips is afraid of his own shadow," Louise smirked. "We can dismiss him as a suspect."

Bess pointed out he had the most to gain.

"He will probably come into both Rosehill and Oakview once Lord Shelby is gone. Money is always a powerful motive, Grandma."

Louise agreed to consider him if they hit a dead end elsewhere.

Viscount Cranford was next. All the older ladies agreed he was incapable of any physical violence.

"If you dismiss every suspect so easily, we will be left with nothing," Bess grumbled.

Vicky sided with the ladies.

"He is too sick, Bess. Striking a fatal blow to someone would make him collapse on the spot. Plus, he was not in the library at the time they found the body."

Bess snapped her fingers.

"Exactly! He says he was in his room but nobody can verify that. The servants were so busy that night, he could have easily slipped out without running into anyone."

Louise nodded to herself, looking pensive.

"You girls might not know this, but Ian, that is the Viscount, had an old grudge against Miles."

"Rather," Perpetua nodded.

"Just spit it out," Hortense clucked. "They were mortal enemies."

Louise told the twins about Mabel's mother. Bess admitted she had not known the whole story.

"You mean he was in love with her?" She looked awed. "Is Mabel …"

"Mabel is a Carrington alright," Hortense dismissed. "It's fortunate she takes after her own mother."

Perpetua had rung for tea while they talked. Barnes entered, followed by a maid. He dismissed her as soon as the tea things had been set out.

"Don't be shy, Barnes," Louise urged. "Any bit you can add will only help us."

One of the footmen had seen Viscount Cranford come out on his balcony that night. It had been around the time someone screamed but he couldn't be sure if it was before or after.

"Thanks Barnie," Bess grinned. "You are the best!"

The butler gave a brief bow and left the room.

"So we know he was in his room," Hortense summed up. "Question is, did he stay there all night?"

Vicky sipped her coffee, grateful that Barnes never forgot her preference. There was a fresh cake flavoured with cardamom and studded with sultanas. Bess cut thick slices and handed them around.

"Have we covered everyone, Grandma?"

"Cecil." Perpetua added a splash of milk to her tea and stirred it. "But we can rule him out, I suppose. Whoever heard of a murderous vicar?" she cackled.

Hortense agreed with her. Cecil had been in the parlour with the ladies when the body was discovered, wolfing down sandwiches.

"Not like him to miss a lavish dinner," she frowned. "But church business kept him away."

Bess told them where he had been.

"He was very cagey when we asked him about the woman. I think he's hiding something. In fact, I am sure of it."

The ladies looked interested. Any woman Cecil brought home would have to be strong enough to stand up to his mother. Vicky almost mentioned what the pub owner had said about the woman but held back.

Hortense stood up and began walking around the room.

"What about that boy who sat near you at dinner that night, Bess?" she asked suddenly. "The one Nigel does business with?"

"Peter?" she frowned. "He is a lawyer, Aunt Hortense. Not a servant but not quite one of us."

"Never understood why he was at the table with us," Perpetua muttered.

Silence reigned for a while as everyone mulled over what they had discussed.

"Let me take the bull by the horns," Louise sighed after some time. "What about Nigel? I believe my son is innocent but we need to be objective and treat him as a suspect."

"That is the only way we can clear his name," Vicky agreed.

Bess understood she wasn't just talking about the present. Their eyes met and a silent message passed between them. They would move heaven and earth to prove Nigel had nothing to do with Philip's death. The time would come when Lord Buxley walked with his head held high, completely exonerated of any wrongdoing. But they needed to focus on Miles and Gordon for now.

"Papa was playing cards with everyone. He went out when they heard the scream and came back in. More than one person can vouch for him, Grandma."

Vicky seconded her.

"I think we are missing something. One of these people has to be lying to us."

They knew Cecil was lying by omission, so was the Viscount. He had acted ignorant about the scream. The ladies proposed talking to them.

"You girls talk to Cecil and we will tackle Cordelia," Hortense declared. "Have Clementine invite her to dinner tonight, Louise. We will break down her defences with a joint of meat."

Bess vowed to talk Mrs. Bird into making a cheese souffle. Aunt Cordelia would not be able to resist.

"What about the Viscount?" Vicky asked. "Shall we visit him at his estate?"

Louise reminded them he was still in Buxley.

"I think you will not need to go to Cranford Hall to talk to him. He is at Primrose Cottage with Beatrice."

Perpetua declared she needed some fresh air. Hortense proposed going for a walk in the rose garden and Louise agreed.

"Let's regroup in a day or two. We can swap notes and see if we have made any progress."

Bess and Vicky agreed.

"Unless, we solve the murder before that, Grandma." Bess winked.

Louise warned them to be careful.

"Two men are dead for no apparent reason. Don't you forget that."

Vicky promised they would watch their step.

The twins left the west wing and headed to the kitchen. The place was a beehive of activity but Mrs. Bird greeted them with a broad smile.

"Mulligatawny soup for lunch, my lady, with grilled trout and apple crumble. I have some biscuits to tide you over until then."

Bess thanked her and Vicky praised the cake. Mrs. Bird couldn't stop smiling, her plump cheeks growing a deeper shade of rose.

"You fancy some curried chicken for dinner, Lady Bess?"

Mrs. Jones, the housekeeper, joined them.

"What is this? Are you making unreasonable demands again, my lady?" The twinkle in her eye suggested she wasn't serious. "I just spoke to the Dowager. The vicar and his mother will be here for dinner, Mrs. Bird."

The cook rolled her eyes.

"You want me to make cheese souffle! Why not just say so, you imp. The vicar likes a second helping of custard with his pudding. I will have to make sure we have enough."

Bess thanked her and declined the offer of a cup of tea. Mrs. Jones asked if the girls had a few minutes to spare.

"Whatever you need, Mrs. Jones." Bess shrugged in response to Vicky's questioning glance.

They squeezed into a tiny room that served as the housekeeper's office.

"May I say how glad we are to have you back with us, Lady Vicky?" Mrs. Jones gushed. "I hope you like the room you are in? Lord Buxley has given orders to redecorate. The upholstery samples will be here soon."

Vicky assured her she was comfortable.

"Everything fine below stairs?" Bess asked, ready to help any way she could.

Barnes and Mrs. Jones often consulted her over minor issues, sure she would be more compassionate than Clementine.

"The scullery maid has a brother who delivers coal," she began. "He saw two men come to blows a fortnight ago." Her eyes widened. "They threatened to kill each other."

One of them had raised his fist and was about to bash it into the other's jaw when he saw the boy hiding behind the bush. The man muttered under his breath and the fight broke up.

"Was it one of our footmen? What does Barnes think about this?"

"No, my lady." Mrs. Jones leaned forward, her voice hushed. "It was Mr. Miles and Mr. Trips. This happened at Oakview, in that wood behind their stables."

Chapter 25

Breakfast was in full swing the next morning and the buffet table groaned with a dozen dishes, Mrs. Bird trying her best to please everyone. Apart from the people who lived in the manor on a permanent basis, there were regular visitors like Gertrude who could be counted upon to be present.

Bess had spent a restless night, going over bizarre theories about what was going on at Buxley. Dawn streaked the horizon when she nodded off, convinced that an unknown adversary was waging a vendetta against the Gaskins family. She woke up with a raging headache and managed to shuffle down, ready to fortify herself with a strong cup of Darjeeling and a generous portion of kedgeree.

"What ho, inmates!"

All she noticed was there was more than the usual crowd. The din of conversation did not improve the hammering in her head. And the food was almost gone. Her eyes sought Barnes who assured her Mrs. Bird was making more kedgeree.

Bess took a seat next to Vicky and closed her eyes.

"They are all here." Vicky nudged her with an elbow. "The Viscount, the vicar and Peter. Who do you want to tackle first?"

Nigel stood up, announcing he and the Viscount were going to spend the day fishing at his favourite spot. He gave a soft whistle to summon his dog.

"But, my lord," Peter stuttered. "I was hoping to go over some papers with you."

Nigel looked like a child who had been sent to bed without dessert.

"Never mind, old boy," the Viscount rasped. "Why don't I go ahead? You can follow later. We have the whole day ahead of us and nothing better to do."

Bess gathered the two friends planned to have a picnic lunch by the stream. Knowing Mrs. Bird, they would be treated to more than just sandwiches.

"How far is this stream from the manor?" Vicky asked, concerned about the Viscount's health. "Why don't you allow us to drive you part of the way, my lord?"

Ian's face lit up.

"You would be doing this old relic a big favour,

girls."

He urged Bess to take her time over her meal. Half an hour later, they set off, Bess feeling sprightly again after having imbibed a hefty amount of tea and food.

The sky was a bright blue as they drove through the grounds, with not a cloud in sight. Sheep dotted the hills in the distance and the lone figure of a shepherd sat under a tree, watching over them.

Ian was curious about life in America. He plied Vicky with lots of questions, expressing a desire to cross the Atlantic and visit the far off land.

"Never took the plunge," he laughed. "And I have run out of time now."

Vicky thought the dry weather was good for him.

Ian shrugged. He had made peace with his fate. Bess could not believe he had ever had a violent thought in his mind. But she was going to be proved wrong soon. Ian inquired after Mabel, concerned how she was dealing with Gordon's death.

"What did the bard say? The course of true love never did run smooth."

Vicky opened her mouth to correct him but Bess

stopped her with a shake of the head. There was no need to divulge Mabel's true feelings.

"So she confided in you?" Bess prompted.

"First love is hard to hide, my dear. It warms the heart and makes it sing." The Viscount had a faraway look in his eyes. "The dear girl doesn't say much, just like her mother. But she wears her heart on her sleeve."

Bess remembered what Louise had told them about Mabel's own mother. She deliberately misunderstood, wanting to bait Ian.

"I confess I have always found Mrs. Carrington a bit cold." Bess bit her lip. "She is not very involved in Mabel's life."

His laughter was laced with a hint of sadness.

"You are thinking of her step mother, Miles's second wife. Marion was the one who gave birth to Mabel. She is not with us now."

Bess confessed she did not remember her.

"I doubt Mabel does either. She rarely talks about her."

Ian's gaze darkened.

"We can thank Miles for that, I am sure. Taking her life was not enough. He wanted to obliterate every memory of her, lest anyone remember the truth."

Neither Bess nor Vicky had to feign interest.

"Are you saying Mabel's father killed her mother?" Vicky voiced what Bess was thinking. "But why?"

Ian's body shook as he dissolved into another coughing fit. Vicky rubbed his back, hoping it would calm him and make it easier to breathe.

Bess had driven as far as the car would go. They were in the middle of a path that led to the stream with not a tree in sight. The sun had risen higher and the heat was becoming unbearable.

Vicky urged Ian to take her arm and lean on her.

"Don't worry about us, my lord." Vicky assured him. "Bess and I lugged dozens of stretchers any given day."

Many of the men on those stretchers had been dead but she didn't mention that. Bess knew, of course. It was a bond they should never have shared.

The path dipped and a valley opened up below them, revealing a swiftly flowing stream. A tall marble structure stood half way down, surrounded by masses of rhododendrons.

"Of course, the sun temple!" Bess exclaimed. "We can rest there, at least until Papa comes along."

Vicky's mouth hung open as she stared at the crumbling structure.

"Gee, where'd that come from?" she burst out.

Bess explained it was a folly, built by one of their ancestors to please his lady wife. It was like an ornament but also very useful for picnics or tea parties.

"Nanny brought me here if I was good."

They proceeded at a snail's pace but finally made it to the temple. Ian lowered himself to sit on the top step with Vicky's help. The girls waited until his breathing returned to normal. He resumed his tale without any prompting.

"Marion was a lamb. Miles must have loved her once but I wonder. They were happy enough when Mabel and her sister were born but Miles wanted an heir."

Marion had suffered in childbirth. But she wanted to please Miles. After a few unsuccessful attempts, the doctor put his foot down.

"Miles was enraged," Ian sighed. "And he made it clear Marion failed in her duty."

She blamed herself, spending more and more time alone until she was a shadow of her former self. Miles told everyone she was leaning toward insanity. When Marion died a few months later from an overdose of laudanum, he called it a blessed release.

"It is easy to get addicted to it," Vicky murmured.

"Mabel never touched the vile stuff," Ian panted. "Miles forced it down her throat, the bounder. He was courting his new wife within six months and was married before the year was out."

Everyone knew the second wife had succeeded in providing an heir.

Bess wondered if an impaired lung could affect a person's brain. The Viscount's theory was ridiculous.

"Do you have any proof?" she asked.

Ian's expression told her everything. He had used his influence to have the police conduct a post mortem. It revealed the excess laudanum in Marion's body but there was no way to prove how she had ingested it. Miles walked free.

"At least I can die happy," he gloated. "Miles got what he deserved."

"And did you help him get his just desserts?" Bess whispered, ready to face his ire.

Ian was stoic.

"Unfortunately, no. Someone beat me to it, my dear."

Vicky patted his arm, not sure what to say. Bess forged ahead.

"Would you care to explain that, my lord? Do you know who murdered Miles?"

Ian shook his head. He had come to Buxley Manor, intending to take a life.

"I have nothing to lose, girls," he sighed. "Marion's death had to be avenged and I was in a position to do it."

He did not have a concrete plan but he carried a small revolver with him, looking for an opportunity to catch Miles by himself. That moment had never come. On the night of the party, his health had forced him to retire early.

"I was in too much pain to sleep," he shrugged. "There was a scream and I rushed to the balcony to see what was happening below."

The men from the library came out on the terrace, Miles among them. He had a clear shot but he hesitated.

"I blamed myself for missing my chance."

"Someone did the job for you," Bess summed up. "Any idea who?"

Ian told them Miles was a villain with a sadistic streak. He took great pleasure in destroying a man, uprooting families. It was a miracle he had escaped unscathed all these years.

A footman appeared in the distance, lugging a heavy basket. Bess hoped it contained some lemonade for her parched throat.

"What about Gordon?" she cried. "One of the theories is that he killed Miles in a fit of rage and took his own life when he couldn't handle the guilt."

Vicky had been quiet for a long time. She broke her silence, asking the question that was uppermost in her mind.

"What about our father, my lord?" Her voice shook. "Do you think he might have been involved?"

"Nigel?" Ian's surprise was genuine. "What makes you think that?"

As if on cue, Lord Buxley appeared a few paces behind the footman.

"He was one of the men in the library that night," Bess replied. "We are trying to be objective."

"Nigel would never hurt Miles," Ian sighed. "They were old friends, even though Miles did some things to upset your family." He held up his hand to ward off Bess. "No, my dear, some things are best left unsaid. But I am willing to bet my entire fortune on this. Nigel is the one person in the room you can rule out."

Bess asked if he suspected someone else. Ian told her they were barking up the wrong tree.

"It's not easy to plan a murder, my dear. I tried my best. If you ask me, this was a spur of the moment thing. One of your party guests came face to face with Miles and acted in the heat of the moment. He was gone before the body was discovered."

Vicky thought it was a plausible theory but didn't explain what happened to Gordon.

"He was smart," Ian chuckled. "And hard working. But he was not from these parts." He took a few rapid breaths. "Must have had a past, poor chap."

"So you don't think the two deaths are related?" Bess pressed her lips together. "Kind of a coincidence though, don't you think, Sir?"

The footman reached them, sweating profusely from head to foot. He set the basket down and opened it, pulling out small bottles of lemonade. Nigel was right behind him, looking cool as a cucumber, Polo at his heels.

"That Peter is a slave driver," he boomed. "Insisted I read every paper before I signed it, what?"

Bess took a bottle from the footman and drank straight from it. She didn't come up for air until she had drained the whole bottle. Vicky waited until the footman poured the lemonade into a glass and handed it to her.

"We are off, Papa." Bess wove her arm through Vicky's. "See you at tea."

Chapter 26

Cecil Chilton boarded a north bound train, praying he wouldn't be spotted. After the disaster at the Laughing Mongrel, he wasn't taking any chances. His mother had handed him an envelope stuffed with pound notes, an unspoken command in her eyes.

"But Mother …" His protests fell on deaf years.

Sometimes, he wondered if she had always been that hard hearted. Losing two sons had taken a toll. She had transferred all her ambitions to him, expecting him to fulfil them.

He disembarked three stations later, in a small village he had never visited before. A porter gave him directions to the local pub. A short walk took him there. It wasn't the most salubrious of places Cecil frequented but he hoped it would serve its purpose.

The place was poorly lit. A lone sun beam shone through a grimy window high up near the rafters. Dirt lined the floor and an unmistakable odour of hops and barley hung in the air. A bald man with a bulbous nose was busy polishing the bar. It was an hour before noon and the place was deserted, except for a scrawny girl who went through the motions of dusting the tables, moving around at a snail's pace. Cecil picked a place at random and sat down.

"What will it be?" the landlord finally paid him some attention.

Cecil's stomach growled, reminding him he had missed breakfast.

"A cup of tea and something to eat, please."

The girl stopped dusting and giggled, fleeing inside when the landlord snapped at her. Five minutes later, Cecil was tucking into a bowl of creamy porridge, flavoured with cinnamon and topped with a generous mound of chopped berries.

She arrived at the given time, dressed in a dark brown frock, a hat pulled low over her eyes. It was as if she wanted to blend into the woodwork and be invisible.

"You came." Cecil poured the tea, adding a good amount of milk and two sugars to her cup.

"I am not in the habit of breaking promises, my lord. Or should I say Reverend?"

Cecil was not wearing his clerical collar. There was no point beating around the bush.

"What do you want?"

"Leave him alone. He thinks his father was a soldier, an honourable man who died fighting for his country."

Cecil felt a low buzzing in his ears.

"It was a boy?" He cupped the mug of tea, desperate to feel its warmth. "I have a son?"

She looked away, refusing to give a direct answer.

"What do you care, after all these years?"

Cecil blanched. Maybe Miles had done him a favour. He might have lived his whole life, unaware he had a son. Why hadn't she asked for help?

"I never knew your name," she reasoned, answering his unspoken question. "The housekeeper turned me out and my Pa refused to take me in."

She had walked for hours, faint with hunger and had collapsed near a cottage on the outskirts of a village, owned by a reclusive spinster. The elderly gentlewoman took pity on her, giving her a roof over her head, earning her loyalty for life. It was a small household, barely scraping through on the old woman's meagre income. The lines between master and servant became blurred as the boy grew to be a healthy toddler and then a strapping young man. The spinster had insisted she learn to read and write and sent the boy to the local school.

Cecil felt he would explode. He had not realized the magnitude of his sins.

"What does he look like?" He licked his lips, finding they had grown dry as sand. "Does he favour me?"

She ignored his questions again.

"Your friend came to our door two or three years later. His horse had thrown a shoe and he was thirsty. He told me you had taken a wife and would not care about scum like us."

Cecil sucked in a breath. Miles had waited for years before revealing the truth. What had he hoped to achieve?

"He lied. I never got married. My brothers died and I …" He choked, unable to go any further.

They both knew they came from different worlds. Marriage had never been an option.

"I saw your friend again a year ago, at the weekly

market," she volunteered.

Miles would never have remembered her. He stopped to admire a wooden writing desk and began haggling over the price. She had felt a foreboding when he stopped midsentence and stared at the small red mark on her son's cheek.

Cecil felt his heart speed up. His hand flew to his own face, caressing the birthmark he shared with his brothers and his father. Miles called it the Chilton stamp.

"He began hinting about it six months ago," he sighed. "I swear I was not aware of any of this, Mary."

Their son had no idea he was illegitimate. She needed time to think.

Cecil considered the wad of notes in his pocket. He would not insult her by offering money. They agreed to meet again in a month.

Cecil stood on the railway platform, waiting for the train, thinking of the sadistic gleam in Miles Carrington's eyes when he delivered the crushing blow. He had come to a fitting end.

***

Nigel Gaskins, the earl of Buxley, sat in his

favourite chair by the fireplace, stroking the dog in his lap. He was overwhelmed by the events of the past few days. His wildest dream had been realized on the night of the party when Vicky made an appearance. Seeing his daughters hand in hand made him so happy he was ready to burst. All they were missing now was Annie. He felt ready to reach out now that Miles Carrington was dead. He had always been a thorn in the side, trying to drive a wedge between him and Annie.

Nigel's eyes filled up as he remembered those turbulent days. He had been in seventh heaven when Annie gave birth to the twins. Neither of them was obsessed with having a male heir. In fact, they had almost decided to emigrate to America where Nigel would look after the Rhodes family business.

Philip's death was a shock. But the bigger blow was being accused of having a hand in his death. Twenty years later, the rumours lingered. There were people in the village who were never quite sure of his innocence. According to Nigel, Philip's death had destroyed his life. He might have gained the earldom but he lost his wife and daughter who were more precious. And he could thank one person for it. Miles Carrington.

The Carrington boys had always been underfoot at Buxley, along with the Chiltons. Even as a child,

Miles did not care between right and wrong. He was willing to be unethical as long as he won. Trips bore the brunt of it, of course. Miles was canny enough to stay in Philip's good books, knowing he would be the earl one day. But Nigel was fair game.

When he started courting Annie, Miles threw his hat in the ring just for fun. Annie was new to British society, eager to please everyone. She was nice to Miles because he meant something to Nigel.

"I hardly know anybody here," she told him. "It's nice to have a friend I can count on."

What could he really tell her? That Miles cheated at cards, laughed when one of them was hurt and kicked dogs just for fun?

They got married and started building a life together. Miles was wooing Marion and rarely made an appearance at Buxley. Then Philip died. Miles came to offer his condolences and began visiting Annie again. He had taken great pleasure in poisoning her mind.

The whole family thought Miles was his childhood friend but Nigel had hated Miles with a passion. He would never have invited him to stay for the weekend but Ian had pleaded with him. He wanted to spend time with Mabel, relive memories of Marion. Nigel could not refuse a dying man's last wish. He braced himself to tolerate Miles and his particular brand of cruelty, itching to teach him a lesson.

In the end, everything had worked out well. Miles Carrington may have duped Annie but he would not lift a finger against Bess and Vicky. Nigel allowed himself a smile and began to plot his next move.

***

He sat alone in the pub, nursing a pint of bitter. Taking a life had been easier than he imagined. Was it because he knew he was doing the world a favour, ridding it of a blackguard like Miles Carrington? The timing had been perfect and his only regret was Miles did not suffer. One blow and he was gone. He would never destroy a family again, separate children from their parents.

Killing Gordon had not been part of the plan. But he had signed his own death warrant by meddling in things that did not concern him. Why couldn't he have bided his time and married Mabel?

The bar maid brought over a meat pie doused in gravy, with peas and boiled potatoes topped with extra butter.

"Want another?" she pointed at the tumbler.

He shook his head and began cutting the pie, a shred of remorse stirring in his chest. An innocent man's blood was on his hands. But as they said, everything was fair in love and war. It was time to move on and think about the future.

Chapter 27

Buxley Manor was dozing in the lull between lunch and tea. The inmates were in their preferred habitats, engaged in resting body or soul. The telephone in the hall trilled, demanding attention. Barnes laboured up the stairs to answer it. The footmen were not allowed to touch the instrument.

The news was bad, although not entirely unexpected. Lord Shelby was dead. Barnes went to the library to apprise Nigel. The news had reached every corner of the manor within an hour.

"You realize what this means?" Clementine asked no one in particular. "Trips is the Baron now and master of Oakview."

Bess mulled over her aunt's words. She had the perfect excuse to go visit Trips.

"We're going for a drive," she declared, smoothing her skirt. "Come on, Vicky."

Half an hour later, they were being ushered into the drawing room at Oakview. The family was having tea. Mabel sat on a chaise, staring out of the window. Clara rushed to greet them, her eyes moist.

"Bess, you came! How kind of you."

Trips added his thanks, looking forlorn. His face was pale but he was trying hard to maintain a stiff upper lip.

"He died asking for Miles," he sighed. "He was Father's favourite, of course." He flung an arm around the room. "Without Miles, this place is a rudderless ship."

Peter Osborne materialized from a corner.

"You will do well, my lord. The tenants on both the estates have a lot of respect for you."

Vicky thought he was laying it on thick. What was he doing there? Bess nudged her, letting her know she was wondering the same.

"I can't handle all this on my own," Trips cried.

Clara suggested the girls step out for some fresh air. Trips followed them, looking so miserable, none of them had the heart to object.

"I was feeling like a caged monkey in there." He pulled off his tie and sighed. "Please excuse me, girls."

Vicky took Clara's arm and picked up the pace while Bess sidled closer to Trips, slowing down a bit.

"We are sorry for your loss, my lord. Papa and Aunt Clem are on their way here."

Trips thanked her, telling her how grateful he was for his neighbours.

"Nigel has always stood by me, and I am grateful. Miles was aggressive and Philip could be arrogant at times. But your father, he was the most sensible of us."

Bess asked if the friends had got into fights.

"We managed to get into plenty of scrapes." His mood lightened as he reminisced over the past. "Miles led us into trouble, then left us to take the fall." He clasped his hands behind his back and paused, gazing at the horizon. "He never changed. It's hard to believe someone got the better of him."

"But you were the heir," Bess protested. "Surely your word was law?"

"Father preferred Miles." Trips resumed their walk. "They never sought my opinion on anything. In fact, we had a big spat over it a few days before your birthday."

Bess couldn't believe her luck. She encouraged Trips to continue.

"It was about Gordon Phipps, poor chap. Miles was furious he was flirting with Mabel and was going to fire him. I told him he was being silly."

Trips believed Mabel had more sense than Miles gave her credit for. She was not going to do anything rash like marry the hired hand. But Miles took it as a personal affront and was making plans to destroy Gordon.

"Miles had murder in his eyes, Bess. He almost punched me when I tried to make him calm down. Funny thing, if that boy had died first, I might have believed Miles did it."

Bess felt her belief questioned. Was the Detective Inspector right? Had Gordon been one step ahead? Had he killed Miles over his obsession with Mabel? Or maybe he had lashed out in self-defence.

They caught up with Vicky and Clara soon and turned back to the house after some time. Nigel and Clementine had arrived, along with some other neighbours. Bess decided it was time to take their leave.

She was quiet on the way back, brooding over what Trips had said.

"Am I holding you back?" she asked Vicky. "When do you need to leave for Edinburgh?"

"The initial response is not encouraging," Vicky admitted. "But I am hopeful."

Although some pioneers had paved the way, earning a full medical degree was still a challenge for women. Bess gazed at her sister, her eyes full of adoration.

"You're the cat's meow, Vicky."

They reached the manor a few minutes past four. Tea was in progress on the lawn and it was a much jolly affair than usual, in Clementine's absence. The great aunts were taking advantage of the mild weather and had decided to join everyone. Cecil sat between Gertrude and Aunt Hortense, balancing a plate of tea on his knees. His attention was fixed on Imogen who sat directly before him, cutting a slice of cake.

"What ho!" Bess greeted, her voice ringing with bonhomie. "Left any tea for us? I am absolutely famished."

The next few minutes were devoted to sampling every type of sandwich, followed by scones slathered with fresh strawberry jam. Vicky found she was beginning to enjoy the ritual and had even ventured so far as to take two sips of Darjeeling.

Bess watched Cecil over the rim of her cup but he wouldn't meet her eye. She wasn't sure if it was because he was hiding something or engrossed in gawking at Imogen.

"I say, am I missing something?"

Cecil squirmed under her gaze, making Gertrude dissolve in peals of laughter.

"When the cat is away, the mice will play."

"Let's do something fun tonight," Bess urged. "How about playing some records on the gramophone after dinner? I feel I haven't danced in ages."

Imogen thought it would not be proper.

"Someone died here, Bess. Two men, to be accurate. It will be in bad taste."

"The cat won't approve," Gertrude smirked.

Bess pooh-poohed their qualms.

"Miles and Gordon were not family. I am tired of seeing all these long faces everywhere I go. What's wrong with living a little, eh? Carpe diem and all that? Eh, Bubbles?"

"Count me in, darling," Gertrude yawned. "This is

the most boring summer imaginable."

Hortense sided with Bess and more plans were made for the evening.

"So shall we see you at dinner?" Imogen asked Cecil. "We have crab voul-au-vents, your favourite. And roast chicken and a brandied apricot tart for pudding."

He gave in.

"I do need to work on my sermon though, ladies, so I will take your leave now."

Bess offered to drive him to the vicarage. He nodded after a moment's hesitation, looking like a lamb being led to slaughter.

"Am I being a pest?"

"No more than usual."

"Could anything be worse than being suspected of murder?"

Cecil chuckled. "When you put it that way … you won't give up, will you, Bessie?" He paused, hoping she would relent. "I was in the parlour when they found Miles. Don't you trust the crusty old retainers?"

Bess asked him about the woman at the Laughing Mongrel. Cecil gave in.

"Someone from another life. She has nothing to do with Buxley, believe me."

He looked away, swallowing a lump, knowing he was a man of God who wasn't being entirely honest. Truth be told, a big weight had been lifted off his chest when Miles died.

Bess told him she had an idea about his colourful past. The vicarage came into view and she stopped the car by the side of the road, making one last attempt to make him open up.

"I'm twenty one and worldly wise. Nobody cares you had an affair all those years ago. You think Momo will think any less of you?"

"How did Momo come into this?" Cecil erupted.

Bess let him stew for a minute, then told him she knew the woman was from a lower class.

"Please, just take my word for it, Bessie. When the time is right, I will tell you everything. But I need you to believe I did not kill Miles or Gordon. The police have done their job. We should all move on."

"Like you did after Philip died?" Bess growled.

"The cloud of suspicion that hangs over Papa destroyed us. I grew up without a mother."

Cecil thought of the son he had never laid eyes on.

"Miles can't hurt us now, Bess. Let's just be happy about it and move on."

He stepped out of the car and left her, shoulders sagging in defeat. Bess banged a fist on the steering wheel, unable to hide her frustration. She wanted to get away from the manor and clear her head. It took her a moment to realize she was equipped to do just that.

Five minutes later, the car sped out of the manor grounds and whizzed through the village. Bess kept a heavy foot on the accelerator, flying across winding roads, over hills and vales until the clangour in her head went down. She spotted a ribbon of water in a lush meadow, festooned with clumps of wildflowers. Sheep grazed nearby but there was no human being in sight. Bess stopped the car and hiked to the tiny rivulet and stepped in, revelling in the cool, clear water flowing over the smooth pebbles. No wonder poets had written odes to the beauty of the English countryside. Was there a spot as tranquil in America? She would have to ask Vicky.

A light wind picked up as the sun moved closer to

the horizon. Bess decided it was time to head back. But first, she would stop at the Buxley Arms for a pint. It had been a while since she caught up on the local gossip.

The pub was crowded. Bess waved and nodded as the locals doffed their caps at her. The landlord set a tankard of ale before her, inquiring after everyone at the manor.

"We heard about Lord Shelby, my lady. He had a good innings, he did. Was good as dead these last few years. It's a release, what?"

Bess agreed and told him she had been at Oakview earlier that day. Most of the people around her were talking about the Carringtons.

"Mr. Trevor is overwhelmed, of course."

Bess whirled around at the familiar voice.

"What ho, Peter!" she walked to a small spot near the entrance. "Coming up to the manor to break bread with us?"

He looked startled to see her.

"Lady Bess!"

Bess asked what he had been doing at Oakview.

"Mr. Trevor needs help with the estate, now that his brother is gone. He has hired me to handle his business."

"Aren't you a solicitor?" she frowned. "Why can't he hire a manager like Gordon?"

Peter explained that would be the first order of business. He would take care of legal matters for the Carringtons, along with some extra duties.

"Trips, I mean, the new Lord Shelby, is like a fish out of water. He has no grasp of how to run things. I will be moving into Gordon's quarters at Rosehill."

Bess knew Miles had kept strict control over the reins, relegating Trips to the shadows. She also knew Nigel trusted Peter, letting him handle business for Buxley. Trips must have asked for help.

"Did Papa recommend you to the Carringtons?" She drained her ale and stood up to leave. "You will be comfortable at Rosehill, I suppose. It's the bee's knees, thanks to Miles."

Chapter 28

"I give up."

Bess lounged in a chair in the west wing, surrounded by the Nightingales. She was feeling so miserable, she had barely eaten a spoonful of kedgeree at breakfast. Alarmed, Barnes called Dr. Evans on the telephone.

"Are you coming down with something, Bess?" Aunt Clem had been most solicitous. "It's not like you to turn down food."

Gertrude asked if she was pining over one of the young men from the party.

"All these silly deaths have kept us busy. Spill the beans, Bess. Is one of those bright young men giving you sleepless nights?"

Bess refused to take the bait, tapping her egg cup with a spoon until Vicky pushed back her chair and declared she was done.

"Come on," she nodded.

They were gone before anyone else took a pot shot

at her. Of one accord, they headed to meet the great aunts, knowing the chauffer had already brought Louise from the Dower House. The older ladies had chosen to have breakfast in their quarters in the west wing.

Three pairs of bright eyes greeted the girls, eager to learn about their progress. Their frowns deepened as Bess and Vicky narrated what they had found out since the last time they met.

"Apart from Viscount Cranford, none of them admit they hated Miles, which we know cannot be true."

Louise pointed out the alternative. They would have to accept the police verdict and move on.

"What are we missing, Grandma?" Bess cried.

Hortense told her to go easy on the dramatics and calm down.

"You forget what you told us about your last meeting with the dead boy."

"Gordon? We ran into him in our library."

Vicky caught on immediately.

"She's talking about the card Gordon mentioned, you dolt. He told us he was trying to trace where it came from, remember?"

Bess straightened and played with the scarf around her neck.

"The Queen of Hearts."

Louise asked if they had ever laid eyes on it, galvanizing Bess into action.

"Oh Grandma, you are the cat's meow. Of course we never saw it because the police took it with them. We are heading to the police station right now, Vicky."

Perpetua told them to stay put for a minute.

"You were in the library when that boy told you all this? Do you think someone overheard you?"

Bess and Vicky tried to think back to the day in question. Neither had noticed anyone around them.

"If we think the card got Gordon killed, we have to assume someone heard you," Louise mused. "Someone inside the manor."

Vicky grew upset. She wondered where Nigel had been at that time.

"You suspect Papa?" Bess fumed. "What is the point of all this if you think he's guilty?" Her ears turned warm as her anger mounted. "He was out fishing, nowhere near the library."

Vicky mumbled an apology. She wanted to establish Nigel's whereabouts so there would be no chance he was anywhere in the house.

"If someone saw him fishing, it will only work in his favour."

Louise had begun to look anxious.

"Wait a minute, girls. I heard something very disturbing from one of my maids. It was the first thing I was going to mention this morning."

The fishing rod found near Gordon's body was etched with a woman's name. Although the police had not found it relevant, speculation was rife among the locals. People in the village had plenty of theories about some scorned lover coming back to take revenge.

"What woman?" Vicky asked.

"Eva," Louise replied, causing Bess to spring up from her chair, her mouth hanging open.

"E, V, A? Those are the initials Papa uses to mark his things, although I have never figured out what they mean."

Hortense enlightened them.

"You poor child! They stand for Elizabeth, Victoria and Annie."

Bess collapsed on a sofa, sliding closer to Vicky. Nigel had a particular style of weaving the three letters together. They could be found on fishing journals and almanacs, anything he laid a hand on. When she was seven, she had sulked for three whole days, demanding he tell her what they meant.

"One day, you will grow up to be a fine young lady, Betsy …" he had stopped midsentence and left the nursery.

Vicky thought it was another nail in her father's coffin. How had the police missed something so significant?

Perpetua spoke up, telling them to focus on the matter at hand.

"Stop second guessing the police. I think we agree that it is all the more crucial we solve this case. What about the servants? Could one of them have been loitering around the library that day?"

The only person who listened at doors was Barnes and they knew he would lay down his life before letting any harm befall them.

"One of the gardener's men might have been outside the window," Louise reasoned. "Or any number of people might have passed it on. How does it matter now?"

They agreed they needed to focus on learning more about the card. The twins were dispatched to the police station post haste. Very soon, they stood before Constable Potts, demanding to meet the Inspector.

"Him?" Potts puffed his chest, pig headed as ever. "Gone back to London. What is it you want from him, my lady?"

Bess asked about the Queen of Hearts.

"Evidence." Potts buried his nose in his newspaper. "Under lock and key. Even for anyone from the manor." He lowered the paper to stare at that them. "Police business."

Vicky promised to be careful.

"Please, can we just have a look? You can hold it for us. We won't even touch it, I promise."

Their pleas fell on deaf years. Ten minutes later, the girls drove back to the manor, defeated. They had hit another wall and this one seemed insurmountable.

Lunch was in progress when they reached the manor. Aunt Clem glanced at the clock on the wall but was mercifully quiet. Bess found she had rediscovered her appetite and gobbled everything in sight. Vicky nudged her when she took a second helping of pudding, glancing surreptitiously at the clock. They rushed to the west wing after the meal ended, hoping the great aunts would pull something else out of their hats.

Perpetua managed to shock them.

"Are you joking?" Vicky asked.

"She's definitely pulling our leg," Bess agreed. "Right, Grandma?"

The three old retainers wore broad smiles, their eyes gleaming with excitement.

***

Constable Potts pedalled his bicycle as fast as he could, ignoring the sweat that trickled down his back. It wasn't every day the likes of him got invited to the manor. The telephone in the police station had rung five minutes after he returned from lunch. The Dowager Countess sought his presence at the manor for tea.

He found himself incapable of speech, stuttering, struggling to form a reply. The call ended before he croaked out a yes.

Constable Potts had not gone to a fancy school but he learned something at a young age. The likes of him did not stare a gift horse in the mouth. He rushed next door to inform the missus. His Sunday suit was pressed and brushed and he set off at the stroke of three, thinking an hour was ample time to cycle to the manor.

Twenty minutes later, he stood on the manor steps, straightened his tie and decided it was now or never. He gave a peremptory knock and waited, adopting his most benevolent expression. The missus had warned him about looking like an offended aubergine. He had a once in a lifetime opportunity to impress the people at the manor, maybe even get a promotion.

The butler Barnes answered the door, insouciant as ever. He was the same height as Potts but managed to look down on him.

"Yes?"

Potts licked his lips and forged ahead. "I'm here for tea."

Barnes told him to use the back entrance. Mrs. Bird was taking a break but he would ask one of the kitchen maids to put the kettle on.

"'ere now." Potts swallowed. "I'm here for tea with the Dowager."

Barnes sniffed, giving Potts a once over from head to toe.

"There was a call from the manor. I reckon she wants to thank me for my work."

Barnes asked Potts to follow him, looking like he was letting a wet dog with muddy feet into the house. They entered a tiny parlour a few feet down the hall, decorated in pink.

"Don't touch anything, " Barnes warned and stepped out.

Potts pulled out a clean handkerchief and mopped the sweat on his brow, wishing he could loosen his tie. He longed for a sip of water to soothe his throat.

After what seemed like an eternity, Imogen entered the room with Gertrude.

"Constable Potts!" she greeted. "To what do we owe the pleasure?"

He stood up and gave an awkward bow.

"I'm here for tea, my lady, just like the telephone said."

Imogen was bewildered. Gertrude burst into peals of laughter.

"Have you been dipping in the bottle, Potts?"

The Constable insisted he had been invited to tea with the Dowager. That's what the man on the telephone had said.

"You know I'm not the only Dowager at Buxley?" Imogen's face cleared. "Grandma Louise must have invited you. I think you need to be at the Dower House."

Potts glanced at the clock, noting it was now thirty minutes past three, still plenty of time to reach the Dower House. He tipped his hat, thanked Imogen and left post haste. Some vigorous pedalling brought him to the Dower House in time for the sacred hour. A similar tableau was repeated with a different butler after he rang the bell. Potts was beginning to resemble a ripe tomato.

He was placed in a yellow parlour this time and left to twiddle his thumbs. Louise arrived five minutes later, looking concerned.

"What's the matter, Potts? And why are you dressed for church?"

"But, but ... your ladyship ..." Potts was truly at a loss for words. "My apologies, my lady. I think someone has been having fun at my expense."

Louise coaxed the story out of him. Bess had not called to give her the green signal yet. That meant she needed to buy more time.

"Tea?" she smiled. "What a marvellous idea, though. I wonder why I didn't think of it."

A ray of hope rose in the Constable's chest. Was his dry throat about to get some relief?

"That is exactly what the telephone said, my lady."

"Are you sure you are not wanted at Primrose Cottage? Beatrice is also the Dowager Countess, you know. Did the telephone mention where you were supposed to go?"

Potts realized his mistake.

"It mentioned the Dowager and I assumed I was wanted at the manor."

"You poor man!" Louise clucked. "I think it was Beatrice. She was telling me how impressed she was with the way you handled the case."

Potts thanked her and rushed out, noting time wasn't on his side. His legs quaked with effort as he pedalled to the cottage, wishing he could go home and share a cuppa with the missus. No doubt she was waiting for him with thick slices of bread and butter and seed cake, with a good strong cup of English tea. But he was nothing if not dogged. He needed to face the third Dowager.

Chapter 29

Bess and Vicky crouched behind a large hawthorn hedge, waiting for Potts to leave.

"I can't believe our granny wants us to break into a police station," Vicky chuckled. "Who says the British don't have a sense of humour?"

Bess was more interested in knowing whether Vicky could jimmy a lock. Their brilliant plan would come to naught if they were unable to enter the police station.

Potts left, dressed to the nines, looking like a stuffed parrot. The twins swarmed the cottage that served as a police station the moment he was out of sight. In a small village like Buxley, it also served as the living quarters for the Constable's family. Fortunately, they did not encounter Mrs. Potts because she had not wasted any time in visiting her sister to apprise her of the great honour that had been bestowed on her husband.

Vicky's lock breaking skills were not tested because the door opened with a slight nudge. Bess looked around for a safe or a strong box, anything which might serve as a repository for evidence. The only thing the tiny room contained was a battered desk and a chair that had seen better days. Bess sat in the chair and noticed the four drawers running down each side of the desk.

"Let's divide and conquer."

The first one Bess opened contained a tennis ball, a piece of twine, a pencil stub and a stained handkerchief among other things.

"Garbage," she muttered and slid it close.

"Wait a minute, Bess." Vicky pulled it open again. "Look at this."

She brandished a gilt edged card illustrated with the Queen's portrait.

"Did someone order the Queen of Hearts?"

They could not believe their luck. Bess wanted to filch the card and flee but Vicky had a better idea. She pulled a pencil and some paper out of her pocket and began drawing. It took longer than expected.

Bess paced around the room, keeping an eye on the street.

"Hurry up, old girl," she pleaded every few

minutes.

Finally, Vicky reproduced every little detail on the card to her satisfaction, one minute before the clock struck four. Bess put the card back where they had found it and tugged at her arm.

They scrambled down the steps and didn't look back. Tea was in progress when they reached the manor.

"Is this tardiness a habit now?" Aunt Clem pinned her disapproving gaze on Vicky. "Dinner is at 8 PM sharp, in case you have forgotten how things work here, Bess."

Potts dominated the topic of conversation.

"Someone played a trick on him," Gertrude chortled, giving Bess a wink.

Barnes, who had been in on the whole caper, didn't bat an eyelid.

Imogen felt sorry for him. She instructed Barnes to ask Mrs. Bird to make up a basket of food and send it over to the Potts family.

"I believe it is already being done, my lady."

After consuming several cucumber sandwiches and a slice of strawberry lemon cake, Bess and Vicky headed to meet the great aunts and their grandmother.

The three ladies sat in a row, looking agitated.

"So?" Louise burst out. "Did you find it?"

Vicky thrust the paper before them, pointing towards a tiny symbol in one corner.

"I wonder what that means."

"Did you draw it right?" Perpetua asked. "I can barely see it, my dear."

Bess rummaged in a writing desk and located a magnifying glass. She handed it over to Hortense. The three ladies perused the tiny symbol one by one and admitted they were stumped.

"It looks like a cross." Louise gave a shrug. "But different. Why is it important?"

Vicky believed it might help them trace where the card came from.

"What if it points to a certain manufacturer?"

"By Jove!" Hortense exclaimed. "I think you hit the nail on the head, child."

They discussed next steps. Bess wondered where

she might find a catalogue of the different playing cards sold in the market.

"Clive Morse collects a lot of things." Louise bit her lip. "He might be able to shed some light on this."

"Aren't the Morses in the south of France?" Hortense asked.

"Lord Morse!" Bess exclaimed. "He's a good egg."

They decided to sleep on it. Louise declared she was going home to have a quiet dinner. She would probably ask for a tray in her room and read a book before turning in early. The great aunts echoed the sentiment.

"Why don't you do whatever young people do?" Louise yawned.

The twins accompanied Louise to the hall and waited until the chauffer was summoned to drive her to the Dower House.

"How about a walk?" Bess asked Vicky. "We have an hour or more before we dress for dinner."

"Let's go to Eden."

"Are you sure you can find the way?"

Vicky shook her head, asking Bess to be patient. She took a few false turns but eventually stumbled upon the wild garden Nigel had taken her to.

Bess looked around, her eyes wide with wonder. "I haven't been here in yonks, Vicky. This is glorious!"

"Our mother's favourite place at Buxley. Untamed but beautiful, just like her."

Bess walked around, marvelling at the profusion of colour, breathing in the sweet scent.

"This means Papa still thinks about her," she grinned. "Oh, this is smashing, Vicky."

Time stood still as Vicky regaled Bess with some anecdotes about their mother. They walked back to the manor, arm in arm, more determined to set things right for their parents.

Gertrude was in full form at dinner, making big plans for her life in London. Imogen looked tired.

"Why don't you girls go to the Riviera?" Clementine asked. "Momo can use a change of scene, I think."

None of them had visited the Mediterranean since the war. Imogen admitted the Morses had written to her, offering up their villa.

"They came back early this year, I am not sure why."

Bess almost shot up, the pork chop she was cutting into forgotten.

"They are back? You mean Lord Morse is back? Are you sure, Momo?"

Gertrude gave her a curious look.

"That's what I gathered," Imogen replied with a smile. "It won't be long before you reunite with Pudding."

Winifred Morse had been born the same year as the twins. She attended the same boarding school with Bess where she had acquired the profound moniker of Pudding, thanks to an unnatural aversion to anything sweet. The girls had been inseparable through their childhood, spending most of their holidays at either estate. Pudding was as much at home at Buxley as Bess was at the Morse family seat of Castle Morse.

"I am driving to the castle first thing tomorrow," Bess declared.

Imogen told her the Morses were spending a week in London before coming back to the country.

Bess sailed through the rest of the meal with a big

smile on her face. She was already planning on taking the 7:20 to London the next morning.

The twins had breakfast on the train and took a taxi to Grosvenor Square. The Morse family had an imposing corner mansion worthy of their name and wealth.

The butler let them in, looking stunned. Bess patted him on the arm.

"You are not seeing double, Norton. Meet my sister Vicky."

He recovered quickly and welcomed her, ushering them to a bright room where the Morses were assembled, engrossed in planning their day.

A petite, skinny young woman with dark glossy curls and large doe like eyes shrieked in delight when she saw Bess. Her mouth hung open when she spotted Vicky.

"Golly! What, what … is this some kind of trick, Bess?"

Lady Morse didn't miss a beat.

"Imogen told us you were back, my dear." She invited Vicky to sit next to her. "How does it feel to be back home?"

"What ho, Mother?" Pudding was most indignant. "And Bess? What …"

"This is Vicky, my twin." Bess shrugged. "It's a long story."

Until she came face to face with Vicky on a battlefield in France, Bess had not withheld the tiniest occurrence in her life from Pudding. She fervently hoped she was not about to lose a friend.

Pudding insisted on knowing the long story. Bess gave her the short version.

"You mean Lord Buxley was lying to you all these years?" Pudding was aghast.

"Not just him," Bess admitted. "Grandma and the aunts and Momo and Bubbles too. And the upper servants. It was a bally conspiracy."

Pudding opened her mouth to ask another question but Lady Morse quelled her with a look. In the end, the two friends embraced each other, eyes moist, trying hard to suppress emotion. Vicky cleared her throat, reminding Bess what they were doing there.

"Where is Lord Morse?" Bess asked, looking around.

"In his study, of course," Pudding yawned. "But what do you want with Papa?"

Bess told her she needed his expert opinion on something.

"Grandma Louise sent me," she added lamely.

Lady Morse looked sharp at the mention of the oldest Dowager Countess.

"Why don't you go and talk to him?" she encouraged Bess. "Meanwhile, I will ring for tea."

Vicky followed Bess down an ornate corridor, past walls lined with exquisite landscapes. She knew enough about art to guess they were original and very expensive. Bess knocked on a sturdy door, pushing it open to enter a cavernous room. A short, slender man looked up from a fat ledger, his dark eyes crinkling in pleasure when he spotted them.

"My dear Bess." He shut the ledger and came around the desk to greet them. "And you must be Victoria. Nigel will be happy you are back in the fold."

"You too?" Bess cried. "I should be going insane by now."

Lord Morse told them it was hard to hide a birth in their tight circle.

"And what's this? Why are you visiting an old fogey

like me instead of going to some disreputable club with my daughter?"

Bess decided to stick to her story.

"Grandma sent us. She found a playing card with an odd symbol in the corner, one that makes absolutely no sense. Aunt Hortense thinks it looks like a cross but Aunt Perpetua and Grandma Louise think it's a key. They have a wager going."

Vicky produced her sketch and handed it to Lord Morse. His eyes widened in surprise for a split second, as if wondering why they had not brought the card itself but he said nothing.

"Grandma says you're a big collector." Bess greased the wheels. "Does this look familiar?"

He took a magnifying glass from his desk and moved closer to a shaft of bright sunlight streaming through a window. The girls waited with bated breath.

"This pack of cards is unique alright. If I'm not wrong, this was a special edition created at the time of the Queen's Jubilee."

Bess asked him about the cross in the corner.

"I'm no Egyptologist, girls, but I think this is a hieroglyph. I have no idea what it means."

He told them about an old bookshop in Piccadilly. The owner pursued Egyptology as a hobby and might be able to shed some light on the matter.

Bess thanked him and rushed out, pulling Vicky along with her.

"Let me know who won." His laughter had a certain ring to it. Clive Morse was nobody's fool.

"I think he's on to us," Vicky whispered.

They said a hurried goodbye to a bewildered Pudding and ran down the steps to the street. Bess let out a piercing whistle to hail a taxi.

"Piccadilly," she panted. "On the double."

"Where do you learn these things, Bess?" Vicky wondered.

To their immense relief, Mr. Brown, the proprietor, was available when they reached the bookstore.

"Do you have a card?" A pompous clerk demanded. "Mr. Brown is very busy."

"Lord Morse sent us." Bess could be imperious when she chose. "Tell him Lady Elizabeth and Lady Victoria Gaskins request a moment of his time on an urgent matter."

Mr. Brown himself arrived before she finished speaking. His eyes twinkled behind thick glasses.

"How can I help you ladies?" he asked.

Vicky produced the sketch of the card and asked about the symbol.

"It's Egyptian alright." Mr. Brown didn't hesitate. "Simply put, it is the key of life and represents life itself."

"But what is it doing on a playing card?" Bess blurted.

Mr. Brown told them the manufacturer was an Egyptologist himself and had the symbol printed on certain special editions. The deck of cards in question was rare and highly valuable.

"I think Lord Morse just bamboozled you."

"What?" Bess gaped. "I say …"

If Mr. Brown hadn't been older than Barnes, she might have punched him in the face. He gave an apologetic shrug, delivering a bolt from the blue.

"I sold this deck to him in 1913."

Chapter 30

Bess wanted to go back to Grosvenor Square and confront Lord Morse at once. Vicky talked her out of it.

"We need to think over it, but my guess is he was just having a bit of fun. Can't blame him though. We lied too, didn't we?"

They decided against going to the Savoy for a proper lunch, choosing to grab some tea and sandwiches at the train station. The bread was stale, the cake dry and the tea weak at best. Bess wanted to get home and go to bed.

The train came in and whisked them away to the Cotswolds, depositing them on the platform at Buxley a few minutes after three. Bess had parked her car outside, allowing them to set off immediately.

"So the Queen of Hearts belongs to Lord Morse?" she mused on the drive home. "How? He wasn't even in the country on the night of our party."

Vicky told her to be patient. There had to be a simple solution.

"How much do you trust this man?"

Bess told her the Morses had always been a part of her life. Lord Morse was like an honorary Uncle. He wasn't ornery like Miles, nor helpless like Trips. He was a benevolent Father Christmas who showered her with gifts and encouraged the girls in their silly escapades.

"He always laughed when we got into scrapes at school, then doled out our punishment with a smile."

The car swerved around a bend at top speed. There was a hissing sound and Bess lost control. She grappled with the steering wheel, trying to stay on the road but her efforts were futile. The car plunged into a field below and crashed into a sturdy beech.

There was a stunned silence. Vicky stirred a few minutes later and tried to move her neck. She had been thrown against the door. The side of her face was sore and she suspected a bruise would form there later. Bess had banged her head against the steering column. Blood trickled from her forehead and ran in a thin stream down her face.

"Bess, wake up." Vicky gave her a gentle shake, afraid to disturb her too much. "Come on, Bess. Talk to me."

She stirred after some gentle prodding and slowly opened her eyes.

"I say … what?"

"We had an accident."

Bess understood what Vicky was leaving unsaid.

"Stop blaming me. The tire punctured and I did the best I could. Must have hit a nail or something."

Vicky dabbed the blood on her sister's face with a handkerchief, relieved that the bleeding had stopped on its own. She stepped out of the car and walked around to the other side to help Bess.

They took a few tentative steps to ascertain there were no broken bones. Vicky decided they were just a bit shook up.

"The aches and pains will come later," she sighed. "And the bruises."

Bess struggled up the incline against her advice to look at the road.

"Good Lord! Vicky!"

A bunch of nails was strewn across the road. Vicky frowned as she took in the scene. This was definitely not the driver's fault.

"They are placed just after that curve so it's impossible to spot them from a distance," she noted.

The twins shared a look, neither wanting to voice what they were thinking.

Bess shook her head.

"No, it's too farfetched."

She clutched the side of her head, dizzy for a moment.

"We better start walking," Vicky nodded. "Aunt Clem is going to be mad again."

They giggled and dissolved into laughter. Being late for tea seemed so trivial after their brush with death. Vicky felt her knee throb but ignored it. Arm in arm, they set off toward Buxley Manor.

The butcher's boy came along in his cart, a few yards after they had entered the manor grounds. He dropped them off at the manor, peppering them with questions until Bess ordered him to shut up.

The servants were clearing up the tea and most of the family had gone back inside. Barnes hastened to meet them, his eyebrows drawn together.

"My lady!" His eyes flew to the dried blood on her

face. "Are you hurt? What has happened?"

Bess assured him they were fine but Barnes rove his eyes over every inch of them, examining them from top to bottom.

"Send for Dr. Evans," he snapped at a footman. "And ask Mrs. Jones to send some tea to Lady Bess's room."

They entered the house via the side door and Barnes insisted on accompanying them to the first floor. Their maid Wilson arrived at once.

"I will take care of my ladies now, Mr. Barnes."

They were ensconced in bed, washed and changed into clean frocks when Dr. Evans arrived. He applied antiseptic on the cuts and bruises and gave them a general examination.

"No broken bones," he declared. "You might still have a concussion, Lady Bess. That's a nasty bump you got there on your head."

Vicky promised to watch her.

"You know what to look for," Dr. Evans conceded. "And no driving for a few days, Lady Bess. Better play it safe, what?"

The tea arrived with Clementine in tow, wringing

her hands together.

"How are you, girls?" She expelled a breath. "You gave me a fright." She pressed her lips together, gearing up for an onslaught. "How many times have I told you to drive slowly, Bess?"

Vicky opened her mouth to defend her sister, then clammed up. Clementine loaded two plates with cucumber sandwiches and fruit cake and handed them to the girls. She poured a cup of tea and added three lumps of sugar and plenty of milk.

"Your coffee is on its way, Vicky."

"Sorry we missed tea, Aunt Clem," Bess grinned, earning a slap on the arm for her cheek.

"Mutton curry for dinner tonight. Now, I suggest you take a nap, girls. You need the rest."

***

Dinner was in full swing later that evening. Cecil had arrived with Cordelia and so had Louise. Dr. Evans had been invited to stay back for the meal.

Vicky watched Bess with growing concern. She had complained of a headache when she woke up from her nap and stumbled on the stairs while they were coming down. She was exhibiting signs of a concussion.

Could the nails on the road be a coincidence? Vicky stirred her consommé, barely taking a sip before the footman whisked it away. She needed to call a meeting of the Nightingales as soon as possible. The fish arrived, followed by a hearty joint of beef and mutton curry.

"There's bread and butter pudding with marmalade, Bess," Clementine cajoled. "And plenty of warm custard."

Vicky sensed Bess was thinking about the Queen of Hearts. Why had Lord Morse given them the run around? Going back to London was out of the question, at least until Bess felt better. Maybe she could talk to him on the telephone.

Clementine provided the answer to her woes, much to her surprise.

"The Morses arrive tomorrow."

"What's that, Aunt Clem?" Bess was looking alert.

"You will be reunited with Pudding," Aunt Clem smiled, unaware they had already met that morning. "The Morse party will stop here on their way home and spend the night. We will have a nice welcome back dinner for them, of course."

"Oh!" Bess looked at Vicky, her eyes speaking volumes.

"Why are you so surprised, my dear?" Nigel asked. "They do that every year. It's when Clive and I make plans for the hunting season."

"Of course, Papa," Bess mumbled.

"The poor girl is falling asleep in her pudding," Louise thundered. "What were you thinking, Clementine? That's it, Bess. You are going straight up to your room. I am taking you there myself."

Vicky sprang up and joined them. Clementine was too miffed to object.

Louise dropped all pretence when they entered Bess's room. She settled into a chair by the fireplace and took them to task.

"You need to watch your back, girls. Clearly, someone tried to hurt you today." Her eyes flickered as she looked at Bess. "It might have been worse."

"How do you know about the nails?" Vicky asked.

"You can't hide something like that from me. I have lived here longer than anyone."

"Not longer than us." Hortense appeared with Perpetua in tow. "We were born here."

Vicky made sure Bess was comfortable under the

covers and sat at the foot of the bed. She narrated everything that happened that day.

"Clive is nobody's fool," Louise sighed. "He must have seen through that cock and bull story you gave him about the bet."

Hortense wondered how Bess had slipped.

"There is no betting book here like they have in the gentlemen's clubs," Perpetua explained. "Plus, Clive is aware how we feel about gambling."

"You mean it was his way of punishing us?" Vicky asked. "He's had his fun. Now he better answer our questions when he gets here tomorrow. "

Louise thought they might have to come clean about the whole murder business before he helped them.

"If he hasn't heard about Miles yet, he will within minutes of getting here."

"So you are not going to ask us to back down, Grandma?" Bess asked.

Louise pressed her lips together and gave her a withering look.

"I would like to think you have more gumption than that, my dear."

"You will not turn tail and flee at the first sign of trouble," Hortense agreed. "That would be a real shame."

Perpetua agreed with them. Vicky realized these ladies would not shrink in the face of adversity.

There was a knock on the door and Clementine arrived with Dr. Evans in tow.

"Are you awake, Bess? Dr. Evans wants to check on you before he leaves. How ..." She noticed the old ladies. "Mama, I thought you went back to the Dower House."

Louis met her gaze but said nothing.

Dr. Evans had finished examining Bess.

"Slight concussion, I think. Stay in bed tomorrow and have all your meals brought up." He looked at Vicky. "Make sure she rests a lot, Nurse."

There was a mass exodus as they all left one by one. A maid arrived with tea.

"It's willow bark," she announced. "For the pain. Mrs. Bird says it's for the both of you. "

Vicky thanked her and dutifully poured two cups, lacing them with a generous amount of honey. She stood by the bed, making sure Bess drank all of it.

"Now, be honest," she urged. "Tell me how bad is it?"

Bess admitted her head hurt and she was a bit woozy, as if she had drunk too much champagne.

"What do you think, old girl? What have we found that has thrown our killer into panic?"

Vicky thought they must be getting close.

"We really need to learn more about that card."

Chapter 31

Vicky kept a close eye on Bess the next day. They went for a brief walk in the gardens and then went up to the west wing to spend time with the great aunts. There was a feeling of anticipation in the air. They were all just biding time until they could talk to Lord Morse.

"It's the calm before the storm, Vicky. We are in for a shock." Bess was sure the man they were looking for was known to them. "You think there must have been a valid reason?"

"There is no justification for murder," Vicky insisted. "That's the difference between man and beast, isn't it? The human mind must prevail and see sense."

Lunch was cottage pie from the Buxley Arms. Mrs. Harvey sent it over when she learned about the accident. Not to be outdone, Mrs. Bird provided fried trout with chips and a treacle tart. Vicky forced Bess to take a nap after that.

"This is the last one," she grumbled. "I am feeling much better now."

Vicky admitted Bess seemed like her usual self but advised caution.

The Morses arrived just before tea. There were a lot of what hos and hand shakes among the men and screeches and giggles among the women.

"Tell me about the latest fashions from Paris," Gertrude urged Lady Morse. "We have been stuck here all summer, thanks to that silly murder."

Pudding huddled close to Bess, darting anxious glances at her every few minutes.

"How terrible!" she exclaimed. "You are not just saying you are fine?"

Lord Morse cornered the girls after tea was underway.

"Meet me in the library. I think it's time you told me the whole story."

Half an hour later, they sat at Nigel's desk in the library. Louise accompanied them, wearing a determined look.

"Just in case they don't take you seriously."

Nigel's eyes popped out when he heard about the nails on the road.

"Good Lord! What were you thinking, girls? Annie would never forgive me if anything happened to you."

Lord Morse stood at a window, puffing on his pipe, his eyebrows drawn together.

"I must apologize, girls." He cleared his throat. "I should never have sent you to Brown."

He had recognized the sketch Vicky showed him and guessed they were holding something back.

"I thought it was a silly scrape, like you and Pudding get into." He had no idea the card had been found close to a dead body.

Louise told him to forget all that and answer her question.

"Did you really recognize that card?"

Clive nodded. "Right away. I bought a deck of cards from the Piccadilly shop several years ago. It was very rare and cost a pretty penny so I was miffed when I discovered one card missing."

"Did you notify the dealer?" Vicky asked.

"Of course!" Clive tapped his pipe. "I don't like to be taken for a ride. I confronted Brown the very next day. Even a single card like that would fetch a good price and I thought he was trying to fill his own pockets by fleecing me."

Brown claimed innocence and pointed him to the person who had sold him the deck.

"Sir Dorian Ridley," Clive declared.

A gasp of surprise travelled across the room.

"Now he might be a curmudgeon, my dears," Clive smiled. "But Sir Dorian is one of the most upstanding men I know."

"Absolutely," Nigel nodded. "Sir Dorian would never cheat anyone."

Clive had come to a decision. Rather than rile up Sir Dorian and make him feel bad, Clive put the matter to rest.

"One card less didn't really make a difference," he shrugged.

Louise thought the time had come to question Sir Dorian.

"This card is our only link to a ruthless killer."

Nigel told her the Ridleys were joining them for dinner.

"I suggest you wait until he has a drink in hand, Mama. And now, Polo and I are going for a walk."

Time crawled slowly after that. Dr. Evans arrived to check on Bess and gave her a clean bill of health.

"No driving for a few days, though."

Pudding kept them entertained with stories from her summer in France.

"I know you're hiding something, Bess," she pouted. "It better be good."

Finally, the dressing gong sounded, heralding the dinner hour. Bess and Vicky changed quickly and took the stairs down to the parlour.

Barnes greeted them. "They are waiting in the library, my lady."

The girls burst in, only to find a red faced Sir Dorian berating Nigel.

"I am not going to wait around for a silly chit."

Bess noted her grandmother was already ensconced in a chair, looking thunderous.

"That's enough, Dorian," she thundered. "You will shut up and listen." She nodded at Bess. "Go on, my dear."

Bess asked if he had sold the vintage deck of cards.

"So what if I did?" Sir Dorian shot back.

He was speechless when he learned about the missing card.

"I had no idea, I swear." His shoulders slumped in defeat. "I won the deck in a game of cards, of course. And the man who wagered it was my friend, an honest man."

There was a stunned silence when Sir Dorian mentioned the man's name.

"That proves nothing," Nigel sighed. "Because he died a long time ago."

Louise thanked Sir Dorian for clearing up the matter and asked him to escort her to the parlour.

"I could use a glass of sherry."

Vicky waited until the door closed behind them.

"You are not going haring off to London to talk to Inspector Gardner," she warned Bess. "Dr. Evans forbid you to travel."

Bess objected vehemently, claiming they could take the train. Nigel put an end to the bickering.

"Girls, girls. Vicky is right. I am not letting you out of sight, Bess. Let me call Sir Edward at Scotland Yard. He can send the Detective Inspector here tomorrow. Then the ball's in your court."

"Don't worry, Papa." Bess narrowed her eyes. "I have a pretty good hunch who committed these murders. I am just not sure why."

Dinner was a blur. Bess didn't argue when Vicky suggested they turn in early. She wanted to wake up with a clear mind in the morning.

The girls had a hearty breakfast and proceeded to the police station in the Rolls. The chauffer stopped outside the tiny building five minutes before ten. Bess took a deep breath and climbed up the rough stone steps, deciding it was now or never.

James Gardner sat behind the tiny desk, his eyes bloodshot, looking like a man who had not slept for days. He made no attempt to hide his displeasure.

"Can we get this out of the way, my lady? I would rather go back to London, to the real world, to chase real criminals."

Vicky told him to stop being prejudiced and listen.

"We almost died, Detective Inspector. It is time to

accept you were wrong."

His eyebrows shot up when he learned about the nails scattered in their path.

Bess started with the Queen of Hearts and explained how they had traced it to its original owner.

"I am smart enough to know when to stop," she admitted. "Don't you think this deserves to be followed up though?"

James Gardner knew when he was beaten. He promised he would investigate further and warned them to be circumspect. Bess grumbled about being put under house arrest.

The chauffer drove them straight back to the manor. The Nightingales convened at the usual hour. The air was heavy with anticipation.

"Is this boy any good?" Louise asked. "At least he doesn't resemble Potts."

"What if we are wrong, Grandma?" Bess burst out. "We'll never know."

The great aunts urged her to be patient.

"I find it's better to be optimistic," Hortense advised.

They suffered through lunch, listening to Gertrude grumble about a dozen things.

"For heaven's sake, Bubbles," Bess interrupted. "Why don't you just buy a ticket and take the train to Paris?"

The afternoon dragged and Barnes and his army had started to set up tea outside when the telephone rang. Bess and Vicky rushed to the library, assuming Nigel would answer it. He was just replacing the receiver when they entered.

"That was DI Gardner." He sounded grim. "He is on his way here."

Vicky and Bess stared at each other, their hearts pounding with excitement.

"Does this mean he apprehended the killer?"

Chapter 32

Tea was underway when Detective Inspector James Gardner arrived in his Hispano Suiza and made his way to the assembled company. Clementine frowned, annoyed at seeing someone she had not invited herself.

"Good afternoon." Her tone made it clear she looked down on him. "Why don't you wait in the library, Inspector? Barnes will show you the way."

Nigel asserted himself for a change, holding Polo in his arms for moral support.

"He is staying here, Clem. Now give him some tea."

James accepted the cup Clementine handed him and thanked her. He took two cucumber sandwiches and a biscuit from a tray and leaned back in his chair, taking a sip.

"Darjeeling, I presume?"

Bess couldn't hold back any longer.

"Stop torturing us!" she cried. "Did you get him?"

James tipped his head, causing Bess to spring up and pump a fist in the air, jubilant. She went to stand behind Vicky and placed her hands on her shoulders.

The rest of the company began to catch on.

"What's going on, Bess?" Gertrude popped a strawberry in her mouth and raised an eyebrow.

James set his plate down and brushed some invisible crumbs off his knee.

"He gave a full confession, Lady Bess. It was easier than we thought, as if he was just waiting for us to go get him."

Clementine had had enough.

"I say, what is the meaning of this, Inspector?"

"It's Detective Inspector, isn't it?" Vicky spoke up. "Give the man a chance to talk, Aunt Clem."

Clementine turned red. Bess, Imogen and Gertrude gave Vicky an approving smile. Nigel preened like a proud Papa.

"Peter Osborne has been arrested for the murder of Miles Carrington and Gordon Phipps," James announced. "And yes, attempted murder of Lady Elizabeth and Victoria Gaskins."

Clementine collapsed in her chair. Imogen had turned white.

James apologized for shocking them and continued.

"He blamed Carrington for destroying his family. Phipps had to go because he posed a danger to Osborne."

Bess wanted to know the whole story. What was Peter's connection to the Carringtons?

James glanced at Nigel. "I think Lord Buxley can give us a better account of their history."

"That poor boy! I tried to do right by him. But I had no idea he harboured so much resentment."

"Tell us the whole story, Papa," Bess urged, slipping a biscuit to Polo who was running around her chair, chasing a butterfly.

"We have to go back to the turn of the century, girls, before you were born." He crumbled a biscuit on his plate. "Do you remember who lived at Rosehill then, Momo?"

Imogen sat up in her chair.

"Oh my God, the Osbornes. I had completely forgotten that."

"That's right," Nigel nodded. "Rosehill always belonged to the Osbornes. I think Peter's grandfather built it and turned it into a flourishing estate. He spent several years in the colonies and came back with a fortune." He had been great friends with Nigel's father.

Bess wondered why she had never known that.

"Miles Carrington," Clementine spoke up. "Nigel is right, of course. The Osbornes were part of our set while growing up. But Miles was living there when I returned to Buxley as a widow."

Peter's father was a second son and chose the law as his profession. Being well connected, he had no trouble drumming up business. His brother was a bachelor and died early, leaving the estate to Peter's father.

"He was a family man," Nigel told them. "And very trustworthy. He only had one flaw. Like many men of his ilk, he liked to gamble."

Bess could guess where the story was going. Miles Carrington won Rosehill in a game of cards. The Osbornes had lost everything overnight. They rented a small cottage in the village and were barely scraping through.

"Things would have been fine, eventually," Nigel mused. "All of us wanted to come to the family's aid. But Robert, Peter's father, was ashamed of what he had done. He died soon after."

James interrupted, telling them Robert had taken his own life. It was documented in the old police records.

"That poor boy!" Louise clucked. "He was always a quiet one."

There had been a trust fund set aside for Peter's education. He was dispatched to boarding school soon after Robert's death. His mother and sister were taken in by some distant relative in Scotland.

"I never knew so much had happened in his life," Clementine admitted.

Nigel tried to be kind to the boy, knowing he had nowhere to go in the school holidays. Peter spent most summers at Buxley, raising hell with Clementine's sons.

Vicky wondered why Peter didn't blame his father.

"I suppose he did, to some extent. But Miles was the real villain. You see, Robert Osborne suspected Miles cheated him. He tried to gather proof but wasn't very successful. All he could ascertain was Miles had marked the cards in some fashion."

Bess asked about the Queen of Hearts.

"What was special about it? Why did he keep it back when he lost the rest of the deck to Sir Dorian?"

James replied Peter had no idea. He just knew the card had come from the deck that sealed their fate. Leaving the card beside the dead body had been a bit theatrical. Ultimately, it sealed his fate.

"Did the boy plan the whole thing?" Louise wondered. "I thought Clementine was not happy about inviting him to dinner that night."

James looked at Bess.

"He was my guest," Bess groaned. "I ran into him in Chipping Woodbury a few days before my birthday and insisted he come to dinner."

That had given him ample time to plan the murder.

Nigel wanted to know about the scream.

"Was that a diversion to get us out on the terrace, Detective Inspector?"

"Just a coincidence, I think," James replied. "Peter claims it was very fortuitous. He couldn't have planned it better."

Vicky wanted to know about Gordon.

"Osborne was in the library when Phipps told you about the card." James frowned. "He was not sure if the card could be traced back to him but he was not taking any chances."

Peter met Gordon at Rosehill and confessed he was in love with a rich young woman. He needed Gordon's advice on how to woo her. They agreed to meet by the river, away from nosy servants. Peter had been late on purpose. He had the element of surprise when he pushed Gordon in. Luckily, he hit his head on a stone and died quickly.

"What about the fishing?" Vicky asked. "According to Mabel, Gordon hated it."

James told them Peter had planted the fishing rod near the body to make it appear Gordon slipped and fell. He flicked one of Nigel's old rods from the manor, just in case.

"That scoundrel!" Bess cried. "He sure fooled me."

Vicky clasped her hand, arguing she had never given up. James seconded her.

"Your persistence paid off, Lady Bess. And the police are grateful. I must say I'm impressed. Even a hardened lawman might have given up after an attempt on their life."

Imogen set her tea cup down with a thud.

"What's that?" Her jaw tightened as she stared at the twins.

"Osborne is most repentant about the attempt on your life, Lady Bess." James accepted another cup of tea from Clementine. "That's when he began to realize he had gone too far."

"I would think so," Hortense broke her silence. "But I don't understand one thing, Inspector."

"Why now?" Perpetua asked. "He must have known about Miles for years. What made him resort to violence and commit the ultimate crime?"

Gertrude thought a lawyer should have known better.

"He was provoked." James gave a shrug. "Peter Osborne dreamed of avenging his father's death but even in his wildest dreams, he never thought of killing Miles. His fantasies had revolved around winning Rosehill back from Miles Carrington, bringing his elderly mother back to her rightful home." James paused. "His sister died a few years ago, in the 1917 air raids in London."

Bess wanted to know more.

"You mean he was just a pawn."

James told them the law would still find Peter

Osborne guilty. There was no gainsaying the fact that he had been fully aware of what he was doing.

"He was of sound mind when he committed those murders and he admits that."

Everyone wanted to know how Peter had been misled.

"He met a man who had lost a big bundle to Miles Carrington," James began. "They commiserated about their misfortune over a pint."

Peter had run into the man a few times at different pubs in the area. They struck up an unlikely friendship after that. Somehow, their angst against Miles had escalated every time they met, prompting Peter to take action.

"Why unlikely?" Bess asked.

James told them the man belonged to the lower class and had nothing in common with Peter Osborne. He had turned out to be an expert manipulator, convincing a highly educated man like Peter to take the law in his hands.

"Good Lord!" Nigel boomed. "Surely the police will arrest this man?"

James replied it would be hard to hold him culpable. All he had done was talk about revenge.

"I must apologize for suspecting you, Lord Buxley. But I was just doing my job. You can rest easy now, thanks to your daughters."

Nigel brushed off his concern. "Ned told me you were a stickler for procedure. But he has complete faith in you."

Clementine wasn't going to let him off that easily.

"You cleared him of this crime, Inspector, but what about the one twenty years ago? Nigel bore the brunt of all the speculation. The rumours haven't died down even after all this time."

James was quiet, not having a suitable response. None that would change the truth. In his opinion, there was no mystery around Philip's death. Even a good rider had an off day. He was thrown because he was unable to control his horse. It might have happened to anyone.

Bess had been trying to get a word in. Vicky sensed her impatience and asked the question uppermost in their mind.

"Who is this man who fanned the fire, Detective Inspector?"

"Joe Cooper. He is the head groom at a local estate, Castle Morse. I doubt you have come across him."

There were a series of exclamations among the assembled group.

"Does that mean you know him?" James asked drily.

He had taught Bess how to ride. Nigel thought he was the best authority on racehorses in the region. Louise had known him since he was a boy.

"He used to be a stable boy here at Buxley," Imogen explained. "Clive Morse poached him from us."

Epilogue

It was the driest August in years. The days were long and bright and the sun shone almost every day. The annual cricket match between Buxley and Ridley had never been held in such hot weather.

The ladies of the house sat in the pavilion, dressed in white summer dresses, drinking lemonade. A delicious lunch had been enjoyed by the players and spectators, comprising of cold meats, salads and pies. The second innings was in progress with the home team on the field. Nigel was still hoping for a win.

"The dry pitch will make the ball spin, you see," he told Vicky while biting into a leg of chicken. "Ridley will never know what hit them."

With two quick wickets in five overs, things were looking good for Buxley.

The constables from the two villages acted as umpires, Potts standing at one end of the wicket while Constable Yates, his colleague from Ridley, manned the other.

"Do you think Potts is on to us?" Vicky asked

Bess, noting his florid complexion, sure he had high blood pressure. "I feel sorry for the trick we played on him. You think Grandma Louise can actually invite him to tea?"

"Never mind Potts. Have you mailed that letter yet, Vicky? Papa was asking me about it."

Bess and Nigel were on tenterhooks, wondering how Annie would react when she learned Vicky had spent the summer at Buxley.

"I did," Vicky sighed. "Yesterday."

The staff bustled around in the tea tent, setting up trays loaded with mountains of finger sandwiches, scones and biscuits. Polo ran around them, begging for a titbit or two. Mrs. Bird had created a magnificent six layer Victoria Sponge and there was a giant trifle loaded with summer fruits and custard laced with plenty of sherry. Regardless of who won the match, neither side would go hungry.

Barnes arrived as Bess plucked a strawberry off the cake, earning a slap on the wrist from Mrs. Bird.

"That was Lord Morse on the telephone, my lady, looking for Constable Yates. Bad news, I am afraid."

Bess immediately thought of Pudding. They hadn't met since a shopping trip to London in the middle of July.

Barnes noted her concern and hastened to reassure her.

"The family is fine, my lady. This pertains to the constable's nephew. The poor man died this morning."

"Yates has a nephew at Castle Morse?" Bess picked up an egg and cress sandwich, intending to sample it.

Barnes frowned and handed her an empty plate.

"Joe Cooper. The stable master at Castle Morse. I had no idea he was related to Constable Yates."

**

Who killed Philip? Will Nigel ever be exonerated in the court of public opinion? And what about Joe Cooper? Does his death have anything to do with what happened at Buxley Manor? Read the next in the series, Murder at Castle Morse to find out.

Recipe – Buxley Manor Kedgeree

Ingredients

1 cup basmati rice

2 cups vegetable stock or broth

1 Tbsp butter

250g or 8 oz smoked haddock

1-2 cups milk

1 bay leaf

2 green cardamom pods

½ cup onion, diced

½ cup green peas

1 tsp lemon juice

2 Tbsp vegetable oil

1 Tbsp butter

½ tsp smoked paprika (see note below)

1 Tbsp Ship brand curry powder

Salt to taste

1 Tbsp cilantro or coriander

1 Tbsp parsley

3-4 lemon wedges

3 hard boiled eggs, cut into quarters

Method

Place the smoked haddock in a stock pot. Add bay leaf and cardamom pods and cover with milk or a mixture of milk and water. Poach for 8-10 minutes until the fish is cooked and can be separated easily with a fork. Lift the fish out and transfer to a plate. Use a fork to break it into good sized chunks.

If desired, use part of the poaching liquid for cooking the rice. Add vegetable stock if needed.

Wash the rice in a bowl until the water runs clear.

Transfer to stock pot. Add double the amount of liquid. This can be a combination of the poaching liquid and vegetable stock or water if you are not using either. Add a knob of butter and bring it to a boil. Cover and cook on medium for 8-10 minutes. Once the liquid is absorbed, check if the rice is almost cooked. Cover and switch off heat. Rice will continue to cook under residual heat and be soft and fluffy after 15 minutes.

Heat oil in a pan. Add the butter and onions with a pinch of salt. Sauté until onions are softened. Now add paprika and curry powder and stir for a second or two, taking care it does not burn.

Add cooked rice to the pan. Mix everything well and fry for 2-3 minutes.

Add in the green peas and most of the flaked fish and gently mix everything together. Season with salt as needed. Add the lemon juice.

Transfer to a serving plate or bowl. Add the rest of the fish on top, along with boiled eggs cut in quarters.

Garnish with finely chopped coriander and parsley and lemon wedges.

Serve hot with more lemon wedges.

Makes two very generous portions of kedgeree. You can

easily double the recipe for four portions.

Notes:

If smoked haddock is not available, use any white fish like cod or tilapia. Be sure to use the smoked paprika since it will impart the smoky flavor that kedgeree is known for.

Use any/ your favorite brand of curry powder if Ship brand is not available.

If you are not a habitual curry eater, start with half the amount of curry powder, taste and add more if needed.

You can add ¼ tsp of ground turmeric to the oil along with the curry powder if you want a deeper yellow color.

Acknowledgements

Who hasn't been charmed by the 1920s? As a mystery fan, I yearned to write a book set in the inter war years in England. It feels like all the others I wrote were leading up to this. The idea for this book and the series came to me one winter night three years ago. Since then, I spent a lot of time doing research, planning the setting and the characters. When I finally began to write, the characters felt like old friends.

My dear sibling cheered me on at every step, providing plenty of encouragement, building my confidence. He read early drafts and gave candid feedback. I will always be thankful for the many words of wisdom he imparts on a day to day basis.

Special thanks to my family for patiently letting me talk ad nauseum about the 1920s and watching reruns of historical movies and shows with me. They are the rock I lean on. All of them held the fort down, allowing me to immerse myself in writing this book.

A big thank you to my editor for pointing out errors and making me think and rethink the different parts of this story, polishing it until it shone. I am grateful to my beta readers and advanced readers for taking the time to read the book.

And most of all, thank you to all my readers for choosing to read this book. Your notes and messages spur me on and your kind words motivate me to hone my skills and make every book worth your while.

I really appreciate all of you.

Thank you for reading this book. If you enjoyed this book, please consider leaving a brief review. Even a few words or a line or two will do.

As an indie author, I rely on reviews to spread the word about my book. Your assistance will be very helpful and greatly appreciated.

I would also really appreciate it if you tell your friends and family about the book. Word of mouth is an author's best friend, and it will be of immense help to me.

Many Thanks!

Author Leena Clover

http://leenaclover.com

leenaclover@gmail.com

https://www.facebook.com/leenaclovercozymysterybooks

Join my Newsletter

Get access to exclusive bonus content, sneak peeks, giveaways and much more. Also get a chance to join my exclusive ARC group, the people who get first dibs on all my new books.

Sign up at the following link and join the fun.

Click here →
http://www.subscribepage.com/leenaclovernl

I love to hear from my readers, so please feel free to connect with me at any of the following places.

Website – http://leenaclover.com

Facebook – http://facebook.com/leenaclovercozymysterybooks

Email – leenaclover@gmail.com

Other books by Leena Clover

Pelican Cove Cozy Mystery Series –

Strawberries and Strangers

Cupcakes and Celebrities

Berries and Birthdays

Sprinkles and Skeletons

Waffles and Weekends

Muffins and Mobsters

Parfaits and Paramours

Truffles and Troubadours

Sundaes and Sinners

Croissants and Cruises

Pancakes and Parrots

Cookies and Christmas

Biscuits and Butlers

Dolphin Bay Cozy Mystery Series –

Raspberry Chocolate Murder

Orange Thyme Death

Apple Caramel Mayhem

Cranberry Sage Miracle

Blueberry Chai Frenzy

Mango Chili Cruiser

Strawberry Vanilla Peril

Cherry Lime Havoc

Pumpkin Ginger Bedlam

Meera Patel Cozy Mystery Series -

Gone with the Wings

A Pocket Full of Pie

For a Few Dumplings More

Back to the Fajitas

Christmas with the Franks

Printed in Great Britain
by Amazon